SOMETIMES I DISAPPEAR

Steve Attridge

A Wild Wolf Publication

Published by Wild Wolf Publishing in 2022

Copyright © 2022 Steve Attridge

All rights reserved. No part of this book may be reproduced, stored in a retrieval system or transmitted in any form or by any means without the prior written permission of the publishers, except by a reviewer who may quote brief passages in a review to be printed by a newspaper, magazine or journal.

First print

ISBN: 9798442146714
Also available as an e-book

www.wildwolfpublishing.com

With many thanks to Jane

1

My name is Alison and sometimes I disappear. I don't know where I go. Then there is a shift, a blinding pain in my head, and I am back. How long has it lasted? A second. A minute. An hour. It feels like forever.

Sometimes I wonder if the Virus mutated me too, like the Ferals, and it is this that disappears me. Or was I chipped, and someone in Dorado strokes a keyboard and I am gone? Perhaps it's a game, or an amusement to while away some bored apparatchik's coffee break. The one certain thing is that there are no certainties. The world is smoke and mirrors. My own guess is that it started when I found them - my husband Joe and daughter Chloe. Something broke. Since then, in a world of vanquished and crushed souls, my disappearing sets me apart, because sometimes I do things when I am gone. In my dreams, what remains is a dark, restless beast that wants to destroy everything, including myself. Then I long to be an enthusiastic architect of my own undoing. Who knows? How can I be held responsible if I am not properly there? And anyway, my disappearing is my protection. Our protection. Sometimes I am tempted to put it on, to act it, but I think someone might guess, and then word would get out and we would be as vulnerable as everyone else.

Our protection. Me and Dad. After I found Joe and Chloe, and came back to myself, I ran. I found a car and started it easily. There are benefits to being an engineer in Beforetimes. All I took was a vest and a lemon silk ribbon of Chloe's and a special coin she kept because she found it under her pillow when she lost a tooth, and a pretty rosewood box with onyx inlay and quartz stones that Joe made for our third wedding anniversary. I drove down here to Kessingland on the Norfolk coast to my Dad's. His small house that looks out on the ragged beach and dishwater Atlantic that often smells of death. I find it a comfort that even the ocean is now only a dream of itself. Dad is my rock and refuge. Seventy five now, which makes him a real Elder, but he has that wistful smile that carries the memory of long gone love and happiness. Most don't even remember Beforetimes when there was work and play and even good laughter, but he carries it in him like a little sun and in the evenings when we hunker down and forget what might be happening outside, it warms me.

If I could I'd get him a ticket to Arcadia, where life is still warm and there is always good food and wine. He wouldn't want to go but I'd make him. It would probably give him a few extra years. Who knows? I might even be able to join him if I survive. But people kill for places. And it costs. One day perhaps. One day. I'm saving a little. It's in the tin box – the one with a picture of the old Queen Elizabeth from Beforetimes - beneath the stairs. And even if I save the tokens I'll have to avoid the Hunt. There are enough people out there happy to scab me to the Protectors. I must watch my back. If you get scabbed it's because someone says you're one of the Others, you've mutated. The guards are meant to check, but often they don't. My disappearings are a contradiction. On the one hand people would like to scab me because of them, on the other they fear that I might have time to seriously damage them. Which I would. Even if I knew nothing of it afterwards. So they both threaten and protect me.

I have to go out to barter. I take my herb knife in case I find anything edible in the dunes. Every day at sundown is barter time. I have three tokens but that's not enough even for a small meal. I'll have to see what is on offer. The tokens are a cheap brownish metal with a number on them, telling you their value. They came in very quickly when real money and plastic disappeared, almost overnight it seemed. Tokens primitivized us even further. Calling them tokens was clever because it showed us we were only now living in a simulacrum of reality. Life and trade reduced to tokenism, a perfunctory or symbolic exchange of things to create the appearance of a functioning society, whereas it had collapsed into itself. Barters are strange brew. Although the virus has gone, at least for now, I still wear a scarf for the barter – a pale pink woollen one that I made for Chloe. It makes me feel a bit safer and is another barrier. I don't like being close to people. The smell of humanity disgusts me. Also, there is the faintest warm clean smell of Chloe and it triggers a memory of putting the scarf around my lower face and telling her a bedtime story of Dick Turpin, famous highwayman. I would stand and brandish an imaginary pistol and say "Dick stopped the coach and, pointing his pistol, say…" and Chloe would shout "Stand and deliver!" and then we would put all the imaginary takings on her bed: a gold fob watch, a ladies pearl necklace (Dick would hold the woman's hand and gently kiss it, for he was a gentleman outlaw), a few gold coins, a shining cane with a wolf's head carved in silver, and a fine leather buckle belt. *His blood spins through his veins; winds round his heart; mounts to his brain. Away! Away! He is wild with joy.* When I die no one will know this story because most stories have been disappeared. By the time I finish the story in my head I am there.

In Barter Square business is slow. A woman sits with a bucket of wriggling maggots. You boil them and then mash them with some wild thyme, but Dad won't eat them. I think they remind him of death. Next to her a man has a tin box full of grasshoppers. They are quite big. You pull off the head and the guts come with it. This reduces the risk of infection. Then take off the wings and legs and roast them. They are crunchy but full of protein. But when I look closely there are one or two brightly coloured ones – yellow and some red. These are poisonous. I move on and approach a boy who has an old cloth full of roly polies. Woodlice. Boil them up to get rid of parasites and they will do. I offer him a token and he shakes his head. He takes two. I wrap the roly polies up, tie a knot in the rag and pocket them. Very few vegetables. An old woman has several stinking onions and some withered beets. A man sitting on an upturned bucket has a few potatoes. I offer him a token and he laughs derisively. He is completely toothless. I ask him how much and he fondles his crotch. I move as if I am about to kick him and he startles and falls backwards off the bucket. People point and laugh and in the confusion I pocket one of the potatoes and walk away quickly.

There are rumours that the food in Dorado, the Capital, is very good. Fresh vegetables and fruits and all sorts of beans. The soil must be different. Here it is either dry and barren or wet and marshy and nothing much grows. There are few trees. Most have become firewood. I find some wild herbs and garlic along the sheltered bits of dunes, but increasingly less so and I have to forage further afield. Sometimes armed Protectors drive a truck loaded with tinned food. They set up a loudspeaker and we all rush down to Barter Square. If you don't queue in an orderly manner they drive away again and whoever spoilt things for everyone else gets a beating. I saw a woman get her arm snapped and an eye knocked out for trying to push in and the truck left straight away. So mostly we behave and each person gets half a dozen tins, usually beans, corn and sometimes green beans. We feel like kings and queens. Dad has an ancient bottle of gin in his room and on the day we open a tin we each have a small glass of gin and toast ourselves for being here, and to those we have lost. Then he sings to me because he knows if I think too long about Joe and Chloe I may disappear.

There is hardly ever meat. The virus mutated and destroyed most animals. Some mongrel dogs survive. Perhaps their complex mix of genes scrambled the virus, but no one eats them because they fear they will catch the virus from them. The same with rats. They are protein but they may carry the virus. I don't know if they do but it isn't worth the risk. So we make do with bugs and creepy crawlies and insects. Snakes too. I forage along the dunes and wetlands and sometimes catch a grass snake, which is sweet eating, and we have another tiny drop of gin. Hardly anyone keeps the dogs. Mostly they live in feral packs and keep their distance. What do they live on? I guess rats, bugs, the weird things that sometimes live in the stagnant waters. The first virus in, I think, 2020, was bad enough, but we got over that. It was the really big one in 2030 that gutted the world to the bone. That and the wars that followed. How long ago was that? Ten years? Twelve? I realise I don't know what year it is. 2040? 2041? I must ask Dad, he has a keen memory for dates. We live in a perpetual outbreak now, and they say the wars are still going on, though I never see bomber planes, and the news is so vague as to be meaningless.

As I leave Barter Square a Protector's van draws up. I hunch into myself. Two Protectors get out, one with an old school gun, a revolver, the other with a laser. They look around. A young woman, thin and lined, sees them, looks at the man next to her accusingly. He must be her brother, same gaunt eyes, receding chin. The Protectors spot her and walk towards her. She turns to run, but her brother trips her and she sprawls, dropping a bottle of maggots. A Protector pulls her half up by one arm and then drags her to the van. Her brother watches, as if recording the scene, until the van drives away, and then crouches and scoops the maggots back in the bottle. He has scabbed her. It could be because it's one less mouth to feed, or because he suspected she might do it to him, or because of some past altercation that has soured the mind into a hunger for revenge. She will either be put in a Hunt or perhaps executed. No one intervenes. I leave.

The beach is bleak, the water a dull grey porridge. Even the tide is a listless goo. About four hundred metres out is the rusting oil rig. Even now it pains me, as an engineer, to see all that machinery going to waste, but even so, its decay is a strange beauty, a reminder of Beforetimes when there was work and industry. A past that refuses to lie down and die. I'm cold. I am almost home and talking in my head to Joe, telling him what I got at Barter Square, when I hear a shout and the twin acrid scents of fear and violent intent almost make me gag.

Ten metres away an elderly man clutches a plastic shopping bag. A tall young man is trying to take it from him. He looks like an Other – that cloudy air of malice and indifference. The old man clings tenaciously and the young man holds a homemade cosh, a sock filled with something, and hits the old man. I run to them. The old man's head is bleeding and his wiry white hair is like the dead bleached seaweed that litters the shore. The young man looks at me. He gives a half smile and then hits the old man again. I think of Dad. Old. Vulnerable. Stupidly I hold out my arm, cock the pistol I almost see, and shout "Stand and Deliver!" Then I disappear.

2

When I return, minutes later because the blood is still fresh, the old man is dead and the young man is more than dead. His eyes have been spooned out and his tongue lolls like a dead dog's. One hand clutches at the wide blood smile on his throat, a perfect arc cut with precision. He has the grey pallored skin of an Other. The Feral kids usually become Others as they grow older. The herb knife in my hand drips blood. I wipe it clean on the young man's grubby coat. I wonder how I got the eyes out. I get on one knee and check the old man for a pulse, then take the bag he still clutches in death. His coat has fallen open and he has a few tools in the inside pockets. A good pry bar, some allen wrenches, tongue and groove pliers, a clawhammer that looks like it was made in Beforetimes, a Stanley knife, a slotted soft grip screw driver and a beautiful TT-03 tap set with handle. Dad will love that. I bloody the Stanley knife blade and put it in the old man's left hand, then pick up the screwdriver and dip it in the dark goo in the young man's eye sockets and put it in the old man's right hand. One hell of a fight in which both died. Any decent Protector would instantly smell a rat and know this is a staged scene, but the chances are they will just register the bodies and cart them away. To where? No one has funerals any more. I look at the old man and say Thank you, and put the clawhammer in the plastic bag, but it clinks on something. I look in the bag. I am so surprised I drop the hammer and gasp.

There are tokens. At least a hundred. A small fortune. I look around to make sure no one is watching and I quickly count them. Ninety eight. The possibilities flywheel through my mind. But one shines brightest. I can send Dad to Arcadia. Not enough for me to go too, but with a bit of luck and on my own I might be able to save, or steal, enough in a year or so. He won't want to go. But even he will know it's the best thing to do. I practically wet myself when there is a gasp behind me and I turn holding the herb knife. A huge blood bubble grows from the young man's lips as he has a delayed death rattle. I smile and pop the bubble with my finger.

"No."

We have finished eating the roly polies and the potato. I wait for the feeling of vague nausea to pass and breathe deeply to keep the food down.

"Dad, it's for the best."

"Not my best. Girl, I needs be with you. Not carted off bugger knows where."

"You know where. Arcadia is the one safe place. You'll eat well. Christ, they might even be able to do something about your legs."

We both look at his withered legs in the wheelchair, which I cobbled together from old bicycle wheels I found and a bucket seat from an abandoned car. I axled the wheels together and then bolted on the seat. Beneath the thin grey trousers his legs resemble a bird's. When I wash him I am frightened they will snap. We don't know what is wrong. Arthritis, nerve damage, muscle degeneration, poor diet. Take your pick. I instantly regret talking about his being wheelchair bound. He hates it so much. The man who used to swim a mile in winter just to show he could.

"I'd be off your hands," he says.

"Don't say that, Dad. You know I want us to be together. You're all I have."

"Then don't send me."

And so we go around for a few days, and then he has a fall. Trying to get to the toilet on his own. Crash. I haul him back into his wheelchair. He is pale, the age spots on his face and hands like little burnt craters in a war zone. My heart feels as if it is weeping tears of blood, but I don't cry. Not now. Perhaps never again. What is the point of tears in this world? His leg is broken. I kiss his head, then make a splint and bandage the leg as tightly as I dare. The papery skin is broken and his blood looks watery and an unhealthy pinkish colour. The pain comes later in the evening. We have no medicine. No pain killers. No doctors or hospitals. I give him a big slug of the gin, then another until it is all gone. I'm helpless. All I can do is love him, and that's not enough.

I look at the old maps of East Anglia pinned to the wall. Dad loves them and prefers to look at them rather than watch TV. I think he sees disappeared places and long-gone lives. The maps are living things to him, but they can't numb his pain. I switch on the crackly old TV to try and distract him. We sit through announcements about the different regions. Things stable in our Eastern regions one, two and three. New outbreak of the virus in Northern regions five and six. I can't even remember when counties were renamed regions and numbered in smaller units. Ten years ago? Then an advert for Arcadia. It shows little bungalows and a few apartment blocks, nothing luxurious, but clean and new. It looks sunny. There are tree lined roads. People look healthy. An elderly man in a motorised wheelchair rolls by and gives a thumbs up to the camera. This could be Dad in a few days. A matronly looking woman walks into view and addresses us. "Arcadia is not paradise, but it's a good safe place for you and your loved ones. Clean water, healthcare, plenty of good food, state of the art security..." And then more blah blah blah about the cost of maintaining Arcadia.

All the old questions form in my mind. Where is it exactly? The official line is that the fewer people who know the exact location, the less chance there is of it being attacked by terrorists or the Enemy, whoever they happen to be now. What if the whole idea is a con? What would be the point of the con? To get our tokens. Frankly, if the Protectors wanted our tokens they could just take them. Perhaps to create a sliver of hope so that we have something to aim for and don't become agitated. That doesn't make sense either because the Protectors clearly aren't frightened of anyone outside Dorado. Terrorists have been easily contained and mostly eliminated. And the virus is real enough. You can't fabricate a pandemic. And if Arcadia was a set up it's incredible that no one has discovered that. And there is audio visual communication with those on Arcadia. Having one bright spot in a grim reaper desert of decay is a clever ploy, like the promise of heaven to a tribe of lost diseased savages. Arcadia is real. In fact its secret location is part of the attraction. Clever.

Now there is an ancient soap opera from somewhere in South America. I wonder if there is still a South America. They all speak Spanish and wear exotic clothes and jewellery. It is like watching aliens. We have become divorced from our own species. We are palimpsests, glimpsing the ghosts of ourselves through a glass darkly. Dad drops off for ten minutes but then he wakes, wincing with pain. Once when he wakes up, I look at the wall and then smile at Dad and nod at the wall. He smiles back and nods a Yes. It's our private joke. I lift my foot and tap with my shoe on the wall in front of me. We wait and seconds later, there is a sudden thunderously loud cacophony of scuttling and tapping and hidden movement, as if a thousand insects are having a mad orgy, dancing in the dark and tapping secret messages to us. Which is exactly what is happening. The layers of wallpaper hardened into cardboard, broke away from the wall, and in the dark concealed gap is a universe of Coleopter, Blattodea, Zygentoma life. Bristletails and cockroaches and beetles and termites and fleas and creatures we call morsemites because it sounds as if scores of tiny agents are tapping secret messages in the dark. Sometimes we try to translate them. 'Help is coming' 'Sorry about the noise' 'Guess what we're building in here' and Dad's favourite: 'Ha! Just when you thought we were dead'. Chloe would have loved this game. The din lasts about thirty seconds and then dies down to silence. A universe of life. We listen and when they stop Dad says "Night, boys and girls. Sleep tight." And we enjoy the moment. Dad winces, closes his eyes and then drifts off into a troubled doze. In my mind I ask Joe what to do. I close my eyes and see him smiling. Crinkly lines around the eyes. Lips I kissed…what, ten thousand times? I think he is telling me to just wait.

I don't have to wait long. The next evening Dad is worse. I look at the leg and it's swollen horribly. Pink and grey. Given his poor health and circulation I'm worried he'll get an embolism. Or the leg will rot and I'll have to amputate. I'm not sure I'm up to it. Even for him. He makes the decision for me.

"If you think it's best…"

"Alright then."

This means a visit to Trash. Not something I relish, but he's the only person I know with a computer.

Trash is a paranoid schizophrenic Aspergers depressive hyperactive sociopath. He's the only friend I've got. I use the term loosely. He lives a mile or so in from the beach on some wasteland in a lock up garage among rusting agricultural machinery. His is the only garage used. The others are in various stages of disintegration. The sole reason he tolerates me is that my Dad is probably the only person with whom he has ever had anything approaching a normal relationship. My Dad was a tool machinist and worked at home. He employed Trash to order parts for him when that was still possible, and to do his paperwork. He idolised my Dad, though of course he would never say that. Perhaps because Dad just treated him like a regular guy and never even referred to any of his weirdnesses. I've never seen him make eye contact with anyone. Occasionally Dad asks me to go and see Trash and say Hi. I haven't seen him leave the garage in a year. No idea where he gets food and supplies. He would hate me to ask, so I don't.

I bang on the lock up door. Then again. I can hear techno music playing – weird stuff that sounds like animals mating.

"Trash. It's Ali. I need a favour. Look, I know you're in there. You never go out."

A pause.

"Trash, this is getting boring."

"Go screw yourself," he says.

"I'll try. Once you do me the favour."

I hear some muttering. Some swearing. Then the door rolls up creakily, shedding cobwebs and dust. Trash looks worse than ever. He wears an old floppy cork hat, his customary homemade glasses – the left round lens from one old pair and the right lens from a thick black framed square pair and tied together in the middle with fuse wire, a sweater down to his knees that bats probably mate in, and baggy cords and odd shoes – one a rubber gardening shoe and one a tasselled golf shoe. He's pointing a gun at me. It's plastic.

"That's a kid's water pistol, Trash."

"Yeh, but it's full of battery acid," he says.

I realise I have no idea how old he is. My Dad met Trash when he was a kid, maybe ten, so that would make him late twenties. He looks about sixty five. Behind him is a floor to ceiling Aladdin's cave of techno junk and mad diagrams. It stinks. He could build a computer from a box of matches and a hairpin. Because he is so outside the ordinary human pale, and that takes some doing now, he has no idea how clever he is. And wouldn't care if he did know. He has music playing constantly. A scary variety of stuff that perhaps shows the eclectic turn of his mind. Rock, old school punk from the dark ages, classical, new wave techno.

"You going to invite me in for cocktails?" I ask.

"What's the favour?" He asks.

"It's for Dad."

Something shifts in him. Wheels turn. He stands to let me inside.

He listens to my plan while looking intently at a soldering iron on the door across two boxes that passes for a desk. His left leg constantly twitches and he thrums the table with his right hand as if playing a keyboard.

"How are you going to pay them?" He asks.

"I made a few good deals," I lie. He knows I'm lying.

"They might refuse."

"They might. But we won't know that until we try."

I'm not stupid enough to offer him money. If I did he would just throw me out. His mind isn't wired like that, or maybe it's become unwired like that.

"His leg is bad. I'm afraid I'll lose him." I try not to get emotional. Trash hates expressions of feeling.

This does it. He logs in on a screen. There is a lot of white noise. Then a message appears: TRY AGAIN LATER. YOUR COMMUNICATION MATTERS TO US. Trash ignores this and tries another route.

"What are you trying?" I ask.

"I'm abstracting physical, spatial, and temporal specifics. Accessing the agent architecture. Decoding the algorithmic interface so I can bypass it and access via a password protected binary code. I have the double-precision floating-point format for most CPUs. You know – the floating radix point," he says.

"Right. That's what I thought," I say.

White noise. A lot of beeps and then a screen with a woman in a white coat. She smiles at us.

"My name is Francine. How can I help?" She asks with a look of phony concern.

"Frigging hologram," Trash says. He types: "I want to send a loved one to Arcadia."

She nods and smiles. "And who is the loved one?"

Trash types in my Dad's name: "Daniel Mace. My father. He needs medical attention too."

"I understand. It's very worrying when a loved one needs help. Our current price is seventy tokens. How much does he weigh?"

Trash frowns. "How is that relevant?" He types.

Francine's look of concern deepens. "We have limited transportation to Arcadia at present, and of course space is needed for foods, medicines and clothing so that all there can have the best life possible. So we have to be absolutely sure of the weight load on each flight."

"About fifty kilos. He's lost a lot," I say.

Trash types it in. Francine looks concerned. Her look changes to abject sorrow.

"At this time, I am afraid we cannot help."

Shit shit shit.

"I'll pay ninety tokens."

Trash types it. Francine considers. "Perhaps with a few realignments we could do something." There is a pause while she smiles and a song from Beforetimes plays – *You are the Sunshine of My Life*. Francine suddenly beams. "Daniel Mace is going to Arcadia. Congratulations. Please pay on collection."

Details are exchanged and I am told to be at Barter Square tomorrow at six pm with Dad. Trash gives me a battered old laptop that I can connect to the TV and talk to Dad when he's in Arcadia. This is generosity that has all but vanished from the world. I am about to thank Trash but bite my lip in time. He goes to a corner of the lock up and starts working on what looks like a transmitter. I have been dismissed. After the initial payment I will have to pay a further ten tokens a month. I'll worry about that when the time comes.

On the way home a dumper truck passes me, driven by a Protector. He looks at me and I acknowledge the look. Two familiar bodies are in the back, loosely tied in and rattling around on the bumpy road. As the truck trundles on I lift two fingers of my right hand to my lips and blow the smoke from my highwayman's pistol. I thank the old man in my mind for the gift that will give Dad a chance to live.

3

There are strange population gaps. When the virus first came things stopped quickly. It's as if the lights in ordinary life went out in a domino effect. Most broadband failed. Mobile phones and tablets were useless. For six months there was nothing, which was a breeding ground for rumour and suspicion and violence. But it was the young who coped the worse. With no screen to live in many fell apart. Depression. Locking themselves in bedrooms. Suicide pacts. They had forgotten how to live in the world, form relationships, take refuge in themselves, how to converse. The worst were the ones who became hysterical. Hospitals were closing so there was no treatment available and many families simply turned them out after months of screaming and fighting. They sometimes formed feral groups. Mad people, little more than children, eyes wide with nothing but hatred for a world that forced them to pay attention to it. They were uncontrollable and dangerous. People called them the Ferals. It was a group of these who came to my house one night when I had gone out looking for work. I think it was a big group. Joe had managed to kill three but the rest overpowered him. I don't know if Chloe had to watch. I think she did because Joe's whole purpose would be to protect her until he could no longer stand. I stood looking at them for hours. Chloe's legs broken, her ears cut off as trophies. Joe disembowelled. As if years of violent video games had suddenly been given a green light in the real world. When I left my soul had become metal. I buried most sympathy and love and concern for others with Joe and Chloe, then torched the house and left. Nowadays I wake up in a sweat and I see them as I found them and work hard to see them as they were alive. If Dad hadn't been around I think I would have stayed in the burning house. All I hope is the Feral group were hunted down by the Protectors. I hope they all screamed. In the Longago macaronic chaos of my heart I try to paint a picture of tender remorse and guddled revenge and sweet kissings and the blood of laughter. I think that I had to start my disappearings to avoid being a pyrophoric killer of the young. The sight of children now makes me shudder.

We saw a group on the beach as I wheeled Dad to Barter Square. Even though he couldn't see me he knew my thoughts.

"Let it go, girl. Let it all go."

"I can't, Dad."

"You have to. Feel it, bury it. Otherwise it'll like bury you."

"I'm going to miss you. Videophone me as soon as you're there. Someone will set it up for you."

"I'll do that."

His leg was worse. But he had spirit, and a doggedness that had endured the death of the world he knew and loved. The group of kids, about eight of them, stood and watched us go by. The worst thing was the unpredictability. You never knew if they were scared little brats who needed a good meal or psychogoblins who would slice you to death for a few tokens. Sometimes a special hunt would be organised as a cull, if there were too many groups in one area. Some liked to watch the hunt and applaud a kill of superfluous Ferals. Not me. I may be a hard-nosed bitch but I'm not a voyeur of murder.

Something aches in me. I realise it is a feeling and I try to squash it. The sight of those Ferals made me think of Chloe and ache to hold her. I swallow hard and imagine the feeling disappearing down a long tunnel. Soon we are at the Square and stand on the corner where the truck will come. I tuck the raggedy blanket around Dad's legs. He looks so frail and cold. His blue eyes are watering in the chill and part of me thinks I should wrap him up and take him home. But this weather, crap diet, no healthcare, his bad leg, this torpid, desiderium life – how long would he last? Gibbosity of despair. And for all I know places in Arcadia may become harder to get, more expensive. I believe in no god and nothing mystical, but the bag full of tokens was a piece of serendipity that came my way and I have to use it for something big, given that the old man gave his life for it. The tokens are in a bag that I've tied inside my coat for safety. It's best to expect the worst and prepare for it. A middle aged woman approaches and nods at me. She has thin blonde hair and scared eyes. Perhaps she is scared because she recognises me as the one who disappears. She carries a little battered valise. A lifetime in a small box. I ignore her but Dad smiles. She's probably on her way to Arcadia too. A part of me is glad Dad won't be alone. I've packed his few clothes, a bar of soap, his little box of photographs – me as a child, Mum, Joe and Chloe, our old dog Rose, his collection of maps that I took off the walls and rolled up for him to decorate his new home.

The truck arrives. A helmeted Protector gets out. He ignores us and opens the back doors. There are three others inside. A youngish man in a battered black suit and two women who cling to each other. They could be twin sisters, in their forties, though it's hard to tell people's ages these days. The Protector looks at Dad's home-made wheelchair and whistles.

"No ramp," he says, lights a cigarette and stands to one side.

The blonde woman gives the Protector her tokens and climbs up on the truck. No way I can lift Dad on my own, and this smoking bastard isn't going to help. If I insult him he'll either taser me or drive away without Dad. The young man inside jumps off and takes one side of Dad's wheelchair and I lift the other. He's in. I hold a wheel to steady him. The Protector flicks away his cigarette and holds out his hand. I give him the tokens.

"When will he get there?" I ask.

"Tomorrow's processing. Flight the following morning. Then a drive to the community. Say two days max. Here's the code so you can get him on vidcall. It's on a timer so you get about ten minutes a day. Sign here."

He gives me a scrap of paper with a code printed on it: MACE72, which is our surname and Dad's age. I sign a paper on a clipboard. I hug Dad's good leg because I can't reach any higher and he pats my head. It is like a papal benediction and I have the hysterical desire to say "Bless me, father, for I have sinned." I hand him the rosewood box with onyx inlay and quartz stones made by Joe. He shakes his head, knowing what it means to me, but I close his fingers over it. He smiles. I'm glad he's not alone. I want him to not feel alone. The young man seems the safest bet. I reach in my pocket and take out my herb knife. It's all I've got on me that's worth anything. I give it to him and say "Keep an eye on my Dad." He takes the knife and nods. I do this only as a bit of security for Dad. I couldn't give a fuck about the young man.

Then the truck is gone and I want to lay down and sleep for a thousand years. I'll get there. Whatever it takes I'll get there and be with him. On my walk back the Ferals are still there, watching. For what? I pick up a stone and throw it at them. They scatter and reform. It was a stupid thing to do. If they follow I'm in trouble. There is a rumour that the ones who have gone seriously apeshit were given an untested version of a vaccine then being used against the virus. The cure was as bad as the disease and created febrile seizures and chronic inflammatory demyelinating polyneuropathy (CIDP), which is a sort of rare neurological disorder where nerve roots and peripheral nerves get inflamed and the fatty protective myelin sheath over the nerves gets destroyed. Their already low levels of self-reliance and concentration evaporated further and we end up with nomadic trasher Ferals of the first order. Then they become Others. I made it my business to learn a lot about this stuff years back for Chloe. So that I could keep her clear of the bad voodoo. Those whom the gods wish to destroy, they first make a fuckwit.

None of the vaccines worked anyway. It was playing catch up with a thing that spread and infected and mutated quicker than anyone could think. So the powers that be just, I think, gave up in the end and consolidated themselves in Dorado. The rest of us hung out to dry. Arcadia is a clever ploy, though. Keeps people focussed, and occasionally working, and making less trouble. Plus it earns. I think Arcadia is probably in Portugal, or Southern Spain, maybe the Canaries. You can see from photos and videos that it's temperate, there are beaches, even palms, and it can't be too far away because beyond the arms of old Europe the war zones start to appear. No point in sending people to a paradise where they get blown to bits. There are Arcadia specials on TV sometimes. Feast days, carnivals, occasionally funerals with sad music and dignified cremations. It's like watching something from another planet. The only attention the dead get here is to rob them and leave the body for collection.

I walk along the beach. The sea spoke to me as a child. I watched the foam chatter its bubbly rumours and the waves were chariots hurling in with the promise of destructive joy and other life beating in ancient wars and lively compact. It enlivened me just to stand and watch the broiling diamond lights and I was breathless in the knowledge that no moment was the same or ever could be and that this living heaving thing before me was magnificent in its indifference to everything but itself. And looking at the sea was like coming home. Crystal shards of light, the little frisky chop chop of smaller waves, the great swells beyond, the mystery of the horizon and the secrets way below where creatures we can only dream of go about their business in the dark womb of the living ocean bed.

The mystery of things in the tiniest organism and the majesty of whales. Now I stare at something like a grey-greenish dead giant slug covering most of the globe and there is nothing to heal in its total demise.

When I get back to Dad's I sit and stare at a wall, feeling the bleak numbness of loss, mixed with relief. That leg was on a trajectory of decay I couldn't control. Now, here on my own, the place seems smaller, the walls dirtier, the scraps of carpet like a dog with mange. My stomach growls but I've forgotten about food. I wish there was some gin left. I rummage through the cupboards under the stairs and find only salt, a jar of pickle, a blunt rusting small axe and an ancient jar of metal polish. I'm tempted to have a swig just to dull me further and give me an hour or two of bad sleep. I take the axe and the polish back and look at dad's empty chair. He would be proud, as I soak an old cloth in the polish and clean the axe. It's blunt but I'll find a flint tomorrow. The axe will be useful for driftwood. I put it under my chair. My other tools are in Dad's old workshop in the small yard. I regret giving away my herb knife. Feeling it in my pocket gave me a spurious sense of security outside. In the kitchen beneath the sink I find a roll of aluminium. I lay it flat on the floor and use the clawhammer I got from the old man to tap the roll until I can get the cardboard tube out, then I keep tapping the foil until it flattens. I light the little camping stove, which is all we have to cook with, and heat the foil, holding it with pliers. Then I beat the foil some more for fifteen minutes until it's hard and flat and the heat cools and hardens it to the consistency of light metal. I finger a shape until I can see it in my mind, and use one of the metal taps and hammer it in the foil all around until I have the rough shape of a six inch hand knife. The chisel helps and soon I can break the knife free. It is ragged edged, so I wedge it between my chair and the wall on the floor and beat the rough edges clean, then I wrap an old rag around the handle. I use the chisel to sharpen the blade a little. It takes an age and even then it isn't sharp, but it is serviceable. Good for vegetables and, at a pinch, it would do human flesh a lot of damage. Tomorrow I will refine it. The knife has taken me two and half hours to make. I put it on the shelf above the old grate and am suddenly overwhelmed with a desire not to be. For my consciousness to be extinguished. I sit and close my eyes. Sleep comes like a drift of black snow.

Chloe comes to me. In my sleep. I guess it's a dream but it seems like something else. It happens every now and then and leaves me with a hole in my heart the size of the dead ocean. *She holds my hand and strokes my arm. I say I wish I could put her back together, the bits they cut and broke and took and that I could put us together too as a family and she says "Silly, we are together. What do you think this is?" I tell her I love her and what I'm doing for Grandpa and she listens but doesn't react. All the things we never said. All the moments not valued like the solid gold they were. She looks sad, then she looks anxious and looks past me at...*

A thin blade of light through a tear in the sack that hangs on the window awakens me. I yawn until my jaw cracks and am aware that my mouth is filthy. I run my tongue over my teeth. I know something is horribly wrong. I am almost too frightened to turn and look, but I do. There are three of them standing in the door frame, one slightly in front. The one with crazy eyes and the knife. My knife.

My first thought is anger. I spent nearly three hours making that knife and now this feral dipbrain has taken it. My second thought is: How could I be so stupid as to leave the door unlocked? I think they may be from the group I threw a stone at. So it's my own ridiculous fault. Which is no comfort at all. The one to the left of crazy Dipbrain looks plain dumb. His face is round, as if someone just painted eyes, nose and mouth on a white blank disc. Thick as a shit pancake through and through. No lights on. The one to the right is a sniggerer. He holds the coats of the big kids and giggles at the violence. But I can see from the way he holds the knife that Dipbrain means violence. I stare him out.

"You want eyes first or tongue?" he says. He means it.

Sniggerer sniggers. And I'm pleased to be right. If I'm going to die it'll be nice to be right about something.

"Tongue. Do the tongue," says Sniggerer.

It's odd how calm I feel. And then a strange thing happens. They start to speak sequentially, one word each in strict rotation as if the same thought is passing through their collective mind: Bleed... her... out... Guts... and... garters... Jizz... this... jugatons... Ogdie... this... booty... Jobby... well... done... Blade... her... bones... Dust... and... stone... Juice... and... sluice... Bitch... now... gone..."

And then they stop. Their expressions don't change, as if they had no consciousness of what they were saying. Even that they were speaking. It was like a litany of intention passing through them. If I survive beyond the next few minutes, which is a moot proposition, I've got food for thought.

"What did that mean?" I ask.

The question doesn't register. They don't know they've done it. Sniggerer sniggers. Dumb looks dumber and Dipbrain just says "Wha' the fuck?" They have no idea of themselves talking their bad rap crap. I sense Dipbrain is tired of this and the kill is coming. Now or never.

"Aren't you going to wait until the show is over?" I say, trying to hide how terrified I am.

Dipbrain frowns. He's going to say Wha' the fuck? Again.

"Wha' the fuck?" He says. Never underestimate the power of human predictability.

"I mean – you don't seriously think I'm alone here. Do you? Why would I leave the front door unlocked? Got my whole family here. You'll never get out alive."

Sniggerer stops sniggering. "Where? How many?" He asks.

"My name is Legion, for we are many," I say.

They are momentarily confused. This is it. High Noon. I reach out my left foot and kick the wall. Within seconds the noise from behind the wallpaper is deafening. The boys and girls are really partying. The Ferals all look uncomprehendingly at the wall. Dipbrain's hand holding the knife drops a little. This is my only chance. I grab the axe from beneath my chair and almost jump at him, raising the axe as I do. He turns and lifts his arm to defend himself but I'm there and swing the axe at his head. It crashes into his skull just above his left eyebrow and with a satisfying crunch cleaves in so fiercely it almost pulls me on top of him as he falls. I yank hard and the axe plops out. It may not be sharp but a human head was no match for it. The knife is on the floor and I grab it with my left hand. Sniggerer and Dumb take a step back. The chorus of creatures behind me feels like applause. Dipbrain is on the floor holding a great flap of flesh with an eyebrow attached from flopping over his eye. I'm pretty sure I got right through to the brain. There is a gloppy stew starting to ooze free. His left leg twitches uncontrollably, heel banging on the floor, and he's wet himself. I hold up the bloody axe and the knife and look at Sniggerer and Dumb.

"Now get the fuck out of my father's house," I say.

The creatures in the wall have stopped. Dumb turns and runs. Sniggerer looks down at the twitching, dying Dipbrain and follows. I get up and close the door. Dipbrain is still alive but has crossed a border and is disappearing into some private darkness. He is stuttering a staccato d-d-d-d-d-d-d- sound and I wonder what he's trying to say. Die? Dad? Deliver me? Then he starts gargling and the smell tells me he's cacked himself. Before I can stop myself I shout "Shut up!" at him, so loud my throat hurts. He looks at me, amazed, and then as if he's thanking me. The hole in his head is pumping his identity out, which is merely a creamy subcutaneous goop. I sit with him while he subsides. I'm amazed when I realise I have put down the axe and am stroking his head. Then he's gone. I shiver and throw up on the floor.

Jesus, it's not been a great start to the day. The look in his eyes. I don't want some feral killer thanking me for putting him out of his misery. It adds another colour to the picture that I don't like. What was hard edged becomes complicated. It softens perception and that's when people weaken. It's the sheer stupidity of things that is a constant reminder of what a failure we are as a species. The ferals would know that in a house like this the likelihood of tokens or food is remote, so the only motive is to do serious damage for the momentary visceral thrill of it. A lightning flash of Chloe a shooting star in my brain, then gone. I spit on the bloodied mess of the feral's head and get to work. I drag the body out to the little enclosed yard and put some sacking over it and tie it tight. At nightfall I'll drag it to the beach and bury it. Maybe prepare a grave during the day and pretend I'm digging in the hope of finding something alive to eat. I don't worry about the little feral band. I think the death of their leader will spook them and they'll probably move on, but I need to be vigilant in case I'm wrong. I clean up the mess on the carpet – his blood and brain and my vomit. I feel shaky.

Where is Dad now? On the plane probably. I hope people help him. The young man with the knife may feel a mild sense of responsibility. I decide to go to Barter Square to see what's doing. I'm out of food and tokens so I need to find something to barter. Occasionally I get a little work for food. Repairing a lock, making a strong box. But it's rare. So far I've resisted sexual favours. Fucking for food is my last resort. I go back out to the yard and search the feral. He has a belt with a faded metal buckle and six notches. In his left back pocket are two tokens. In his right a pencil stub. I take them all.

Barter Square is almost empty. A man with wolfish eyes has a few tins of fish. Mackerel. Ten years past their sell by date, but he still wants five tokens a tin. An old woman has a cardboard box full of what look like conkers from Beforetimes. I look at them. Old and withered and no memory of the shine as they once fell and cracked open their green Viking casing. How many years ago? Then a memory comes. A fire. A Christmas tree with silver fronds of tinsel glinting in the light. A raggedy old doll on top as our fairy. We called her Elsie. Dad wearing a huge white beard. Mum Laughing. I hold a plastic sword that flashed different coloured lights – never much of a girly girl. I'd forgotten about Christmas. And the smell, the smell, sweet and nutty. Not conker. Chestnuts. Of course.

"Chestnuts," I say to the old woman.

She holds out a handful and then two fingers on her other hand. Two tokens. I shake my head. I offer the belt. She examines it. Approves. I stuff the chestnuts in my pocket. On the way back the tide has gone out, leaving its grey-green greasy slime on the beach, like the sheen of dead plasma. I don't think anyone ever seriously thought whole oceans could die. It started during the wars following the virus.

Chemical dumps to spoil food sources for the enemy, but once you start trying to kill on that scale you've already lost control. The oil rig stares defiantly in its decay at the shoreline. The ghosts of workers and engineers haunting the rust.

I stop near the house, find a spatula shaped chunk of tin and start to dig a grave. You can sometimes find something living. Larger phyla on the littoral zones. Lugworms. Smaller bivalves. Even a hardy sand crab whose lineage has somehow escaped Armageddon. Probably full of infection so you boil the thing to hell and hope for the best. No one passing would know I'm digging a grave for a shit-brained feral who just wanted to see someone's blood. I guess he got his wish, in a way. Beware of what you wish for. As I dig I feel a tug in my solar plexus. A strong physical feeling. It happens sometimes, as if I am being reeled into something. Or someone. A pull in my gut, sometimes in my brain, as if someone stands on a hill a hundred miles away with a giant magnet and is pointing it directly at me. It has a slight dizzying effect. I concentrate on the pudding textured, slightly putrid sand, and wait for the feeling to pass.

The chestnuts are full of memories and I sit in Dad's chair savouring both the nutty sweetness and the past. When it's good and dark outside I open the front door and look outside. It's quiet. I go to the yard and grab the bottom of the sack and start to pull the dead body through the house. It's not as hard as I thought. He was pretty skinny. When I get to the door I check outside again. Clear. I drag the body as quickly as I can across the road and bump it down the steps onto the beach. Across the sand to the hole and dump it in. Then I fill it in as quickly as I can and stamp on the sand to pack it down. Whatever mutated microbes are down there will feast well.

I'm sweating heavily and straighten up and wipe my brow with my sleeve. There's a cool breeze and I shiver. I find a flinty stone to sharpen the knife and axe, turn to go back and that's when I see her. Standing ten metres away on the beach by the little roadside wall. Shit. A girl of maybe eleven. Stick thin, ghost white, eyes like dark circles, raggedy reddish hair framing her face. A living doll with dirt smudged cheeks. How long has she been watching? Did she creep up or was she there all the time and I just didn't see her? Is she alone? Is she from the same feral gang as the boy I've just buried? What will she do with what she has seen? I need to know.

"Hi," I say.

Nothing.

"How long have you been watching me?"

More nothing. She doesn't even blink. If she's that far gone perhaps there's no problem. But I can't take chances. I move towards her. She lets me take a few steps then she moves back, one hand on the wall.

"I don't want to hurt you," I say. Unless you mean me harm, of course. Then I'll be digging another hole in the beach. I've had my fill of uppity kids for one day. "Did you see me digging for food? Worms? Crabs? Snails?" She just stares. This kid is flipped out big time. "Just get lost, will you?" I say and head back to the house. When I reach the door I look back and she's gone. I don't think I need to worry about her, but I keep the knife in my pocket just in case. There is more than enough craziness orbiting this cracked world.

I ransack the kitchen cupboards and find a packet of soup powder and two potatoes hiding in the dark. The white sprouts are like starched triffids. I cut them out, boil the potatoes and stir in the soup powder. I have three cooked chestnuts left and add them. It will have to do until tomorrow. As I eat I try the laptop. I key in the code: MACE 72. Nothing. White noise. Then grey noise. Then black noise. The Protector said two days max, which is about now, but maybe I'm jumping the gun. Things are never what you are told. I sharpen the axe and the knife. Good solid tools. I miss seeing my tools all in their rightful place in my little workshop. I should have got them before I torched the house but I just wanted to leave as quickly as possible and do my mourning away from the bleeding carnage. I'm just entering a darker than usual mood of bitter goblinry when the screen bleeps, flashes and there he is. Dad. He's smiling.

I press the record button so I can rewatch this. We both start talking at once. Both stop. Both start again and then laugh. He is sitting in a smallish room, walls painted white, a print of Turner's *Storm at Sea* on the wall behind him, the light coming from a window or glass door on his left, some fresh daffodils on the desk before him. God, I'd forgotten how much flowers enliven a room. When did I last see flowers like these growing, and not the ragged chickweed and briar that mostly grows now? I drink in every detail. He's had a shave and his hair has been combed. I can almost smell him. Not an old decaying smell but something warm and seasoned and reassuring that was the essence of him. There is a crutch leaning against his chair. I tell him to go first.

"Got here few hours ago, Ali. Nice room. And we had a d...." his voice trails into static.

"Can't hear you, Dad. Have they fed you?"

He seems to strain to hear. There's obviously a relay delay.

"Yes. Wonderful food. Some sort of soya thing but with onions and greens. Gravy. And fresh apples." And he holds up a rosy red apple as if he's a conjuror producing a rabbit from a hat. We both laugh.

"How about your leg?" I ask.

With some difficulty he uses the crutch to haul himself up and shows a fresh white plaster on his leg. Thank God for that. Without those tokens he'd be in real trouble now.

"Is that sunshine outside?"

"Yes. Lovely and warm here."

So maybe it is Spain, Portugal, the Canaries, Ibiza?

"Dad, the boys and the girls were partying heavily last night. What do you think they were saying?"

The picture goes fuzzy, then a countdown message appears: 9.57, 9.58, 9.59...and the screen goes blank. That was a quick ten minutes. But at least I know he's there. And safe. And looked after. Now I need to get myself there. Seventy tokens.

Tomorrow I need to find work. Or another magic bag.

4

The raggedy beach sloops around my feet like grey pus. Occasionally people try to swim but they are usually people with either a death wish or who have parted company with their wits. Enough of those to start a small country. I wonder if far out and under, leagues and leagues beneath the surface, way below the photic zone, some creatures might still live. Mutations perhaps. Or glass sponges. Frilled Shark. Fangtooth Fish. Vampire Squid. Pacific Viperfish. Giant Tube Worms. Waiting until we are gone and the great oceans sluice their sicknesses away over millennia and then these creatures will swim, float and grope up, or send their spores towards light where they will grow, finger by finger around a brain and guts and then break surface to take that first terrifying, spittling squeezebox gush of air in new lungs made from ancient tissue. I cannot talk much to people, except Dad, so my thoughts dive deep and solitary into myself, which is like this dead swill of gutwater. I live far inside myself, except it is more like a long dying. Sometimes I think I am this dead ocean.

Barter Square is pretty full, but in terms of supply and demand, the demanders outnumber suppliers probably five to one. There are often a few grabbers hanging around watching. These are people on the make. Most are criminals but sometimes they are offering or looking for something like real work used to be. I walk slowly past them, looking at each face. A tall man with straggly, grey long black hair and wearing filthy overalls and a torn leather biker jacket meets my eyes. He looks me up and down.

"Work?" He asks.

I nod.

He turns and walks away. I follow him to an old van. He doesn't look back and gets in the driver's seat. I feel the knife in my pocket. I'm not getting in that van without knowing more. We have a one minute standoff, and then he sighs and speaks, still looking ahead.

"Up coast. Lowestoft. Food processing. One day. Fifteen tokens."

Fifteen tokens is a lot. For one day's work. There must be a catch. Either it's something else altogether, for which I could get shot, or raped, or it's something illegal and must be done quickly. And what does food processing mean anyway? He takes five tokens from his pocket and holds them out.

"On account. Rest when it's done."

I need the money. I take the tokens and minutes later we're bumping along the pitted road to Lowestoft. He's not a conversationalist, which suits me fine. I wonder where he gets petrol. There are no filling stations and it's expensive. Five tokens for a litre bottle at Barter Square. It's a while since I've been in a vehicle and I'm astonished at how the roads have deteriorated. Pot holes everywhere. Cracks like old scars. Rubbish strewn on the kerbs. As we approach Lowestoft there are more people on the street. From the A12 we cross the Inner Harbour onto the A47. No one begs anymore because there's no point. A gang of ferals watch us as if their eyes are on one string being pulled. Every time I see a gang of them I wonder: was it you? Or you? Or you? Or all of you, taking turns on Joe and Chloe. Then, irrationally, I want to gut them anyway. When all law and all good feeling goes, there are only the rules you make up for yourself. I improvise mine, moment by moment. I am a constant surprise to myself and never know what I am capable of. The sooner I get my seventy tokens the better. Dad will regain some health and whatever time is left we can spend together.

We turn right at a roundabout and then left towards Gas Works Road. I memorise the route in case I need to make a quick getaway. Gutted warehouses and workshops everywhere. Anything of any use will have been taken long ago. The harbour has a metallic stink with undertows of organic things rotting. Sometimes people in coastal towns just dumped their dead in the sea because it was easier and funerals had died out – no pun intended. We are going towards Ness Point, the most Easterly point in the country. We arrive at a large lock up and the driver parks on the side facing the sea so we won't be visible. He gets out and looks around. Keys the lock up open and looks at me.

It's dark inside and the smell is so horrendous I start to gag. How many dead rotting things are there in here?

"You get used to it," he says, and lights an old fashioned kerosene lamp. There are metal bins lining the walls and two swab tables. A small camping gas stove, some little machines I don't recognise and kitchen utilities – a colander, saucepans, sieves, knives, ladles, graters. He gives me a mask, which I fasten on. It has a menthol impregnation which masks some of the rotting smell, but he doesn't put one on himself. He takes the lid off one of the metal bins and smiles. His teeth are like brown tombstones. I look in the bin. It is full of decomposing fish, with a few eels and what look like sea snakes. These creatures must have been dead a long time because you can't find fish in any bartering place that I know of.

"Where did you get these?" I ask.

"Found an old fishing boat along the coast. The hold full of dead fish and stuff. Was so cold they hadn't rotted down. So I bring them here. Freeze them and then unfreeze them. Now we cook 'em."

"But they're all completely rotten. Eat these and it's a death sentence."

"Yeh. No. We cook for the oil. Then I sell it."

"To cook with?"

"Mebbe. Mebbe not."

"Chatty bastard, aren't you?"

He shows me. Scoop a saucepan full of fish out and boil them for fifteen minutes. Then pour off the liquid from the top into another saucepan. Wait until it cools little and the oil separates from the water and rises to the top. Spoon out the oil into jars and then when they are completely cool, seal them. It takes a hell of a lot of dead fish to get one jar full of oil, and the work is hot and arduous because he has locked us in and there are no windows and no air coming in.

After four hours I stop. He looks at me quizzically.

"I'm going outside for ten minutes," I say.

Outside the air is cool. I've taken off the mask, of course, and I grab lungfuls of air. There is the stench from the harbour but it's like primrose paradise compared to inside the lockup. A few minutes later he joins me and smokes a cigarette. It smells like herbs soaked in petrol. People will smoke anything these days. He takes a crust of bread from his pocket and scrapes a light ash of mould from it. He breaks off a small piece and offers it to me. I take it and chew. It tastes like cardboard. He continues to smoke while he chews.

"You been to Dorado?" I ask.

He looks sideways at me. "Close. They got food there you wouldn't believe. Vegetables so fresh they talk to you. Even some animals they saved from the virus. Pigs mostly. Chicken. Big and plump."

"You've seen them?"

"One time. Making a delivery. Forget going there. Lockdown on Dorado's tougher than ever." Charmer that he is, he flicks the butt into the soupy water, spits after it and taps his wrist. "Playtime's over," he says.

I get into a rhythm of scoop, boil, sieve, cool, ladle. And get more done by cooking one batch while another is separating. After four more hours of sweaty work we have ten jars of oil. Then he opens another metal bin that is full of sunflower seeds and shelled nuts. All old but priceless.

"Where did you get these?" I ask.

"Friends in low places," he says, and shows me how to warm up an oil press by igniting a heating lamp, and then hand cranking a press filled with nuts and seeds, and slowly the oil collects below. We each have a press and work for two hours. He wipes his brow, spits in a saucepan of mushed fish, and says "Clocking off." We put the jars in two cardboard boxes and take them out to the van. He locks up and we are on the way back to Kessingland. It is starting to get dark and what I know will happen does. He pulls off the road and stops the van in a deserted alley.

"You worked good," he says.

"I know."

"Now it's playtime," he says. And moves towards me, puts his left arm around me and his right turns my head for what would be the most disgusting kiss in the history of this misbegotten ruined world. He pulls back as he feels the point of my homemade knife against his belly.

"Meet my friend," I say.

"Alright. Only a bit of fun."

"Said the spider to the fly. Now. Three things. One. Given me my tokens. Now."

He takes ten tokens from his pocket and counts them out in my free hand.

"Two. Drive."

He backs the van out and we joined the road. I keep the knife against him. We drive in silence for a few minutes.

"What's three?" He asks.

"The oil. It's not for cooking. There would be easier ways if it was for a machine. So I'm stumped. What's it for?"

He looks at me and smiles.

"Hell, you wouldn't understand."

"Try me."

An extraordinary transformation takes place. His face metamorphoses from being an ugly chancer with tombstone teeth to something like an intelligent gerbil.

"The vegetable oil. If you want a method for producing an emulsion device having a viscosity greater than 240,000 cps and which is essentially free from high shear induced crystallization, you need a melt or aqueous phase solution of an oxidizer salt. Then forming a liquid, water-immiscible, organic fuel phase which comprises at least about fifteen per cent vegetable oil. This increases the viscosity, and the resistance to high shear induced crystallization."

He looks at me, smug as a cat in a cream factory. Now I get it.

"Explosive device. You're making fucking bombs," I say.

His jaw literally drops. "How'd you know?"

"And the fish oil. To make nitro glycerine. You are a one person explosives factory. I was an engineer. A good one. Who buys them?"

"No idea. I get a call. An order. I meet them on a dark night."

We arrive at Barter Square. He looks at me.

"You know that if you tell anyone you're dead. I mean, you inform the Protectors they'll assume you're involved and just trying to cover yourself and you'll be the first one with a goodnight forever bullet in your head. Or worse, they'll put you in a hunt."

"How about I come and steal your stuff?"

"I use different lock ups in different places."

"Alright then."

I get out. He gives me a scrap of paper with a number on it. Also a name. Jez.

"Ring me in say two weeks. I'll have more work if you want it."

I jingle the tokens in my pocket. Five, maybe six more work days like that and I'm on my way to Arcadia. It'll be a few months but I have something to work for now.

Whom the gods would destroy they first make mad.

5

It is crackly. The picture fuzzes at times, but he's there and looks like he's recovering. We talk about his leg, and about what he does there – reads, a lady in the next room brings him a cup of chocolate (I make a joke about romance in the air, which he ignores). He says it's nine o'clock there in the evening, so an hour ahead, which gives me clues as to his whereabouts. I have a theory that there might be pockets of places that have escaped devastation, whether because of tidal patterns, or lack of Covid infections, or just good luck, and obviously Arcadia is one of them. But I also think there are very few, maybe only one or two, which is why they are kept secret. I tell him I've been working and will apply to join him as soon as possible. There is something about the room that doesn't seem right, and then I realise what it is. The maps. They would be the first thing he put on the walls. Perhaps they have rules about stuff like that. Or perhaps they are pinned up where I can't see them. I ask him where the maps are but he clearly can't hear me. I ask again and there is static, then he's back.

"Dad. Have you got your maps?"

"Yes. Got them."

"Where are they?"

"I think they're in my bag still."

"Alright then. High five." I raise my right hand and he raises his. Yes, it's him, there is the crooked little finger that broke and never healed. But still…"Dad, have you got the picture of Rosie safe?"

He looks baffled.

"Rosie. Our old cat?"

He smiles.

"Yes, Rosie's picture safe and sound in my drawer."

"And the maps. I didn't forget any? You've got the one of the old Welsh borders? Your favourite."

"All safe, Ali."

"Good. I love you."

"I love you."

The countdown starts and the call ends. My heart is frozen solid. I can barely breathe. I stare at the screen, wanting to put my foot through it. All is through a glass darkly. Ash in my mouth. Everything unreal. I look at my hands and wonder who they belong to and what they will do next. As if in reply they reach up and cradle my face as I lean forward and rock in the chair. Someone is moaning and I realise it is me. Hours go by. I stand and look out of the window. In the moon-dry night a faint spectre. I breathe her name. Chloe. But it is the saucer-eyed redhead girl standing staring at me. I open the front door but she is gone. The cool night air biles in my throat. I go to the kitchen and gulp down a glass of water, then lie on the floor and roll into a tight ball, as small as I can make myself. I want to disappear. I ask the great nothingness all around to make me part of itself, part of the vast indifference which is our true home. Something like death comes and I ask Joe why things happen and he smiles and says "Because they have to." Chloe floats by and says "Stand and deliver!" and I see Bess, Dick's beautiful horse, her sweat gleaming in moonlight, the cold dragon mist spraying from her nostrils and a beautiful light in the big eyes. *His blood spins through his veins; winds round his heart; mounts to his brain. Away! Away! He is wild with joy.* I long for the oblivion of riding away and of not being. Do I prolong the suffering for Joe and Chloe by carrying them in the rags of my heart? But how do you let them go? Only by following them into the dark.

Trash is even less communicative than usual. It takes fifteen minutes of pounding and pleading before he opens the garage. Some old fashioned English folk music is playing. He blinks in the light behind his ridiculous glasses. He points the water pistol at me, looks around and lets me in. I realise that I don't actually know what he does all day. He fiddles with computers and gadgets but is there some overriding purpose?

"What do you really do all day, Trash?" I ask. "What's it for?"

This is too up close and personal. He looks around suspiciously. Says nothing. When someone has deliberately dug a cave for themselves, the last thing they want is some nosey parker shining a torch in it. He's breviloquent at the best of times but now I'm not even getting grunts. I pick up a chip from his worktop and he snatches it back.

"That's the Brahms. Violin Concerto in D major, Op.77. Only gets played on a day like no other."

"Alright then. I wait for that day. Watch," I say.

I open the laptop and we watch me talking to Dad. The whole ten minutes. Trash grunts.

"What do you see?"

"Your dad. You and him talking."

"But you know how he loved those maps and they're not on the wall. And I asked him about his favourite map of the Welsh borders. There is no map of the Welsh borders. I ask him about Rosie the cat. There was no Rosie. When I ask him anything too specific the screen goes fuzzy."

Now I've got Trash's interest. He watches the whole thing through again. Then he starts to enhance the picture. Then he brings up an inset corridor on the screen of numbers and signs. He hisses through his teeth.

"What?" I ask.

"Heuristic algorithms. Smart digit classifier network. Copies pixelated neural pathways," he mutters almost to himself.

"Plain language, Trash."

"It's fake. He's not in that room. They filmed him somewhere, probably in front of a green screen, got his voice and body recorded, created digital neural networks to track and replicate his mouth movements. Synched audio and visual so that video of him is generated just by sound. Hologram it into this room, and your voice stimulates it into action, and within a limited range of information it can hold a conversation. Because it's smart it learns too, so what he gets wrong in one conversation he'll get right next time. I mean it, not he."

It's only what I knew, but the brutality of confirmation drives a spike deeper in me. I need to know and I need to cause someone a lot of pain.

"So where's my dad?"

Trash shrugs. "He's sure as fuck not in Arcadia."

"Bastards."

"What will you do?"

"Find out where he is."

"Good luck with that. You start making trouble they'll get you."

"Thanks. Vote of confidence is what I need right now."

"Watching. Making connections. Joining up the dots."

"What?"

"What I'm doing. You asked."

"And what have you found out?"

"A lot of possibles. About…" he waves a hand vaguely, indicating everything and nothing.

"Will you tell me what they are? If I come back when I feel less like murdering someone?"

"Maybe."

I turn to go.

"Your dad. You know he might…"

"Don't say it."

Walking back I realise that a part of me never trusted Dad being taken to Arcadia. I thought I'd been cured of hope but any chance of him living a slightly better life than in this diseased shithole of a country seemed worth taking. Who was I fooling? Since when have people been given a break? When you're desperate you start to think there might really be a tooth fairy. Perhaps they sift out only the old sick ones and just take the money. He could be stuck in some god-awful hole somewhere. I must believe they didn't just kill him. If they kill everyone they take surely word would have escaped. A rumour.

Chinese whispers. Do we really know nothing? He's probably in some hideous dormitory with a lot of infected deadbeats. I feel someone watching me but whenever I look around there is no one. I have the awful sensation again of being pulled somewhere and I sit on the beach wall for a few minutes until it passes. My first step when I get home is to make contact and ask a few questions.

The same hologram Francine in a white coat smiles out at me.

"How can I help?" She asks.

"It's about my father. I paid for him to go to Arcadia."

"If you have any questions it is best to got to our central website."

"I want to know where he is."

"Arcadia."

"No. He's not. I just want to know."

"If you have any questions it is best to got to our central website."

"Where is he?"

"If you have any questions it is best to got to our central website."

Alright then. Stand and deliver, bitch. If I must I'll go to Dorado. I owe it to Dad. He didn't want to go and I forced his hand. He could be sitting here with me. We could have at least watched the world go to hell together. Why is it that you feel love for someone most acutely when they aren't there? I spend the rest of the day feeling hungry but I can't be bothered to go to Barter Square. I crawl into bed and shiver. Somehow sleep comes. A door opens and as I pass through I am a little girl again and there are green things in the garden and butterflies. I skip and stop in front of a stranger. What is he doing in my garden? He has black trousers and a white shirt and wears a black hat with a wide rim. Watching a little away is the wide eyed redhead girl. She nods to the man and he crouches down and looks in my eyes. I feel that he knows my thoughts, my secret self that no one should know.

"Remember this," he says, and opens his hand to reveal a shiny blue pebble. "Everything is a key to something else. Even this."

I laugh and say it's not a key, it's a stone. He closes his fist and opens it again and instead of a pebble there is a silver key. I look up into his face and he's now Joe, my future husband. He gives me the key, looks sad, stands and walks away. As he does so the garden drains of colour, as if someone has pierced it and the world's bloom is leaking out. I look down and the key has turned to ash. I feel rain drops on my hands and face and legs. Angry dark clouds ravage the sky and suddenly a lightning bolt zig zags down like a fresh scar and hits the tree at the bottom of our garden, and coils back into itself and a cannon of thunder booms across everything. And again. And again. I cannot understand why the thunder booms so persistently until my eyes flicker open and I know it is not thunder at all.

The banging on the door continues as I stumble downstairs. I hold my knife in my pocket. I open the door and two Protectors stand there, helmets on, visors down. They do this ostensibly to protect from infection but really it's to maintain anonymity. If you see the face and eyes clearly, you might spot a weakness, or that it's a person like you, and they don't want that. Given that we've all been stripped of most of our humanity I can't see why it matters, but oftentimes it's a mistake to look for logic. It is the very illogicality of many things that blinds us to the real.

"Alison Steel. Formerly Mace?"

I nod. He hands me an envelope. The other looks away at the beach, bored. I take the envelope and am about to close the door, but he wedges his foot in it.

"Open it now."

"Why?"

"It's an invitation. I need to report back that you accept. It's protocol."

"Pro-to-col" the other echoes, still looking away.

I open the envelope, assuming it's about Dad. It's not.

Dear Alison Steel,

Congratulations. You have been chosen to be a participant in the next Hunt in your region. It will be a great challenge to your powers of invention and courage. Protectors will collect you on the morning of April 9th at 8 am. You will be provided with everything you need for this momentous day. It will, as convention decrees, be televised to everyone in every region.

Our most sincere regards

The Hunt Committee

The spit dries in my mouth. "This is a death sentence," I say.

The Protector shrugs. "You have to say you accept."

"Pro-to-col," says the moron watching the beach.

"Why me? It's usually Ferals and known offenders."

He shrugs again. "Say you accept."

No point in arguing. "I have no choice."

"That's an acceptance. Have a nice day."

They both turn and walk away to their van. There on the beach is Chloe, her back to me looking at the sea. My heart stops. She turns around and it is the redhead girl. I start towards her but she walks quickly away, calling out something to the breeze that I can't make out. I shut the door and lean against the wall and slowly slump down. "Dad. Dad," I whisper.

If Trash is annoyed that I'm back yet again he hides it well. His small glittering dark eyes widen behind his home-made glasses when I show him the Hunt invitation. He flicks his hand derisively at the word 'invitation.' He asks what I did when I last left him. I tell him I went online to find where Dad is.

"Did you get heavy about it?"

I nodded.

"This is your punishment. Open dissent or criticism. Bad idea."

"What can I do?"

"You're screwed. No choice. They'll sling you in anyway. And if they have to force you there will less in the bag of tricks. It's a lose lose situation."

The hunt works like this. You are collected in a van and driven blindfold to the location for the hunt, which is different each time. It covers an area of several square miles and you know when you reach a perimeter because there's a force field that stops you. Before you are released you are given a bag of tricks. They are not obvious things like weapons, but clues. So a single shoe might be telling you to find the other shoe and inside that will be something to help you. Or a small pot of paint may be telling you to find a building that has the same coloured door or walls and inside will be something useful. In the bag will be a few rogue clues, things that have no helpful meaning at all, and you can be sitting still trying to puzzle it out when a Protector's bullet says hello to your brain. There are ten hunter Protectors and ten hunted. The Protectors only have three bullets each and then they are on their own, but that's still thirty chances of getting killed. The last survivor is set free. Most people watch because there's not much else on TV and because it has all the fascination of a car crash. You can't help yourself. Dad refused to watch and I was glad for that.

Trash had closed the lock up door and was sorting through a jumble of boxes. How was it possible to cram so much crap into one lock up garage, and live there as well? He holds up a small old school mobile phone. Few people have mobiles now. No one can afford them and signals get blocked and scrambled anyway. You're not allowed any contact with anyone during the hunt. Trash tells me to hide this in my bra and wear a small wireless earpiece. He says he'll be watching the hunt and can communicate with me. It's on such a low frequency it flies below the official and standard wavelengths. He tells me that in the bag of tricks nothing will be what it seems and I have to think tangentially.

"There's something else. Do you sometimes have the feeling that you're being pulled? Or called? Summoned in some weird way? And you feel slightly sick when it happens."

I look at him. This man is full of surprises.

"How do you know?" I ask.

"You've been chipped. They can pull you in any time they want. But I think they sometimes use it in the hunt to locate someone. It's why the Protector bastards seem so frigging adept at hunting down people."

I suddenly feel unclean. Violated. Are my thoughts really my own? Does someone in an air con office know what I'm thinking? Everything in my life in unravelling further just when I thought I'd peaked on the crapometer.

"How would they have done it?" I ask.

"Vaccinations against the virus were the most common way. Did bugger all against the virus because when it ran into an enemy it simply mutated. But people who had it got chipped. It's pretty rudimentary. Just a homing signal. They can't do anything else with it. But it's a fucker in the hunt."

"So my chances go from zero to minus zero?"

"That's about it."

"I was being sarcastic. You're meant to reassure me, Trash."

He ignored me and started rummaging through another box.

"So these are the dots you're joining up?" I ask.

"Some. Not all."

"And is your overriding purpose to save the human race?"

He splutters and I realise it's his version of laughter. I've never seen him do it before.

"Why the fuck would I do that? The human race is a mistake. I just want to know what's happening."

"Alright then."

He's found what he's looking for. Some sort of handheld scanning device. He blows dust off it and bangs it on his worktop. A dead cockroach drops from inside the rim. He checks the batteries and replaces one that has corroded. He switches it on and starts scanning me.

"If it's in a major organ or nervous system or, fuck forbid, your brain, there's nothing we can do, but….ah, here we go cheerio."

He holds the scanner over my foot and it beeps.

"It's under your little toe nail."

"How does it help to know where it is?" I ask, fearing the answer.

Trash reaches into a box and takes out a rusty knife. He wipes it on his sleeve. Then he finds a pair of pliers.

"I won't lie to you. This is going to hurt you much more than it is me."

The piece of cloth I chew on and scream into is foamed and bloody and my teeth ache. I bit into my cheek and practically clawed a hole in the workbench. As the pain abates from screaming agony to a piercing throb I open my eyes. Trash is smiling to himself as he scrutinises something on a tiny glass plate. He has ear plugs in, presumably to block my screaming. Being as far on the spectrum as he must be means you don't have to waste time on gratuitous empathy. He takes the plugs out and hands me a greasy rag to wipe my sweaty face. I decline.

"See? Like a pin head."

I can see a tiny white dot. He wraps it, still on the glass, in a bit of rag and places it in a matchbox.

"Take this on the hunt. You might be able to use it to distract them. If they try to track you leave it somewhere."

I pocket the matchbox. My little toe is minus a nail and bleeds freely. It hurts like a bastard. No point in asking if Trash has any bandages. I just hope it doesn't get infected. My stomach growls and I feel faint.

"Do you have anything to eat? A biscuit?" I ask.

He looks around helplessly, as if I'd asked for a golden mermaid. How does he survive? "However bad you think it's going to be, it'll be worse. And you'll be shit scared. And most people watching won't care if you live or die," he says.

"Is this your pep talk to inspire confidence in me? If so, it's made me feel worse."

"Listen to your fear. It will help you. And don't forget, you have a secret weapon."

"What's that?"

"Moi."

"You've just ripped off my toe nail."

"In a good cause."

"Alright then."

6

I walk back slowly. My toe sends a new shard of pain through me with each step. I'm dehydrated and my tongue is swollen. I spit blood from where I bit my cheek. I have two days before the hunt. I need rest and food if I'm going to have any chance of survival. At home I bathe my toe and bind it, drink a litre of water and lay down for an hour. I suspect Trash is right. Putting me into the hunt is a punishment for asking where Dad is. Why are they so frightened that they have to kill me? What are they hiding? Or maybe it's simply that any nuisance is promptly scotched. I'm under no illusions that my life has any significance to anyone other than Dad. I close my eyes and picture Joe and ask him to help me find food. He smiles and shrugs. I trace the tiny scar on his forehead where a bramble caught him. It was before Chloe and we had walked in a woods and made love and as I looked up at the sky I thought This is a perfect moment, I must always remember it. Sun, sky, warm breath of the man I love, the ache of desire, the wet melting pleasure and a smell of mint and blackberries. Fucking my good man while the sun warms the curls in the nape of his neck and my fingers clawing hungrily at his back. A time between the viruses. Covid 19 had dissipated but we had other scares and then Covid 24 came like Armageddon. Conspiracy theorists were seen as either prophets or lunatics. Some were disappeared under new emergency laws against dissent. People became frightened of saying anything controversial, frightened of each other and frightened of themselves. How quickly humanity crashed. Seems like a lifetime ago.

    I'm awoken by a gentle knocking at the front door. I rouse and open it. No one. At my feet is a cardboard box with a withered piece of ragwort placed on top. Jacobaea vulgaris or Stinking Willie. And a seashell with beautiful whorls that curl like tracer comets in a far off long dead universe. Chloe loved shells. We imagined the creatures that once inhabited them and gave them names and identities and stories. And it would always end with Dick Turpin flourishing his pistol, and saying, "Keep your gold, but stand and deliver your shells!" and we'd both laugh. I think people leave their own whorls of being, a ghostly palimpsest that speaks through the living if we let it. Could the ferals have left this box? Will I find a dead thing or a live and stinging thing inside? I take out my knife and gingerly lift the top of the box. What is this? A trick? A joke? Inside is half a loaf of bread, two tins of beans, an onion, and a small pack of biscuits. I look around again and then take the box inside and close the door. Is it poisoned?

    Trash is the only person who could have left it, but I dismiss the thought. He never leaves the lock up. I've never seen him eat. And if he was going to give me food why not do it when I was there and asked if he had anything I could eat? I try a little of the bread. It tastes fine. If it's poisoned it's too late now. I open one of the tins of beans and eat them with more bread. I tie Chloe's lemon ribbon around my neck and try to sleep. If I don't wake up it will be no great loss.

They come just after eight on the morning of the ninth. The same two Protectors who delivered the 'invitation.' The second one who never looked at me is yawning behind his visor. Let me call them Number one and Number Two. Number One frisks me and removes my knife. He tut tuts. "Can't take nothing to the hunt. All you need will be provided."

"Ev-e-ry essential," says moronic Number Two.

I get in the back of the van and I am blindfolded. The moron tells me if I take off the blindfold or try to escape he will break an arm, which will severely reduce my already non-existent chances of survival. Then he starts singing an old song *All You need is Love*. "Nothing you can do that can't be done, nothing you can sing that can't be sung…doo dee doo dee dee something or other…All you need is love, doo deee doo deee doo, All you need is love, All you need is love, love, Love is all you need. Don't write 'em like that now."

"They don't write nothing now, you twat."

"Shame in a way. Bit of a sing song. Anyways, I reckon this one, gone in the first four."

"Two tokens?"

"Done."

I realise they are betting on how long I will last in the hunt. I have the chip in a flattened matchbox and the little mobile phone taped inside my bra, but these now seem like pathetic bulwarks against death. I'm surprised I am not more terrified. The idea of sustained pain frightens me more than the thought of dying. Except I want to see Dad one last time. Something in me believes he is alive. Somewhere. I shut off the Protectors' voices and summon Dad when he was younger, when I was a girl, but somehow me as a little girl keeps conflating with the redhead girl, and then with Chloe, and I must dispel the butchery and carnage that often chase on the tail of memories of my daughter. I realise now why it was so crucial for me to get Dad to Arcadia. It was a validation, if not a redemption. A small atonement for the husband and daughter I could not save. I was doing it for myself as much as Dad.

We drive for about two hours. The van stops and a checking of numbers and huge metal gates are opened. Then we are on a bumpy track. The van stops and the doors open. I am led out and I blink tears when the blindfold is taken off. I look around. We are in an abandoned factory. A toy factory. There are aisles full of boxes, some spilling things — tractors, puppets, game consoles, fluffy bears. It is an eerie child's paradise gone sour, for everything is dirty and rotting. A smell of dust and faeces. There are rat droppings everywhere.

"Happy fucking Christmas," says Number Two cheerily, looking at me for the first time.

"Twenty four hours we'll be back."

"To take me home," I say.

They both laugh at this. Number One gives me a backpack, my bag of tricks, and they both walk away. I look around. Quiet. I walk to the middle of an aisle stacked with dolls three metres high, where I have a good view of both ends, which are a long way off. Maybe sixty metres. I sit down. Inside the bag are six things. A large oak leaf and I wonder that there are still oak trees anywhere. A little wooden flute. A silver painted key, like the key to an old fashioned door. A box of matches. A biscuit that looks like a dog biscuit. The last thing makes me gasp and choke back a sob. A photograph of Chloe, not long before she was murdered. She is smiling straight at the camera. At me. What perverse slice of cruelty is this? Where did they get it? What does it mean?

A movement next to me makes me start. I am sitting next to a doll with bright pink cheeks and a cloud of curly golden hair. She has one huge blue staring eye and one brown eye that is moving. A large cockroach is poking its head through. Probably a whole family of them in there. I put the things back in my bag and think about the phrase bag of tricks. Tricks mean someone gets fooled. I must make sure it isn't me. There is dark magic at work. I open the top of my shirt and switch on the phone in my bra. I assume I'm being watched so I have to be careful with it. I know it's a mistake to stay put. The Protectors will be making decisions about who to hunt first. They usually work in threes so they can pincer-trap people. I walk around to the next aisle, which is full of games consoles. I try one and it's dead. So is a second. But a third works. I think of the fish bomb man, Jez. I open the games console and it's got a lipo battery. I find another working six and take out the batteries. Three are highly charged. I find a sharp piece of wire, like a pin, take a chance and pierce the ends of the batteries, and then put them in a games box and pack bubblewrap from toy boxes so that the batteries are tightly compacted. I leave the box among the dolls because they are plastic and many have highly flammable hair. I need to move and wonder which thing in the bag of tricks to consider first. I wish Trash would make contact. A low growl startles me and I turn and face the biggest dog I've ever seen in my life.

A Doberman standing five feet high with great mucousy trails swinging from its' jaws. Mad eyes. If I run it will be on me in a second. It emits another low growl like a train shunting. I wonder how long it takes to die with a dog chewing on you. Quick is probably best, so absurdly I'm hoping that when it comes it comes fast and efficient, tears my throat out and releases me. The thought also comes that this is unusual. I've never seen dogs used in the hunt before. Maybe they are adding a spice of novelty. Keep viewers sharp. The dog takes a step forward and seems to be shimmering with murderous intent. How could a dog get to be the size of a horse? Suddenly a voice whispers "Throw the dog biscuit!" I freeze and then realise it's Trash. I open the bag, take out the dog biscuit and throw it at the dog. He catches it in his mouth and swallows it, and then almost seems to smile. The tension leaves its heaving muscular frame and it shimmers, as if its whole biological structure is undergoing some huge internal transformation. Was the biscuit poisoned? I can't believe what I am seeing. It seems to shrink. No. It is shrinking. This beast is actually getting smaller. I wonder if I've been given an hallucinogenic. The dog keeps shrinking. Now the size of an Alsatian, now the size of a poodle, now a westie, now a chihuahua, now a mouse. Gone. Just the biscuit on the ground. What the hell is happening?

"Hologram," Trash whispers. He's actually enjoying this.

"How can you see what's happening?" I ask.

"Carrier-neutral datacentres are by definition served by multiple ISPs. So what I did…"

"Forget it."

Sometimes they loosen you up with fear. Prime you for the kill. That was the purpose of the dog psychologically. Other than that it was just good old fashioned entertainment for the viewers. The bag of tricks at its best.

"You have company," Trash says and then the signal goes. I look behind and at the end of the isle is a Protector. I know he won't shoot from there. This is a TV realtime show so they want to let the drama build for a while. I take out the matches and light the box containing the lipo batteries. I have no idea if it will work. Ideally they would be fully charged. I slowly back away to the other end of the isle. I am assuming there will be at least one other Protector, probably two. I'm caught in an alley of mad dolls piled twice my height. I'm right and a second Protector appears at the other end of doll alley. This must be the easiest kill they've ever had. And I'm probably the first of the day. The first Protector has reached the box I lit and looks down at it curiously. A pitiful little flame splutters. He pokes it with his foot and the box detonates. The sound is deafening. The second Protector is distracted and I launch myself into doll wall and scramble inside. I know there will be rats and cockroaches but I am almost swimming in the dark through a tightly packed wall of dolls. They become so dense that I can't breathe. I start to panic and punch in front of me and keep squirming forward, then I somehow turn myself round and start kicking. I hang on to my bag of tricks. Light breaks in and I'm through. I look around. No one. There is a sickening smell of burning plastic and something else, a smell I don't recognise.

I need to be out of here. I creep to the end and turn left. As I pass doll alley smoke starts to billow towards me. I see a screaming Protector in flames and writhing on the ground, surrounded by thousands of tiny bodies igniting in a doll genocide and their hair sparking up in mad illuminations, the second Protector torn between trying to put out the flames consuming his fellow Protector and saving himself. Then he is gone in a blast of acrid black smoke. I run to the end wall and turn left again. I push through the main door and look around outside. Is there a third Protector? Maybe they thought two would be enough for a scared wimp like me. Open space in front. I turn right and keep to the wall of the warehouse and then come to a car park with a dozen or so rusting cars. Protectors could be hiding in or behind any of them. On the other side of the car park is a cluster of buildings with broken windows and graffitied walls. At least they will offer cover. I decide it's worth the risk and run to the first car. Look around. Run to the second. There is a noise from inside the abandoned car. I get ready to run but there is a whimper. I stand slowly and it is a woman of about fifty trying to hide in the back of the car, on the floor in front of the seat. She looks at me in startled terror. I make a shhh sound and run to the next car. If she tries to wait it out there she'll die. Everyone knows you have to keep moving. Two more cars and I reach the buildings. They look like they were once offices. One is missing a door and I run inside. No one here. Then there is the mother of all explosions.

The toy warehouse is now a volcano, flames and black smoke mushrooming from the top. No one can say I haven't given them value. I assume both Protectors are cooked, not to say a hundred thousand dolls and a universe of rats and bugs in toy heaven. Briefly I get a perverse flicker of the satisfaction an arsonist must feel. To play god. Angel of fire. To do a small thing and then retreat to watch it expand into a destructive immensity. Is this how the universe began? And will end?

Now I will be a prime target. My phone crackles. A strange human sound. It is Trash laughing. "Je-sus. You showed them," he says. All the time I am frightened we will be heard, and I'll simply be exterminated with a drone for cheating. "What next?" I ask. A pause. He's thinking. I look in the bag. I avoid looking at the photograph of Chloe. The leaf intrigues me. "The leaf," he says. I look at it. What is it telling me? Or is it a dud, a trick, a nothing that will occupy me until I am hunted down? "What's the source of a leaf?" He asks. A tree. An Oak tree. I must find an oak tree. Alright then.

I go outside and look around. I see two Protectors standing a safe distance from the inferno and then looking around, so I duck back into the building. They start walking towards me through the cars as if they know exactly where I am. They both take out their guns. Shit. There is no other way out of this office. And if I stay I'm dead. I clutch Chloe's lemon ribbon and close my eyes. I conjure Joe and Chloe and Dad. Goodbye my darlings. I hope I can make myself disappear when the Protectors come, but I am not always in control of it. A scream outside. I peek through the broken window. The Protectors are dragging the woman from the car. One holds her and forces her to her knees. The other holds the gun tight against her forehead. I get out of the office and run behind it and away. A single gunshot. They don't like to waste bullets. I am in a pock marked road with long abandoned houses, even a few shops, so this place really is longago Beforetimes. Even the skeletal remains of a pub called The Urban Fox which boasts of having its own well in the garden. I keep to one side, close to the buildings, and mark doors and broken walls where I can get inside if need be. Of course it might be that the Hunters are inside and I'll be ambushed. Every move and every decision are a risk. So I mustn't let it paralyse me. And I have my secret weapon. Trash. I get to the end of the road and look around. There is absolutely no sign of a blade of grass, let alone a tree in this urban death zone. Then there is a click from inside a house I have just passed.

I freeze and wait for a shot. A bearded skinny man in the rags of a pair of overalls appears. "I lost my bag of tricks," he says forlornly. "Dropped it when I ran from them."

I'm not sure what to do. You'd think that there is safety in numbers, that by joining together there is a better chance of survival, but it doesn't work like that. For one thing, people no longer trust each other and are more used to scabbing on others than forming alliances. Only one can survive anyway, so groups are out. Third, one of the tricks played in the hunt is that sometimes there is a rogue prey introduced, someone who appears to be like you but actually stays with you in order to expose you. So everyone figures it's best to be solo.

"Tough," I say. I can't believe this lost soul is a rogue prey, but you never know. Plus, he looks like he'd be more a liability than a help. The problem solves itself when I see three Protectors come from the direction I've just left. That fire, which is still smoking and blackening the sky, must be a magnet for them. They are perhaps seven hundred metres back but they must have seen us.

"Run!" I say.

We both run. The man veers to the middle of the street, which is stupid as it makes him an easier target, but maybe that will draw the fire away from me. Shouts far behind tell me they are after us. Adrenalin helps me keep up a good pace, but skinny man is starting to drop a little, so much so that the Hunters risk a shot. This seems to galvanise him and he starts flywheeling faster than I thought possible from his appearance. He catches up and we are nearly at the end of the street and beyond that what looks like a truck graveyard. Good hiding places. "Faster!" I shout and we run for all we are worth.

And then there is a searing pain and a galaxy of red and yellow flashes.

7

I pick myself up. My nose is pouring blood but I don't think broken. My forehead throbs but the cobwebs in my eyes clear. We ran into a force field. Something pings above me and it is a bullet rebounding off the force field. I get up, test my balance. Skinny is still on the floor a few metres away. "Get up!" I shout. Behind, the Hunters are maybe five hundred metres away. Stupid to waste a bullet when we are sitting ducks. Skinny shakes his head and gets to his knees, then his feet. He holds his left arm with his right and looks at me helplessly. "Arm busted," he says.

"You can still run. Come on," I say and decide, on pure whim, to go right.

"What about…?" But he never gets to finish the sentence. A bullet finds a dead centre spot in his forehead. He looks amazed and flattens against the force field, which bounces him forward and onto his face. His feet and head on the floor, backside in the air, he makes a perfect triangle. Then I am gone. I swing right to the back of the street and then take a left into an alley. I decide that to zig zag is best. There are little alleys on left and right and I choose randomly, third next on the right, second next on the left.

Two hours later I am exhausted, shaking, dehydrated and hungry. What finishes most people on the hunt is disorientation from those things. I stop and take stock. The most pressing need is water, then food. My lips are cracked, my nose is caked with dried blood, my head aches. I try the phone. Nothing. None of the buildings will have running water. There might be an old tin of something maybe. I also realise that some of the alleys and buildings are familiar. I've come more or less in a circle. I guess the Hunters will have moved on. They won't need to be tracking my chip just yet. And there is something in the back of my mind that won't go away. It's a long shot, but who knows?

I retrace my steps to the force field and work along. Skinny's body is still there. They like to leave the bodies until the end. If there is a lull in the action they can always show shots of them. Sometimes rats appear and create a new level of horror show viewing. That people watch this crap shows how far we've fallen. Perhaps the capacity to be reduced has always been there. I go back up the street, keeping to the side, and stop at every new house to listen. I haven't heard from Trash in a while. I hope the signal returns. I hope he's there when I need him.

There it is. The Urban Fox. Twenty years since I've been in a pub. Relics of Longagotimes when people wanted to socialise. I peer through a broken window. All looks dark inside. A few chairs covered with dusty plastic sheets. A pool table with a broken leg. The door is intact but padlocked. I go to another window that is completely out and climb through into the gloom. A hundred red dots shine on me like miniature lasers. Rats. I walk through to a door at the back and push it open. A cascade of ancient spider webs and dust falls. I step back until the worst clears and go through. I step on something and my foot goes clean through and crunches on something. It's a body. Long gone dead. I look around and see at least a dozen more. They must have herded or were driven here. Virus victims. I've lived in the shadow of Covid too long to be panicked, and these pilgrims died so long ago the virus is gone too, or it floated on to fresh pastures.

The sign outside said a well. And there it is in what used to be the garden. Walls on three sides that are intact, so I'm hidden from view. It's a small ornamental brick built well. Wire mesh over the top, which is good as it means rats cannot get in. I remove the mesh. I peer down but can see nothing. I drop a pebble, count and when I get to three there is a splash. I'm so excited I look around as if there was someone or something I could share the moment with. There is a pulley with a chain still attached. I turn the handle, which squeaks into life and bring up…nothing. The bucket has gone. Probably down there in the water. I hunt around and go inside to what was the bar and find a metal bucket. I empty as much of the dust out as I can then go back to the garden and tie the chain to the bucket handle. I lower it, swirl it around at the bottom to fill, and then pull it up. A bucket half full of water. It's cloudy but not putrid. Smells OK. I'm so thirsty it's tempting to gulp down a stomachful but I know better. Bad water and you get the cramps, or worse, and can't move. I don't want to send up smoke signals, so I go inside to the bar area, break another leg from the pool table, stamp it into bits and use another match to light a small fire, and then place the bucket in it. While it's boiling I look around.

A small kitchen area off the main bar. Another dried out body on the floor. "Excuse me, Bonesy," I say and step over him. A row of cupboards – all empty bar dust and droppings. An electric cooker that no longer works. A fridge that I won't even open. Anything in there would be into fifty stages of rot and if anything organic might still harbour Covid virus spores. There is a pull-out metal drawer at the bottom of the cooker. It's rusted but I yank it free, expecting to find cooking trays, but I have to blink twice to believe it. Tins. Seven tins. Two beans, one vegetable soup, two sardines and two mushy peas. If there was still a lottery I have just won it. I discount the sardines. The date on the back is BBE April 17 2021. Twenty-year-old fish, even in a tin, would not be good news. I take out the others and put them in my bag of tricks.

The bucket of water has boiled. I find an old plastic bottle with a screw cap, sluice some of the boiling water around it and leave it to dry and the bucket to cool. I stamp out the fire. There is a cellar door off the kitchen area and I go to explore. I tear off a piece of tarpaulin, roll it up and light it as a torch and go down. An ancient boiler and lots of tins of paint. Chairs, some beer barrels and a few bottles of Chianti and some litre bottles of whisky. Tempting but not a good idea. A pile of stair rods, lengths of plastic for window frames, and what looks like a few entangled bodies in a corner. Think out of the box, Trash said. I remember when I first qualified as an engineer and Dad would play a game with me. Take me to his workshop and say – "Look in the scrap box and make something. Surprise me.

You've got an hour" And sometimes I did. I made a door latch from scrap, a Morse code tapper from the innards of a clock, a screwdriver from a stair rod by filing it to an edge. I look at the stair rods again. The edges could be made sharp. I grab ten and a few lengths of the plastic.

Upstairs I tie two of the plastic lengths together – now the strip is a metre long, durable but still flexible. I smash a bottle and hold a sharp piece in a piece of tarpaulin and groove four indentations, two at each end, and then bend the plastic taut and tie a length of string, courtesy of my bag of tricks, tight onto both ends. It looks silly but holds as I pull back the string. I have a working bow. I stop and drink a pint of water straight from the bucket. It had cooled sufficiently and tastes sweet. I pour the rest of the water in the plastic bottle and put it in my bag of tricks. The arrows are trickier. It takes me twenty minutes to make the tiniest groove on one end to fit the string, using the glass, and twenty minutes to make something resembling a point on the other end, by filing it down on the concrete floor in the kitchen. I use my new arrow to puncture a tin of beans in several places so that I can empty them into my hand and eat. I make one more arrow and then hear shots. Five in all. Not outside but close enough to be a green light. I have to go.

Outside I stop and look both ways. Two more shots, probably a quarter of a mile south. I turn left and start travelling north. I have two arrows and my makeshift bow, water, food and my bag of tricks. No sign of a tree anywhere. I pass a small church with broken stained glass windows, a bent steeple that points accusingly at me, and a huge closed door. I try the door but it's locked. Must be three inches thick. Windows too high up to get in. Why would I want to go anyway? What sort of sanctuary did the church provide to the millions of dead? God himself probably died of the virus. I move on.

"You're becoming a bit of a star," Trash suddenly says. I bow my head to listen and whisper back. He tells me that the two hunters in the toy factory were spectacularly incinerated and the footage is now in the top ten favourite hunt clips. The downside is that the rest really want to get me. Another hunter fell through some rotten stairs and is now out with a broken leg. Five prey have been killed, so that leaves me and four others. The odds are tightening. He thinks they will start using the tracker soon to locate me.

"I haven't seen an oak tree anywhere. I doubt there's been anything like a tree in this hole for a generation," I say. "Maybe it's one of the duds and I'm just wasting time."

I can feel him thinking.

"Maybe it's not a tree. Think leaf. Green. Think things growing. Think…what? Oak. Tree. Wood."

"Wood. Things made of oak. The church. It's got a big wooden door. Maybe oak."

I turn and head back to the church. As I'm walking it's as if some mad encyclopaedic switch has been triggered in Trash. "Oak. More likely to be struck by lightning than other trees. This enhanced their significance for Druids who seek 'arwen' or inspiration which they believe can come through lightning. They called this 'courting the flash'. The most important texts in western history - including the Magna Carta, Newton's theories and Mozart's music - were written using oak gall ink."

"Trash! Are you reading this?"

"No. I'm remembering it."

"You're weird."

"Thanks."

I reach the church. Touch the wooden door. I tell Trash it's locked. I look through my bag of tricks again. The silver key. Old school. Has to be for this door. I try it. No fit. Perhaps the key is a dud. Perhaps the whole leaf-oak-door connection is a dead end.

"Maybe the flute is an open sesame," says Trash unhelpfully. I take out the flute and blow on it. No sound. It's a dud too. I look carefully at it, the odd shaped mouthpiece. I push it into the keyhole, turn and…I'm in. Trash is still talking about the oak as a symbol of strength, morale, resistance and knowledge. I wonder if he's been drinking furniture polish. Then I realise, he's getting vicarious kicks from this. His whole life is spent in a cold dark cavern of a place experiencing everything second hand. Because he knows me this is one step further towards the real. I'm almost like an alter ego for him, out here in mortal frigging terror, and it's a turn on. Even so he's been helpful. Maybe even lifesavingly so. Alright then. "Shut up. I'm in." I say. I close the door behind me.

The church is musty, cold, damp. A forlorn looking Christ on a tapestry hangs like a wet rag from a pulpit. A golden eagle holds a bible that turns to ash and dust when I touch it. Several dried out dead bodies in rags sit up in a mezzanine gallery that looks out over the whole church, as if they have been waiting decades for the service to begin. A few bell ropes hang from the ceiling. According to the rules there is something for me in here. Where? I wander around, looking and touching. The alabaster wing of a cherub breaks off in my hand. I look in the vestry and on the floor is a dishevelled rat-chewed set of liturgical vestments and it takes me a few moments to see there are the rope-like remains of a priest killed by the virus. "Hi father," I say. "If you could tell me where my prize is I'll leave a few matches in the poor box." No response. The angels must have died with him.

I walk back out and to the front of the church again. On a table is the poor box. The lid has no dust on it, as if recently opened. I open it and there inside is a cardboard box with the word *Congratulations* printed on it. Inside the box is a pair of odd looking goggles. I take them out and wonder what the hell use they will be. "Infra-red" whispers Trash. So I'm still on camera, which is a bizarre feeling. I realise how useful these might be. Unless the hunters have infra-red goggles too. For the sake of the drama they probably don't. They have guns and invariably make all their kills with very rare losses, so the viewers' interest needs to be spiced occasionally. And I'm it. Give the bitch a chance. Maybe one in twenty.

"What now?" I whisper.

"Hunker down. Rest. Let them come to you this time. Which will surprise them."

Perhaps he's right. And I'm near to collapse. I realise the muscles in my neck and shoulders and lower back are rigid with tension and fear. My body has been disguising this from me, enabling me to carry on, but now it is telling me to stop. For a while. I drink some water. Eat the tin of soup. The door is closed. Unless they also have a key, I'm safe. I lie between two pews and am asleep in seconds.

"Stand and deliver!" Says Dick, flashing white teeth at the nizzled postillion. Bess is glossy in the moonlight and her coat sheens like wet coal. The postillion thinks of going for his pistol but Dick smiles and shakes his head. He gives Dick the strong box containing twenty guineas. Dick throws the box back and then nudging Bess alongside the coach, he leans forward and looks inside the carriage......

...Joe and Chloe sit looking straight ahead. They do not even see Dick smiling in, nor the warm steamy breath from Bess's flaring nostrils. As if they are in the grip of some terrible allure. The effect on Dick is immediate. All confidence and daring gone in a macaronic enchantment. He is baffled and speechless. He looks across and realises they are not staring at the awful void but at a child sitting opposite, who turns her orbed eyes at him, pale face framed by crescents of red hair. She half smiles and hold up three fingers. He seems to understand, but through a glass darkly, and on the gallop home that night his thoughts never quite collect, as if he has looked in a mirror and been dazzled and chastened by what he saw and has an imperfect connection with himself. He longs for the warmth of the inn, the thick taste of the wine and the flesh of a willing girl. There is always a willing girl. He feels things will never be the same.

I gasp and awaken. They are coming.

8

It is dark. I must have slept for several hours. The phone beeps.

"They're coming!" he says.

"I know."

"How do you...? OK. You've got about..." and it goes dead.

About what? A minute? Fifteen minutes? I get up and my legs wobble. I take a deep breath. Try not to panic. It's dark. I'm so stupid. Why didn't I prepare earlier? I put on my infrared goggles. All I can see are a few reddish blobs in the corner. They don't work. Then I remember that they work through heat. The red blobs are rats. Alright then. Think think think. What have I got in here? Me. My bag. Dead bodies. Dead bodies? I light a match and grope my way to the altar. There is a broken candle. I snap it in two and light half with a match. I close my eyes and think of Chloe and see her laughing. What is she laughing at? It's me with a silly hat on pretending to be Dick Turpin, and holding a wooden pistol at Joe, who pretends to be a terrified duchess I am about to relieve of her pearls. Sometimes the best moments were when life became theatre. So it shall be.

I go up wooden steps to the mezzanine. There are four dead bodies. I lean over and get two of the bell ropes. One I loop around one body and then a second and tie it off. Then I do the same with another rope and the other two bodies. I reach out for a third rope and twine this around the other two ropes, and then tie an old robe to the end of this rope so that it is long enough to hang down to the church floor. On the ground I drag the dead priest in a cloud of dust and fluff to the pulpit with the golden eagle and prop him up so he looks like Death himself delivering a hell fire sermon. I wrap his skeletal arms around the eagle so it looks as if he is leaning forward to the congregation to make a point. *See what happens if you don't repent. The wrath of the Lord will burn you to dust.* I squat on the floor behind the pulpit so I am hidden. I have my bag of tricks in my backpack, my goggles on and my handmade bow and two arrows. Suddenly my attempts at saving myself seem pathetic. Is everyone watching laughing at my foolish self-destruction? Look at this crazy bitch with her theatre of death. And I am a ludicrous spectacle in my own reckoning too. Seven of them could come in with loaded guns, torches or infrared goggles, and laugh at my homemade theatricals and take turns in making me endure a slow death for the watching millions. Millions? I realise I have no idea what the population is now. A billion? Ten thousand? It doesn't matter. Nothing matters. I close my eyes and summon first Joe and then Chloe and then Dad and kiss them goodbye in my mind.

Someone tries to open the door, then there is muffled discussion. Then an almighty crash that makes me start. They have an axe. I breathe deeply and look up at the dead priest in front of me. You and me, father. Brimstone and fire. Clickety clack those old bones for me. Crash crash crash. Splinter as the wood cleaves. Five minutes later the door is smashed down and torch beams scatter around the church like miniature search lights in a war zone. So maybe that means they don't have infrared. Good. I see one two three reddish lumps start to move. Three. Alright then. I wait until they are in the middle of the church, then pull the robe attached to the rope. Nothing happens so I yank again and with a strange whoosh three of the bodies are launched and swing down towards the Hunters. Who panic.

"Fuck! They're flying!"

"What the bastard hell are they?"

Gunshots. One. Two. Three. Four. One of the bodies crashes into a hunter, who falls in a paroxysm of disgust and fear. There is a confusion of torch beams, curses and crashes. Then things calm. There is so much dust and flotsam in the air now that the hunters' torch beams only serve to create a surreal landscape of whorls and phantasms. Only two torch beams now. One was dropped and broke, I hope.

"It's all right. It's just dead crap. Get a frigging grip, you tosser."

"You two work the sides, I'll go up the centre."

"I haven't got a torch."

"For Christ's sake, there's nothing to be scared of."

"Christ!!" I say, deepening my voice. I push the pulpit gently so it looks as if the dead priest is moving. Both torch beams swing in my direction.

"Fuck. That bastard just said…"

"Christ bastard says the vengeance of the Lord is mine. Stand and deliver!" I say. This is so demented I almost want to giggle. A pile of ecclesiastical bones in rags spouting a bafflegab of terrifying threats.

Another shot and the priest's skeletal head shatters. I lean from the side, where they cannot see me because they are still looking up at the priest, I put one of my home made arrows in the bow and take careful aim at one of the glowing red shapes. I take a breath and hold it, pull back and release.

I can't believe it works. The shape stops, then sways and then falls. There is a noise like a deflating ball.

"Aaron's been shot. What is it?"

"Fucking steel."

Another shot. That's six.

"I'm out of here," says one of the shapes, and is gone from the church. One left. He is breathing heavily and holds two torches. He knows where I am and he knows he's been fooled. Now he's angry. I can feel it. He ducks low and creeps along one of the pews. I move to the back of the chancel and behind the altar and wait. He's taking his time. I load the second arrow. He is doing a slow sweep with the torches, one in each hand. I wait until I am steady and he has reached the pulpit and stops. I stand and take aim. A torch beam blinds me momentarily. I take a breath and fire. The stair rod clatters to the ground as the string breaks. My one chance gone. Now he has my position, he comes forward slowly, keeping both torch beams ahead on the altar. I have no weapons. I crouch down and decide that as soon as he is there I will make a run for it. I put my hands on the floor to steady myself and my fingers brush against the brass candle holder. I hold it. It feels good and solid in my hand. I hold the steel rod in my other hand.

I have no idea which side of the altar he will come from so I move back a little so I can get a good swing either way. He does neither. He jumps on the altar and then shines the torch down on me. It takes me by surprise and I drop the candlestick.

"Bitch!" He says and jumps down at me, a flying lump of reddish heat. Adrenaline floods me and I disappear.

Everything moves so quickly. We are lying backs to the ground and it is bearing down on us. Chloe is trying not to scream but I'm not sure how much longer I can hold it off. This hideous pressing weight that wants to flatten us and then what — gorge? But is it even alive? It is like pressure personified, almost an abstraction of matter that will crush us. As if we are in a quantum world where nothing is understood. Pressure. Force. Physics with an appetite. All I know is I must keep my hands steady. But why? I look at them. So that's what it is…I twist my hands and delight in the low, gruff, scream.

He is on top of me, a pile of struggling, stifling flesh. His breath smells of something rancid, rotting onions, stale fish, and he has his hands around my throat. I am holding tight to the steel rod, which he impaled himself on when he jumped at me. I keep twisting and wrenching it and he moans. I can't breathe. My strength will go soon. I bite hard into his cheek. He loosens his grip and I roll as hard as I can and push him off. I pull out the rod and jam it down into his head. It goes straight through his left eye. He screams and clutches it and I roll away and get up, choking and coughing.

I drink a little water, fix my bag of tricks tight on my back. I pick up one of the torches and flip it off. I also take one of the guns. No bullets but it might scare someone in a tight corner.

"Help, help, help," the Hunter begs.

I leave him to die.

I walk along street after street, hiding if my infrareds pick up any heat movement. By the time a smoky dawn begins I am tired and everything aches. I want this to be over. My throat must have swollen internally because I find it hard to swallow. The hunter's finger marks are on the lemon ribbon around my neck. Chloe's ribbon. I know there are four hunters dead. I heard shots and have no idea how many prey are gone.

Trash speaks into my dark reverie.

"I bow to thee, queen of the hunt," he says.

Trash doesn't do irony. In fact he barely does anything as a personality so what is all this new stuff that's been unleashed? "Apparently viewing figures have gone up by…a lot. We couldn't see in the dark but when you walked out of that church it was like the Second Coming."

"I can't tell you how much I couldn't give a fig," I say. "Do you know how many prey left?"

"You. Two others. They're working together. Four hunters down, five with the leg man, is not quite a record, but getting there. What's up with your voice?"

"I nearly got choked to death."

"OK. I've got to go. I'm working on a biometric speech technology chip and a bit behind."

"Sorry, don't let me being hunted to death interfere with your day any more. Trash?" He's gone. That's fine with me. We are in danger of becoming friends, which is a form of intimacy, something I have spent years avoiding. Intimacy means pain and I prefer solid concrete numbness. Dad is the exception.

I hear shouts about half a kilometre north. I hide in a house and watch. A few minutes later two people, a youngish man and younger woman, come running down the centre of the street. I've never understood that. If you are trying to escape from someone why run in the most conspicuous place? I should shout to them to get off the street and zig zag down the alleys but already the hunters are in sight. If I shout I give my position away. It isn't noble but I haven't come this far to sacrifice myself for a couple of dickshits who are determined to die. They aren't even weaving as they run. A shot and the man coughs a fountain of blood as his lungs explode and he falls face down, trembling fitfully. Another shot misses the young woman.

Involuntarily and against my better judgement I stand and shout to her, "Over here!" She turns, wild eyed and terrified and runs towards me. Straight into my arms. "It's alright. You're alright. I've got you." She gives a loud sob that carries all the pain of the world and collapses into me. Another shot close to and she convulses and I feel my hands grow wet and sticky on her back. She looks up at me and for an instant I see Chloe.

She tries to say something but only an incoherent gurgle comes out and she exhales loudly.

I gently squat and ease her to the floor. "Goodbye, my girl," I whisper. My hands are hot with her blood. I hear something and look up. A shitforbrains hunter is slowly clapping his hands, sardonic and smirking. A second hunter raises his pistol and aims at my head. Then a siren sounds and they look at each other. I am the last one. I've done it.

"Fuck it. Do her anyway," says shitforbrains.

"Right. And get executed," says the other.

"Protocol," I say.

They both look at me.

"You can't break pro-to-col."

The one with the gun considers for a second breaking with protocol and blowing a hole in my brain, but as he just said, he'd pay for it with his own blood and pain. This is sport and sport has rules, of a sort, even if they are loaded against you. I feel lightheaded, as if I might throw up, and I still hold the dead girl in my arms. I will show nothing. All those watching would probably like a show of emotion now, a bit of heat to finish off the fucked up spectacle of fear and gore they've just watched. I wonder where all this anger comes from. For years I have lived in quiet stoicism, and indifference to how the world has fallen into its own shadow.

The hunter holsters his gun. "Let's go."

It's the same two Protectors who brought me here, as they promised. Clearly they are surprised and annoyed. It ruined their betting. I see my knife in the passenger side compartment and while they are talking to the hunters I pocket it. I worked hard to make that blade and these bastards aren't keeping it.

My throat still burns and while I was in the hunt I now realise there was something that removed me from myself. A shift of being so that I wasn't overwhelmed by the moment. I have learnt that fear can make you strong if you let it keen your senses and awaken your thinking. It is a primal energy. But you have to befriend it and use it as a tool. If you let it grow beyond your control you are lost. You cannot function if you shake with fear.

Number Two looks at me for the first time.

"Think you're fucking Queen of the dicks now, eh?"

What does that even mean? It isn't worth replying. He blindfolds me and I'm bundled in the back of the van and we are away on the bumpy road home. I try not to fall asleep. The adrenalin has long since drained and I now feel like a filthy rag. I cannot even summon Joe or Chloe. I drift into nowhere and float there like a dream of myself.

I'm aware of when we are approaching Kessingland. Some sixth sense alerts me. I also know something is wrong. When we go as far as we can instead of turning left to Dad's place we turn right on Beach Road, past the old long ago closed holiday park and on, bumping over the ground to Hundred River and Benacre, what used to be a nature reserve but is now a fetid wasteland of mud, slime and dead land. I must keep alert. The van stops.

I take off the blindfold. It's dark. Too dark.

"Why haven't you taken me home? I'm free," I say.

They both laugh.

"Free you ain't, fruit drop," says Number One.

"But I won."

"That's the problem. Bit of a star, you was. And they don't like that, our bosses."

"The powers that be, as it were," adds Number Two.

"They like everything normal. The hunt, the winner's some lucky sod usually with nothing special about 'em. But if you make a splash. If you show a bit of bollocks…"

"It's a problem-o," says Number Two.

"People might think you're a heroine. Someone who might make a fuss. A bit of trouble."

"A frigging dis-senter."

"But if you disappear. Nice and quiet. You know what people are like. They'll forget you in a week. Two weeks max. You're just a replay."

"So your job now is to kill me?"

"We like to think of it as providing a public service," says Number One. He takes out his gun and points it at me. "Outside. We don't want to have to spend unpaid overtime cleaning your slop out the back."

"I've got a suggestion," I say.

They both look at me.

"If I'm going I want a last request."

They wait.

"I'm feeling concupiscent."

They look at each other. None the wiser.

"It's been a long while since I've had a good fuck. Any sort of sex. Being in the hunt has got me horny. Maybe, just maybe between the two of you I can at least have one decent screw before I check out. Go out with a bang. Together or one at a time. I'm not fussy."

This surprises them. They expected pleading or begging. Number Two is already excited at the prospect. Number One less so. Perhaps he swings the other way. Perhaps he's impotent. Perhaps he's scared. Number Two looks at him.

"Let's have a go. Why not, eh? Good way to round off the day. You want to go first?"

Number One looks slightly sheepish. "Can't. Bleedin' hernia."

"Oh, tough one. Mind if I...?" He gestures in my direction.

Number One isn't sure.

"Won't take me long."

Number one nods. Number Two gets out of the van and comes round to open the back doors. He clambers in. Takes out his gun and places it at the back by the door, furthest from me, and then takes off his helmet. He has a ratty unhealthy face. Most people have bad teeth these days but his are in a class of their own. Like a filthy broken wall. He sits upright, unbuckles his trousers and wriggles out of them and starts fondling his crotch.

"Let me do that" I say and shuffle over.

I start rubbing his groin with my left hand and kissing his neck. He grabs my left breast. Then pulls my shirt open. I manoeuvre so that he screens me from Number One at the front. I open his mouth with my fingers and kiss him. He seems surprised at this. I nearly gag but it means he can't talk. Then I take out my knife with my right hand and jab him quickly three times in the neck. I get the main carotid artery with the third thrust and the blood fountains out over me. I lock my mouth over his so that all Number One can hear is some desperate moaning. He grabs at his neck and I stab him in the side. His left leg is twitching uncontrollably and thumping on the floor.

"Keep the noise down and get a bloody move on!" says Number One.

Number Two can't say a word now. He is drowning in his own blood. I start moaning loudly and reach to the back of the van and get Number Two's gun. I've never fired a gun before but I stole one during the hunt so know where the safety catch is. Now it's off. Number One turns around and realises something is wrong. I shoot him twice. The first shaves his ear, but the second goes clean through his right eye. The blood fountains in a perfect arc all over me.

They have several bottles of water in the van. I get outside and wash as much blood off me as I can. I gag and the little that is in my stomach retches up until there is only a hot bile burning my mouth. I have no idea what to do next but already the plasticity of a possible plan is forming in my mind.

I get in the van, push Number One down on the floor and check for food, tokens and anything else. Then I check the pockets of the two dead men. I have quite a haul on the seat – packets of nuts, which I haven't seen in years, some chewy bars made of roly polies – good protein – twenty five tokens, maps, lists of contact numbers, their ID cards, barcode passes into various buildings in Dorado, three bottles of water, two guns and thirty rounds of ammunition and a laser pistol. I put them all in my bag.

I start the engine and just hope I don't meet any night patrols. It's low on petrol. You can switch it to methane but that is empty, or switch it to electricity but that too is low. I put on one of the Protector's helmets to disguise my face. I haven't driven since I came down to Dad's – how many years ago? A lifetime. Since then I've become a killer. No longer a wife, no longer a mother, no longer a lover, no longer an engineer. What is left? I hope still a daughter, but a solid gold killer is what is coming into stark relief. I know that putting a bullet into the fat face of Number One gave me a thrill. I enjoyed putting full stops to these two lives. And the ones in the Hunt. How quickly we tread a path once a million light years away.

I can't drive to Dad's. It will be the first place they look and the van will be conspicuous. I wonder how long before they realise something is wrong. There are built in speakers and microphones in the van. Various lights on the dashboard are flashing. Perhaps they are meant to confirm the kill. For now, I just have to get off the road and hidden as soon as possible.

I arrive at Trash's garage. I can see a light through the cracks at the side of the door so he's still working. I don't know if he eats and now I wonder if he sleeps. The garage to the right of him has no door but to the left there is a rusted frame panel propped against the opening. It's heavy and it takes me several minutes to pull it to one side, then drive the van inside and pull the panel over the entrance. I'm too tired to bother with anything else tonight.

I tap the metal pull-over door on Trash's place and, to my surprise, he immediately opens it.

"I've put a van next door," I say.

"I know. I saw. Micro surveillance camera on my roof."

"Then why didn't you help?"

He looks puzzled, rendering the question redundant. I go inside. It's even more of a mess. I sit on top of a pile of flat screens. One of them breaks.

"I need to sleep," I say.

"Then sleep."

"Where?"

"Anywhere."

"Alright then."

I find something that might have once been a blanket, scoop a pile of rubbish away from a corner and lay down. My bag of tricks, now very full, acts as a hard pillow. I think I am asleep even before I close my eyes.

"I think we'll be safe on this road," she says, clasping my hand tightly.

The wind in the trees does not sound right. As if everything is trying to warn us of a calamity that sleeps in all things, living and dead, and awakens like a kraken to consume us. I wonder where Joe is.

"Anyway, we don't have to worry about robbers and highwaymen, because this is Dick's patch, and if any harm befell us he would demand a smoking vengeance with his pistols."

She seems so happy and sure that I am ashamed of the saponaceous terror that clogs my veins and wearies my heart. I should be reassuring her.

"And anyway, we have her." Who? I look around and can't see anyone. "And she'll be a Lot of help. A Lot." And she peals into laughter. I smile and feel that a great sickness has entered me. I understand nothing.

"I thought you were dead," Trash says indifferently.

"And you were grief stricken and tearful," I say.

"No."

"I was being sarcastic."

"I know."

"Alright then."

Classical music plays. I think it's Bach. Swirling organ that creates delightful order in a black chaos. Trash tells me that my winning the Hunt has created a real stir on the Shadow Web, an Internet space that shows the weird and wild and keeps getting closed down by Protectors, and springing up again, like a virus itself. In Beforetimes this would be my twenty minutes of fame.

"Thanks for your help. In the Hunt. It saved me," I say, instantly regretting it. This show of emotion switches him off. Odd, because he seemed so animated when he was helping me during the Hunt, but it was just vicarious adrenalin kicking in. He starts examining some tiny circuits under a microscope. I drink some water and eat a bag of the nuts. They taste like heaven. I don't offer Trash any because he'll say No and we are way beyond polite protocols. Then he talks.

"While you were asleep I went to the van. I took out the tracker in the dashboard and destroyed it, otherwise this place would now be overrun by Protectors and we would be dead. Speaking of which, what plans do you have for the terrible twins. They will start to stink soon."

I tell him any suggestions welcomed but I'm keeping the uniforms.

"Why?"

"They might come in handy."

"Why?"

"I'm going to Dorado in that van to find out what happened to Dad, and any fucker gets in my way will be sorry."

He stops scrutinising his miniature world and looks at me. Perhaps for the first time. "It's a death sentence. You're mad."

"No. We are mad. You're coming with me."

9

We don't argue. He tells me that he will not come, out of the question, and just gets practical. I realise that although he lives in one garage this is as an empire to him. Breaking with precedent and leaving his lock up he takes me to where there is some sodium hydroxide, or lye, in a nearby lock up and then shows me how to mix it with water. We do this in an old oil drum and then drag the two bodies from the van, take their clothing and put Number One in the drum, where Trash tells me he will dissolve nicely into a brown mush. Number Two can wait his turn. Probably a few hours, he says. He's not sure because he's never done it before, which is something of a relief.

My plan is to utilize the uniforms and the van to get as close to Dorado as possible. I might even be able to use the terrible twins' IDs. The radio will be useful. Then I go on foot when it's no longer possible to use the van. I have two hand guns, a laser pistol, a flare gun, water. I tell him I could really use a techie. He repeats that he's not coming but he could help at a distance. He says he will put different license plates on. He's already removed the digital tracker. He might be able to steal the codes for another van and create a phony tracker. He says a few hand weapons will be useless if they use drones but he might be able to interfere with their frequencies. Also, there is little fuel in the van and getting petrol is like squeezing juice from a stone. I tell him I've already thought of both the weapons problem and the fuel and have a possible solution. If he's impressed he doesn't show it.

First, I need to find a boat. Trash says there is probably a couple in one of the lock ups but they'd be in bad repair. He shows no curiosity as to why I want a boat. I find one in the fourth lock up. Battered old carbon fibre rower, but no oars. It's light. I can carry it on my head. I scavenge and find a piece of wood that will makeshift as an oar. Trash says he will take care of the second body when the first is nicely sludged. He gives me an old mobile phone in case there's a problem. I already know what I will use it for.

Close up, the sea is even worse. Inflorescence of putridity as if a scum-laden, diseased ogre the size of a small moon has bathed and dissolved in its own effluence. I push the boat and the sea is so scummy it instantly sucks to the sides. Tides are smaller because the water moves less fluently, more like a solid doughy mass. I get in with my oar and my bag of tricks which I have now filled with some of my tools.

The oil rig has been left to rot. All the workers got the virus and died. The living threw the dead in the sea and then the living became the dead. The economy crashed, petrol stations closed, people killed for fuel, so there is no chance of getting any on land. My hope is that there will be a store of petrol there. Methane gas is probably all gone. It's highly flammable so would probably have burnt out years ago. Also the symmetry of its molecule makes it hard to liquify. You could in principle store methane in a tank in the gas state, but methane has such low density you could not store a usable amount. Stupidly I haven't brought any cans, but a little bit of luck might go a long way.

It is like paddling through glue. I'm sweating and only about ten metres from shore. Each paddle stroke churns up a new wave of puddingy stodge, the colour of sooty snot. The smell is a rank, odoriferous, lively reminder of what a dead world we are. Perhaps it is only cockroach stubbornness that endures us towards a mephitic Armageddon. I stop to retch but there is too little in my stomach to respond. I used to find hunger pangs unbearable. Now they are a comfort that my body is claiming attention. I am still here. The well fed can never understand the hungry. It is another country.

After an hour I am almost there. My shirt, an old tartan working one of Dad's, clings to my back. The sweat has poured between my breasts and down to my groin. I stop to gulp down water and force myself to eat a few nuts. I start paddling again and reach the oil rig. It is like an ancient becalmed beast that fought its final battle aeons ago and is now only a rusting memory of itself. The rotting sea has made valiant attempts to bring it to heel but despite holes in the metal the four columns, like those of a classical temple, are holding out. I find a metal ladder still intact, tie my boat to it, and climb up. There are three layers to the rig, like a giant wedding cake, and a large central derrick and casing that holds the drill bits. The first layer is storage and some rooms for workers. The second layer has the generator and mud casings pit on one side, where mud and shale are separated from the drilling, more worker galleys on the other side. The top layer has the engines and turntable. I go up the little staircases to the top layer just to get a perspective. It is a long time since I've looked back on land. I can see Dad's house. The whole vista looks grey and funereal, even with a pale sun doing its best through scuddy cloud banks. The other view out to sea is just sludge and more sludge to the horizon. I am amazed that some hybrid creatures live in the sludge, but these are wormy bags of liquidity that even we, who gobble crushed maggots and roly polies, would baulk at. The sea's swampy consistency means the tide is tortoise paced.

Enough sightseeing. I go down to the first layer and search the storage rooms. Some beautiful drilling tools, many of which I don't even recognise. I wish I could photograph them and show Dad. One room is digitally padlocked, but I find a metal pole and prise the weathered door. When it finally gives I fall over with the effort, which is just as well. A brownish putrescent cloud of gas escapes. I gag at a smell that was born in hell. Bodies piled high inside. I see that it was some sort of refrigeration unit for dead virus victims, and when the power finally outed, they rotted over the years in a vacuum that semi preserved them. I close the door quickly. Further along is a storeroom with oils and petrol cans. Promising. I shake the cans. Three are full. I open one and smell. Diesel fuel. Intact. The two others are fine too. I take the three good cans outside, plus some oil, and decide, given that I'm here, to do a thorough search.

In one of the sleeping quarters, a tiny room, a dried out husk of a corpse, wearing an engineer's cap, sits upright on the bed, looking at a curled old photograph he holds. Like disappearing ghosts the fading images of a young boy and a dog looking at the camera. "Love from Timmy and Ben xxx" still discernible on the back. Our words and images long outlive us. I look through his bedside cupboard and take a torch, a lighter and an old school Swiss knife. On the next layer I find a kitchen area and a Plato's cave of tinned food. I fill a holdall with tins of things, some of which I've forgotten the taste, like pineapple and olives. As I pack them I find I am salivating uncontrollably. Gastro memories kicking in. I open a tin of chickpeas and scoop out a few handfuls, chewing slowly and savouring the protein. I wonder if there are such things as pineapples growing in the world anymore.

Along the corridor is another locked room. Two digital key pads. I use the crowbar again but the door is solid. A sign says AUTHORISED STAFF ONLY. What could be so important on an oil rig? More dead? I look around and poke the ceiling with the crow bar. Metal sheeting on narrow steels about a metre apart. I go up the next level and find where the locked room is directly below. I wedge the crow bar in a lip of alloy sheeting on the floor and use my foot to lever it down. The panel comes away a little from the steel, then a little more. In ten minutes I have one of the floor panels sheared away and I can see down into the room below. I shine the torch and have to scan the room twice before I believe what I see.

An arsenal of weapons. Still beautiful and shiny. A soldier's dream. I ease myself down and soften my knees as I hit the floor. Old school Glocks and

Kalashnikovs. M4 A41 assault rifles. 725 shotguns. PKM light machine guns. I know women aren't supposed to be nerdy about guns but as an engineer I always admired craftsmanship. I sort through them. No explosives. Which is clever. On an oil rig even a small explosion could mean a thousand tons of oil beneath you turns your immediate world into a tsunami of fire and hell.

Why are they here? When you move into a plague world where oil is diminishing it becomes worth dying for. Oil rigs weren't just workplaces. They were plunder. So they became fortresses. There is an override button to open the door from the inside. I open it and look around outside until I find a couple of canvas bags. Go back and select ten good weapons, two grenade launchers, a box of grenades and as much ammo as I can carry.

I carry all my plunder down in stages to the boat. On a whim I go back and get 6 MP7 submachine guns. I'll need them for phase two of my plan. I scan the inland roads to ensure there are no white vans, then begin the tedious row back to shore. Given the dead water people rarely bother to look out to sea, so even a few stragglers walking along the beach have eyes down and shoulders hunched. I head for a part of the coast away from houses. It takes me two hours but I find the spot I was looking for. Piles of dead branches will create good cover.

I hide most of my things under branches and fill my bag of tricks with tins and one Glock pistol and one of the PKMs. The rest I put in canvas bags and hide them further away under branches. I drag the boat a little away, upend it and cover it in mud so it looks as if it has been there a while. Then I phone Jez. I tell him I'm the woman who said No and he laughs. He says he is too busy to meet me until I say there will be a profit in it for him.

We sit in his van a hundred metres from Barter Square. I have made my pitch to him. He throws his cigarette butt out of the window and spits after it. I know that soon, if not already, the Authority will know that I am responsible for the disappearance of two Protectors and a van. I know they hate me for surviving the Hunt. I know that if I try to find out the truth of things I will be seen as a terrorist. I am a walking dead woman. I have a war on my hands. In a war you need weapons. Guns certainly. Explosives a bonus. I have offered a trade to Jez – a lot of explosives in return for all 6 PKMs. I know he's going to say yes, but we have to go through bargaining motions.

"I have to see them all," he says.

I know he's looking around to see if there are more weapons, which is why I hid the PKMs separately. Finally he seems satisfied. It's a deal. He takes the PKMs and we drive to pick up the explosives. I ask the question that has been bugging me since I last saw him.

"It's too vague. You sell to whoever asks you. Too risky."

"Everything's a risk."

"You must be in touch with groups. Renegade groups."

"I thought there weren't any. That's what the Authority tells us. Everything under control."

We drive in silence. Through the deserted village of Giselham and then on to Carlton Colville, past the old abandoned transport museum, then left to a few derelict cottages. Jez drives down an alley to the back of the cottages, stops the van and shushes me. He listens. Silence except for his raspy breathing. He unlocks one of the cottages, and we enter. He shines a flashlight in the gloom. The place is damp and airless, curtains closed. He opens a door and goes down into a cellar and returns with a large box. Then goes down and returns with another. Each box has two metal clasps. He undoes one box and a chilled steam emits. There are about twenty glass containers inside. The glass is frosted so I can't see inside them.

"Nitro glycerine. Refrigerated. Once it warms up it becomes unstable and it's liable to blow at any time. All a question of timing. You've got to think ahead. Take one out in advance and I'd say – an hour to thaw, then another hour before they become unstable. These boxes are good to stay cold for at least another week, so that's how long you've got before the whole mother rocks."

"Alright then."

He drives me back with the boxes. I'm nervous about letting him know where Trash lives, so I get him to drop me half a kilometre away. I stand on the verge with the boxes. "I'm going to Dorado," I say, "to find out what's happened to my dad. If you have no loyalties, why not come with me? I could use a man who can think ahead and knows about explosives and questions of timing."

"What's in it for me?"

"The truth of things."

"That old bitch. She died years ago. There is no truth, there is only what happens and none of it has any meaning."

"Just thought you might want a change from boiling up dead fish. But if that's enough excitement for you, good luck. Plus, if we make it back I'll let you know where there are enough weapons for a small army."

He looks at me thoughtfully. Then drives away. I phone Trash and ask him to come and help me with the boxes.

10

When you prepare for something it's always a surprise when the moment arrives. If there was anything to think of, Trash had got there before me. Number plates changed on the van. Fake Protector ID – with the helmet on I can pass for a man unless someone really looks. He'd listened in to radio signals and had written down much of what I needed to know. There's an alert out for the missing van so there might be roadblocks, though they'd still be relying on drones. He showed me how to work the vid satnav screen. He'd also found a way of charging the fuel battery electrically so I have plenty of juice. Dorado was a hundred and twenty miles away. The van was loaded with weapons and food and water. It's time.

I get in the van wearing my Protector suit. The helmet coves the whole cranium and part of the face with a bullet proof visor. I hate it. Trash is nowhere to be seen. My guess is he doesn't do final goodbyes, which is what this may be. I start the van and am about to drive away when the passenger door opens and Trash gets in, wearing the other Protector suit. He stares straight ahead. He has a different pair of glasses – large tortoise shells that magnify his eyes, but at least he looks slightly less demented. He pushes his chip into the console. Moment's later music starts.

"Brahms?"

"Violin Concerto in D major, Op.77."

We are quiet for a few minutes.

"I'm testing a hypothesis."

"What?"

"Why I'm coming. Test a hypothesis. Several actually."

"Alright then."

My phone rings. I look at the number and answer.

"Alright."

Trash shows no curiosity.

I pass Barter Square and then take the road inland. Jez is waiting at a corner, carrying a holdall and a small bag. I stop. Never underestimate the profit motive. The thought of an arsenal of weapons had kept him awake and he couldn't resist. He gets in the back seats of the van and shows me the holdall that contained about ten bottles.

"Few more home-mades," he says.

"And you can think ahead and have a gift for timing. This is Trash. Jez."

Jez holds out his hand and Trash stares ahead, ignoring him.

"Good to meet you too, old buddy. What's this crap playing?"

"This is special day music."

We drive another few miles, each in our own thoughts and Brahms' notes so sweet they should break a concrete heart. Ludicrously I feel something odd. It takes a few seconds and then I realise it's joy. Or something like. It feels good to be doing something. Not always on a passive back step. I want to see Dad, wherever he is. And take him home, no matter what. I summon Joe and tell him what I'm doing. He half smiles. It's a tender smile, the one he reserved for when I told him something true and heartfelt. As if he wanted no other gift ever. I kiss him adieu and summon Chloe. She seems ghostly. I start to tell her I love her.

"Shit!"

I slam on the brakes and just avoid hitting her. Jez shouts from the back. I look at Trash.

"Why didn't you tell me someone was there?"

"You're the one driving," he says.

It is the little girl, large orb eyes, red hair framing her pale face. Skinny legs. In a one-piece shift, no socks and black slip on shoes. I almost killed her. The van is millimetres away. She stands in the road looking up at me.

She doesn't move.

"She's feral. Probably turned. God knows what. Run her over," says Jez.

I get out of the van and we look at each other.

"You keep turning up," I say.

She nods.

"In my dreams too."

She looks at me.

"What do you want?"

"I'm coming with you," she says.

"No. That is not going to happen. Good luck."

I turn.

"You have to take me."

I turn back. Look curious.

"I helped you. Tit for tat," she says.

"How did you help me?"

"In the coach. Stand and deliver. I told you. Three. And that's how many came into the church. The Hunt. I told you. Three."

This kid is weird and then some.

"Look. I give that you're special in some way. But you can't come. I don't want…"

"I know. You don't want the same thing to happen. Like before. Finding them both."

"How do you… but I'm not sure I want to know how this freak knows things. I turn again to the van.

"She wants me to come."

"Who?"

"You know who. Tie a yellow ribbon."

I touch the place where the ribbon is inside my uniform. Too many questions to ask. On impulse I tell her to get in the van. She sits behind next to Jez. She looks surprised to see him, but says nothing.

"What's your name?" I ask.

"Lottie. Call me Lot."

"I'm Ali, but you probably already know that. The quiet brains trust is Trash and this gentleman is Jez."

"Shouldn't bring a kid," says Jez.

"Well, she's here. Let's go."

I don't rightly know why I am letting her come on what is, after all, something of a suicide mission. I am going because I have to know, Trash is coming because he has some theories he is clearly desperate to test. Jez is coming for money. I have no idea why this girl is coming, but I feel I cannot refuse. She is like a compulsion.

Trash has a small screen on his lap and is making constant adjustments to it. I ask what he's doing and he says he is blocking Protector signals, and that if other Protectors actually see us he can send false signals so that they think we are another crew altogether. Without him I'd probably be dead by now. We make good time and travel about forty miles. We stop near a vale of dead trees that rattle like bones in the breeze. Dedham Vale. I turn off the road and into a dark copse where we won't be visible from the road. Trash says he can block drone searches.

We eat a few tins of beans and corn and drink water. Trash mysteriously produces a bottle of viscous, pale liquid and offers it to me. I take a swig and my tongue cleaves to my palate.

"What the hell is that?"

"Home brew."

"But what's in it?"

"You don't want to know."

It certainly warms everything. Jez takes a swig and approves. Lot sits hunched against her knees and withdrawing into herself.

"Where are you from, Lot?" I ask.

She glances at Jez, then at me. "We shouldn't talk like that."

"How should we talk?"

She shrugs. This little one was a mystery top to bottom. We were all tired and subdued but full of the tension of unknown things to come. Our plan for tomorrow was to get closer to Dorado, then try to hunker down somewhere, maybe even establish a base, and Trash would try to get some sort of picture of activity, population density, by bouncing a signal from satellite shields, or even tap into drone surveillance. What I wanted was some sort of clue as to where people are kept – labour camps, prison, and the rationale for it. The ideal scenario would be if Trash could actually get into a database and we could find Dad's name and ID and location. I realise that without Trash this whole venture would have been futile. I want to tell him how grateful I am but he would hate it. He might even want to go back. Perhaps it was a mistake to bring Jez. Time will tell. Lot was something else altogether. It's hard to reject someone who finds their way into your dreams.

The heath is full of mist and strangeness. Bess stamps the ground and neighs and snorts, a sure sign of stress. "Easy girl, easy sweet Bess," he says, but knows he should heed this warning. Bess is the cleverest of the two of them by far. He has the reckless heart and peacock courage and she has the brains and the muscle. The coach will trundle by soon. He checks his pistols. Tips his hat at a rakish angle. Feels the sword scabbard down Bess's flank. He had flirted with seven years transportation when the Essex verderers found him dealing in contraband venison and horse stealing. He had dodged powder and ball twice and some say the shadow of chains and hangman's noose darken his footsteps now. There is only so much luck afforded a man. Very well, he would ride his luck as he rode Bess, with a curse and a wink and a holleroo.

The wheels of the coach and the horse's hooves clickety clacked. Turned a corner and from the darkness, from nowhere it seemed, a tall figure on a proud horse. All in shadow and daring and the <u>irriguous</u> breath from the horse. Penumbra of silhouettes threatening in the night.

"*Stand and deliver.*"

The carriage door opens and two troopers with pistols are in the road facing him down. A trap.

"*Right again, my girl. When will I heed you?*" *he says quietly.* "*Is this where our story ends, Bess?*" *He imagines epitaphs and eulogies.* '*Turpin was the ultimus Romanorum, the last of a race... no name worthy to be recorded after his own. With him expired the chivalrous spirit which animated successively the bosoms of so many knights of the road; with him died away that passionate love of enterprise, that high spirit of devotion to the fair sex, which was first breathed upon the highway by the gay, gallant Claude Du-Val, the Bayard of the road—Le filou sans peur et sans reproche—but which was extinguished at last by the cord that tied the heroic Turpin to the remorseless tree.*' *But he knows that the true glory is due to Bess. And all is in peril, but not lost.*

"So put your hands on your head before I put lightning through it."

I am still half in the dream. I see Lot sitting placidly, hands on her head, looking up at the Protector who holds a laser pistol. One blast will put a fiery hole straight through you. Trash sits, looking slightly baffled, hands on head. I put my hands on my head.

"Where's your vehicle?" Asks Trash.

The Protector looks at him curiously.

"Is everything working? Satnav. Broadband?"

"What?"

"Is everything working? It's not, is it? You've got a phone but the stuff in the van is kaput."

"How do you know?"

Trash looks satisfied. Redeemed even. They got to us under the radar – a bit of luck on their part.

"You are all under arrest. Illegal possession of weapons and uniforms of the Authority. You're using a Protector van. Suspicious circumstances. You are terrorists. We may execute you on the spot. Hang on, you're that witch bitch from the hunt. Oh boy, are you going to be skinned." He turns slightly, "Rob! Got a catch here. Robbo!" And he lurches forward spastically and then falls on the ground twitching and clutching at imaginary demons. His eyes roll and he's salivating white foam and blood. Jez stands behind him and has shot him through the back of the neck with a laser pistol. He coughs a fountain of blood which arcs and speckles Lot like hot rain drops. Then he subsides, twitching. We watch until he is no more.

"Other one's dead too," Jez says.

"He might have been useful," says Trash.

"And now he's dead. These apparatchiks know John Joe shit. I've done business with them. I know."

I wipe the blood from Lot and she looks at me.

"It's alright," she says.

I look at her big eyes.

"He got away."

"What?"

"In your dream. What happened was – Dick laughed and one of the troopers fired but it flash'd in the pan and the other trooper turned to see what had befallen his comrade and Dick fired blue thunder at him, winging him in the shooting hand, and Bess flew into the night. In his company you could mount the hill-side, dash through the bustling village, sweep over the desolate heath, thread the silent street, plunge into the eddying stream. He kept an onward course without fatigue. With him you shouted, sang, laughed, exalted, wept. Safe."

I'm gobsmacked. "Where do you find all this stuff?"

"It finds me."

"But how do you know about it?"

"It knows me."

"Fucking kid's weirded out. Probably feral. She'll turn."

He wants to kill her too. She is on another planet, but no one is killing her. She knows things. She looks at Jez without fear.

"All I'm saying is..." he starts.

"I know what you're saying. Leave it. More important, we need to clear up this mess and move," I say.

Trash is examining the Protector's van. He comes back with a log book.

"Useful," he says.

Now we have important decisions to make.

11

We take the Protector's weapons and their uniforms, so now Jez has one. Too big for Lot, but at a pinch it might help. They had water and food in the van so we stock up, and siphon off their fuel. We put their bodies in their van and cover it with dead bracken. The software wasn't working properly, which is why Trash didn't get a signal from them, and he makes sure everything else electrical and digital he doesn't need is dead.

I anticipate getting to the outskirts of Dorado by dusk, which is ideal. Then we stop and see what we can gauge from the lie of the land and from Trash's wizardry. He is improvising a new signal detection device from equipment he found in the Protector's van. I go off a little in the bracken to wash from a bottle of water and get myself ready for the journey. When I return Jez is sitting next to Lot and whispering to her. Perhaps he is comforting her. When I get closer I get the gist of it. "So when a bloke puts it to her, she usually squawks a lot because the first time it really hurts. But then she gets a taste for it. Some women like it rough."

"Jez."

He turns. Smiles. "Just chatting," he says.

I smile back and tell him to come and talk, away from Lot.

"You can talk like the dirty prick you are to whatever morons you usually mix with, but in front of her keep a civil tongue or I'll slice it off."

"I saved your miserable lives. You owe me. And she's weird. Feral. I was just telling her the facts of life. If she lives she'll bump into them soon enough."

"She's a child. Probably no more than ten. If you can't shut up leave. Go now. Well?"

He looks sheepish. Surly. He mock salutes and goose steps away. He did probably save our lives, albeit with considerable relish. We do owe him. I need to be on the alert with this strange little band I've gathered.

Much of the land is uninhabited. We pass whole villages and towns abandoned to the odd group of ferals. Occasional pack of wild dogs. A line from an old forgotten poem comes to me: *I had not thought death had undone so many*. Dante's *Inferno* and Eliot's *Wasteland*. It is remarkable that less than two generations ago the problem was overpopulation. Now we are often in a ghost world. How did it all come to pass? In BeforeTimes I had a passing interest in mathematics. Probability Theory. Is it true that randomness is all around us? Probability theory is the mathematical framework that allows us to analyze chance events in a logical fashion. The probability of an event is a number indicating how likely that event will occur. This number is always between 0 and 1, where 0 indicates impossibility and 1 indicates certainty. With a coin toss it's easy. A chance of one in two it is heads or tails and the 50% ratio probability increases the more you toss the coin. When Covid really started to bite into society and the deaths and infection rates were spiralling, and you could see Armageddon in a scarlet cloak riding into town, I started to calculate probable outcomes in terms of societal mortality rates. Numerically it got scary as percentages rose until I realised that Chloe had a one in two possibility of dying, as did we all. Then it started to narrow more until the figures on my computer were like little black harpies heralding imminent disease and death. Almost a one in one chance. No parent wants to live in the shadow of those odds. That's when I realised I had no faith in any form of authority and every stranger I met was a potential nemesis. Joe asked me to stop my calculations. He said they were making me weird and him weirder, but I was hooked. Mathematics is addictive. I then started calculating the likelihood of the new strain of virus being deliberately introduced as opposed to poor hygiene and bad luck. One in two. The probability that the death rate would rise when we ran out of protective masks. One in two. The probability that the human immune system would develop a natural resistance to Covid, but that then had to be set against the fact that the Health care system had collapsed, and against food becoming scarce and getting more so. Probabilities started to turn in on themselves until I knew there was a one in two possibility I would go completely off my head. Which might be a blessed relief. Then I found a dog eared copy of a play by Tom Stoppard called *Rosencrantz and Guildenstern*. At the beginning they play a coin tossing game. After Rosencrantz has successfully bet heads seventy seven times in a row, Guildenstern proclaims that, "A weaker man might be moved to re-examine his faith, if in nothing else at least in the law of probability." He ends up flipping heads 92 times in a row.

This illogical and mathematically highly unlikely sequence symbolizes both the randomness of the world and the play's exploration of oppositional forces. The coin flips suggest that the world is ruled by randomness and the occurrence of highly improbable events. So I came to the conclusion that shit happens and we are in the land of Job, where the probability of one miserable thing following another is one hundred per cent, a one in one dead cert. Mathematics is no comfort for the hopeless and lost.

Then we arrive at Gallows Corner and it's a whole new story. Just before the A12 intersection blue black smoke billows in front of us. We approach slowly a wall of burning tyres in the road. In front are six men, two black, two Chinese, two white. They all wear red bandanas and drip with thin chains decorated with tiny skulls. Others appear, curious. Lots of different nationalities and some faces and colours I've never seen before: a man with a greyish skin and two women with a bluish hue. It doesn't look like face paint. Perhaps some illness? One of the women holds a home-made blast gun made from a drainpipe. I wonder what it fires and how the blast is achieved. She points it at us, but then waves us to drive to the side of the tyres and onto some wasteland. As Protectors we are not worth stopping or trying to steal from. The fires of hell would be unleashed on them, as they may be on us.

I drive around the tyres and through the blue-black acrid smoke, then re-join the broken road on the other side. All around is activity. Some houses demolished and ransacked, some painted in gaudy colours and hung with insignia and flags bearing messages: Gallows Gin; FFS; Hope Hurts; Die on Demand. Raggedy tents and caravans like a forgotten circus. People sleeping on the ground. Ferals stand watching everything and nothing. It is a grotesque carnival town of misfits and miscreants. I drive slowly. I don't want to knock anyone down and risk having to get out. There is the whiff of mischief and violence here. A pack of dogs follows the van, barking and snarling. Quickly, and before anyone can react, Lot opens the back doors and a smallish sized sable coloured dog leaps inside. Lot closes the door quickly. I stop and look behind.

"What the hell are you doing?"

Jez points his pistol at the dog but Lot sits in front of it, her arms outstretched. "Get out of the way, you little bitch." But she is defiant. He tries to grab her but I tell him to stop. He turns on me, spittle on his lips. "A dog? A fucking dog? They're walking plague traps. There isn't a dog outside of Dorado won't give you every shit hopping disease you can dream up, and then some. This dog is dead and then out."

"This dog is different," says Lot, her arms still out protectively. The dog sits quietly behind her.

By now a little crowd has gathered outside, drawn by the spectacle we are creating. A Protector van stopping to pick up a dog. Must be something wrong here. They are growing suspicious. A woman picks up a large stone. Others follow. We need to get out of here. Clearly some of these people are beyond concerns of personal safety, indifferent to everything, even Protector guns.

"Throw the dog out!" Jez shouts.

A thump as a rock hits the windscreen. It's bulletproof so it bounces off, but still. I safety lock all the doors. A crash makes me turn. A feral child with glassy fish eyes has hit the windscreen with a sledgehammer and is lining up to do it again. A hairline crack appears in the glass. I drive away and accelerate. If anyone gets in the way – tough. I wonder how far this horror show extends. Just beyond the crossroads on a sports field to our left a tooth and claw pitch battle is going on between feral children and about a dozen adults. Sticks, knives, stones. Next to it is a wicker fence, broken down in places. Inside, are dozens of bodies lying down. Some still. Some coughing. A Covid compound. Put them in there, let them die, burn them. Then three hundred metres beyond the crossroads we rejoin the A12 and everything is suddenly quiet, as if we had driven through an invisible wall that separated collective madness from the usual quiet and dead land.

Trash is shaking his head.

"What?" I say.

He looks straight ahead. I pull over and stop. Trash is now investigating some hand held electrical signal device. His way of blanking out what is happening. I turn and Jez is staring at Lot, now petting the dog, who has the prettiest collie type face, fronds of gold brown hair trail from her ears and she licks Lot's hands as she is stroked. We've got a problem here.

"Dog has to go," Jez says.

"Lot, tell me what happened back there. Why did you open the door?"

Lot looks at me, as does the dog.

"To let Emma in."

"Emma?

"That's her name."

"You know her?"

"I do now."

"I don't understand."

"She'd explain, but it would take too long."

"Alright then."

I turn and start the engine. Jez erupts. "I am taking that dog outside now and shooting it. You're insane. You think you can bring a mindfucked brat and a rabid dog on something like this? We have a one in a hundred shot at finding out what's going on in Dorado and you want to make it a zero shot? "

"That's my plan, Jez, so why don't you stop whining and make sure the weapons are all clean and ready? And check on the temperature of your home made Armageddons."

We seem to be expanding into the strangest brew little band of insurgents, if that's what we are. I remind myself that my sole purpose in this quest is to find out what has happened to my Dad. That is all. What price am I prepared to pay for that? The better question is: what price doing nothing? I may as well be dead. And I tell myself that the others are here through choice. No one forced them. So they take their chances. And that now appears to include Emma the dog.

A few hours and we are driving through what was Hackney marshes, now a grey sea of wet sludge with the A12 snaking through it, full of potholes. Then we swing left with Victoria Park on our right. Trash tells me to pull over. He has been busy. He is scrolling through data on a phone. He starts voice swiping through a tablet too. *Right right left. Enhance.* I think again what an extraordinary person he is and how I need him here. Lot is asleep cuddled up with Emma in the back. Jez in a strop and playing patience.

"OK. Here's a map. Half a mile to our right is a force field. You need a code to get through, which I have. There is also a city fence, five metres high, razor wire, another quarter of a mile in. I guess in case there's a power failure and the force field fails."

I point at what look like rows of hangars just beyond the fence. He says these are where the Protectors live. They are like army barracks. He rolls the map around for a 3D ground view. Then further in from there are clusters of small buildings and then what look like large stadia or factories. Trash says they must be manufacturing units – perhaps weapons or luxury goods. Or maybe prisons, I think. Beyond these is a vast agricultural and farming area that extends down to the river, where it looks as if there is still water, but in a series of dammed lakes. Then going west there are what look like suburbs – roads with cars and actual trees. I long to get close to a proper tree again. Hear the wind whistling the leaves, feel the healthy bark. Something that isn't dead or dying. Much further in is an area referred to as The Park. Trash says this used to be Hyde Park. It is fenced all the way round. Trash keys in a few numbers and gets a response. "Second electrical fence, plus drone and satellite surveillance," he says. Some large buildings. And then rows of villas. Admin buildings and housing for the elite.

I wonder who lives there. It occurs to me that when I was young and gobbled up dystopian stories – *Brave New World, 1984, The Hunger Games*, there was always a figurehead, the big cheese, someone to supposedly unite people and keep them down, but the reality here is there is no one in particular, no Big Brother or Sister to frighten us, nor an inspirational charismatic figure to comfort and guide us and promise us a better tomorrow. Just voices and different grey figures, often holograms, on TV and the Internet. Perhaps that is why we have become so weakened and eviscerated, because there was no bogeyman oppressing us, and whom we could both fear and hate and perhaps rebel against, nor was there a future beyond the meagre, disease-ridden life we had. The human landscape was not a tragedy. Merely a tedious sludge. A dying world administered by a grey bureaucracy. Perhaps that was the truth of things. If only I'd known then what I know now. I notice an ancient spider web across a corner of the windscreen. Life goes on. Until it doesn't.

Trash was still talking while I'd vamped out in my own thoughts.

"How do you know all this stuff, Trash?"

"I'm a genius. At finding out how things work. I learnt a lot from your Dad."

He looks aslant at a kamikaze fly determined to concuss itself on the windscreen. An uncomfortable moment. Things unspoken.

"What?"

He almost looks at me. He scrolls further on the map and points much further down the river. Most of the old bridges directly into the city are gone. A few on our side of the force field, and then right over on the south west there's Putney bridge. He points to a large area.

"This. The airport. Not many planes. I've been monitoring them. They go up. Three hours later they're back. Never longer."

The implications start to sink in.

"They don't go far," I say, my throat squeezing tight.

"Probably just to other parts of the country. For supplies or personnel. Who knows?"

"So no warm climes? No Arcadia?"

He shakes his head. "And if you think about it, all the oceans roil around into each other. Ours are dead. It's unlikely any others are alive. Chances are, the number of times the virus has gone round, there is no Europe. What saved us is that we're an island."

"So there might be other islands that had that natural protection where people have survived?"

"It's possible. But it means that if your Dad is anywhere he's probably here. In Dorado."

"Let's find somewhere for the night. Make a plan."

I decide we are safer south of the river. We stay on the A12 across what was the Thames, then right into Blackwall Lane. On the A206 keeping the Thames just to our right.

"Where are we going?" Jez asks.

I suddenly know. "Back into the nineteenth century. Ahoy."

Lights in the distance beyond the force field and the fence, but eerily quiet here. The ancient timbers creak a little as I climb up. I help Lot up and Emma nimbly pads up a fallen timber onto the main deck and starts sniffing around for scraps of anything interesting.

"What is it?" Lot asks.

"The Cutty Sark. A clipper ship. Cargo ship. Fastest ship of her day."

"What day was that?"

"Many days. Two hundred years ago."

"And now we live here?"

"For a little while."

"And Emma can be our lookout."

"Alright then."

We go right down to the lower deck and explore. Rats scatter. Old tarpaulins. A box of tickets, memento of the days when there were tourists, people who pay to look at something that is already there. Some photographs of the Cutty Sark. Lot picks up one and scrutinizes it. I believe she can see high seas and squalls and tea and spices from China, tobacco and coco beans from the Americas. Exotica. Frankincense. Myrrh. Things departed in our brave new world. Long gone lives mend ropes, scrub decks, paint with tar, haul sail and dream of land and ale and gold and love. All dreams are crooked now.

We decide to sleep on the 'Tween deck. A few of the port holes have rotted so we can escape if anyone comes from above. We are not visible to the outside.

Trash and Jez unload what we need for the night from the van and bring the explosives aboard, and then find some filthy old tarpaulins to hide the van. Trash switches off all communications inside the van. Another reason I chose this as a base was because we are close to the Greenwich foot tunnel. If we get stuck on the other side for whatever reason it's at least another escape option.

Emma has her nose to the floor and is following a cockroach the size of a mouse in ever more thoughtful circles. We eat some tins of mush that were perhaps beans at some time past – the labels long gone so no way of knowing. Then we make a plan for the morning. Drive back and through the force field, hoping Trash has got the algorithms right. I have no doubt he has. Then through the fence at one of the check points. We have digital passes. I want to get to the big units to see if there are prisoners there, or an admin centre that can give us information. Which is all I want. If I find out Dad is nearby I'll let the others go and try to get him out. That's my responsibility. Lot and Emma will stay here. I'd prefer an adult to stay but I need Trash for the tech stuff and Jez for the explosives. Besides, I don't trust leaving Jez with Lot. He argues that Lot should go too, but I refuse.

We hunker down under tarpaulins. Sleep is a long time coming. I watch Lot stroking Emma and finally, sometime in the early hours, I am gone.

The wind was a torrent of darkness among the gusty trees.
The moon was a ghostly galleon tossed upon cloudy seas.
The road was a ribbon of moonlight over the purple moor,

And the highwayman came riding—
 Riding—riding—
The highwayman came riding, up to the old inn-door.

Chloe and Joe in the shadows, trying to get my attention. What are they saying? Obdurate world where all is confusion. I long to hold them but am stuck fast in the moment, the pull of myself against an invisible tide. Joe is looking through me. Am I invisible? No. I realise he is looking behind. Look behind! But already it is too late. Too late for looking. Too late for salvation. Too late for love. There is only...

"Surrender! surrender!" said the chief of the officers. "There's five hundred pounds for your apprehension, dead or alive. Surrender, or I fire!" The only reply Dick made to this invitation was to give Bess the reins, and dash off along the road in the direction of the common.

Lot looks down on me, Emma beside her cocking her head to one side and also staring. Morning.

"You were talking. We were worried," she says.

"It was only a dream," I say.

"Nothing is only a dream. You needed to look behind, didn't you?"

I never know what to say to this child. I stroke Emma's soft ears and she licks my hand. Tears spring to my eyes. I am not used to this kind of affection. I wipe them away. It's not a time for feeling.

We eat a little, gather weapons. Jez checks the temperatures of the explosives. Decide on the order of things. If Trash has got his digital homework right, we could get way into Dorado without even having to speak. Lot plays with Emma, throwing a ball made of rags. They have a little food and water. I tell them to stay in the Sark and imagine they are on a voyage. Hide if they hear anyone around.

"Or blow blue thunder through them," Lot says. Trash hides a few weapons, a machine gun and two pistols, on a cross beam just out of sight. If we have to leave in a hurry we may need them here when we return. If we return.

"Let's go," I say.

12

Jez drove west along the Thames and then right over Tower Bridge. I sat in the back. On the other side of the Thames there is traffic, some Protector vans and a motley crew of old cars and motorcycles. We drove along until Trash says a Gateway is on the left through the force field. We stop and he used a phone he took from one of the Protectors. Seconds later a blue fire hologram door showed the way through. We drove through and there was a slight ripple in the air as the field closed behind us.

This was a different world. As if a giant hoover had sucked up all dirt and dust and filth and decaying rubbish. Mostly only Protector vans here, but a few cars so state of the art I had no idea what they were, like giant toys. People walked in decent clothes. Then something I thought didn't exist anymore. Restaurants. Shops selling clothes. Grocers with fine vegetables and fresh fruit. A butcher shop with giant hams on display. Trees lined the streets. Flower displays in huge tubs. There were drones overhead, a discrete distance so that people did not feel oppressed by them. Trash's signal blocking, or signal diversions, seemed to be working.

We came to the fence and drove until we found an entrance, a gold framed gate. Trash pointed his phone and keyed in a signal. Nothing. He looked puzzled. Tried again.

"Shit. What's wrong?"

"I don't know. It should work."

"Come on then!" Shouted Jez.

"Shut it, Jez. We're OK," I said.

I saw two small drones come down and hover around us like mosquitoes. They would be taking constant photographs.

"Don't look directly at them," I said.

A loud bang on the side window made us all start. A Protector stood looking in inquisitively. Jez lowered the window.

"What you trying to do?" The Protector asked.

Jez looked at the gate. "What do you think?"

"What unit you with?"

Jez showed his ID card.

"You should have got info from the signals. This gate's kaput. Fuel's down. New supply coming in so should be up in hour or two. Use number three."

Jez raised a hand in thanks. Where the hell is number three? Jez gambled and drove to the left. A few minutes later we came to a gate – Number three in gold letters. The gods of chance had favoured us so far. Trash keyed in numbers and the gates slid apart and we're through. We stopped in a general parking area of vans and trucks and got out to look. We left the explosives in the van but took hand weapons and some grenades in holdalls. We left the big explosives in the van. We were all surprised. I was expecting more opulence but this was an abaundant world – to our left fields of fine vegetables, beans, peas, sprouts, cabbages, carrots, corn, and orchards that go down to the river – apples and pears and cherries, peaches and blackberries and huge greenhouses with grape bearing vines, berries and lemon trees. Heat lamps played over the scene furnishing all with a deeper gloss green than seems natural. It was an Eden of freshness and pasture. There were goats and pigs in big enclosures. The smell of ripe manure was overpowering. Creatures treated like royalty. Some of the apples seemed unnaturally large, but then it was so long since I'd seen things growing that my sense memories were probably shot. On the right a utilitarian landscape of giant factories and behind them admin buildings.

Trash looked at the lushness and whistled through his teeth, then started to mutter, almost to himself:

"But he grew old—
 This knight so bold—
And o'er his heart a shadow—
 Fell as he found
 No spot of ground
That looked like Eldorado.

 And, as his strength
 Failed him at length,
He met a pilgrim shadow—
 'Shadow,' said he,
 'Where can it be—
This land of Eldorado?'

 'Over the Mountains
 Of the Moon,
Down the Valley of the Shadow,
 Ride, boldly ride,'
 The shade replied,—
'If you seek for Eldorado!'"

I stared at him in amazement. He looked sheepish, apologetic. "Edgar Allen Poe. I'm not illiterate, for Christ's sake."

This was a journey of amazement.

It was surprisingly easy to move around incognito because there were so many Protectors, walking, in vans, on hoverbikes. I wanted to see inside the factories and then get to the admin buildings. That would probably be where we might run into trouble. Our ID cards got us into one of the factories. We entered a lit corridor and then there were various metal grille steps leading up, like entering a giant sports stadium. Jez was alert, hand in pocket on his gun. Trash touched my arm. I started because this was the first time he had ever touched me. Hell, it might be the first time he'd ever touched anyone.

"Are you sure you want to do this?" He asked.

"What do you know?"

"I suspect a great deal."

"I want the truth."

"Lead on, Macduff."

We climbed the metal stairs, which echoed tinnily, and in front was a door which said AUTHORISED PERSONNEL ONLY. We opened it and emerged onto a platform. We ducked down behind a handrail with a grilled wall and looked through at the scene below. It took at least ten seconds for the full horror of what I saw to sink in.

I feel bile rising and have to swallow hard to stop me throwing up. My skin feels clammy and then itchy, as if an army of ticks and ants are crawling and biting beneath the skin itself. Below us are giant vats, the size of trucks, on a belt three metres wide. Hollow metal tubes feed naked dead bodies down into the vats, people in grey prison garbs wearing rubber gloves are sorting the bodies above and feeding them into the tubes: old, young, male, female. Once the vats are full a liquid chemical spray is turned on and a hideous yellowish steam rises. The stench is horrendous. The bodies start to putrefy into mush. Some things so push the boundaries of what you already thought was as bad as it can be that the mind takes longer to compute the images, in case you are overwhelmed with horror. The industrialising of human beings into slop on such a scale. Large lids are pushed over the vats and once every vat is full, I count twenty five, the belt turns and the vats are slowly conveyed out through a large hatch. I see there are valve taps on the side of each vat. A line comes to me: *Through me you pass into the city of woe.* I am covered head to toe in sweat, as if a sudden sickness is plaguing me. All this flesh boiled down into…what?

Next to me Trash stares implacably.

"You knew," I say.

"I guessed."

"How?"

"The planes that seem to go nowhere. The fresh fruit and vegetables."

I look enquiringly.

"These people are a form of human composting. They are harvested, if you like, and rather than being left between layers of wood chip to naturally putrefy into compost they've found a way of fast tracking the bodies into manure. Hence those orchards and fields outside," he says.

"But they need a constant supply of bodies."

"Some natural deaths. A lot of virus deaths. Hunts. The culls of Ferals."

"And the myth of Arcadia."

He looks at me. "The myth of Arcadia."

Bastards. I want to kill everyone involved. Every last piece of scum. I start to recoil inside myself. A live wet thing that wants nothing to do with the world around. I start to gag but swallow it back.

"There's more," he says. But behind him, a hundred and fifty or so metres, a Protector striding towards us.

"Time to go," I say. I expect Jez on be on my right, but he isn't. Has he been caught? Did he not even come up the stairway? We stand and run to the stairway. If we can get outside it should be easy enough to get lost in the melee. I open the door and there is Jez, smiling, with a Protector on either side. They point their laser pistols at us.

"Welcome to Dorado," he says.

The delayed shock at what I've just seen bubbles into despairing anger. I can feel my whole body trembling. Then I disappear.

It hurts but I can't seem to find where it hurts. As if I am simply pain. The very form of suffering. God's fool. My eyes feel gluey but I force them open. Shadows and stripes and ghosts. Someone wipes my face with a cool wet rag. I try to move but my left shoulder screams and my neck feels brick solid. I breathe deeply until I can feel my heartbeat and am ready to be in the world again. I blink a few times and see Trash. He fades and shimmers and then comes into focus.

"Take it easy," he says. Blood on the rag he wiped me with. I touch my head and feel the wound. Not deep but it will do for a few hangovers. My neck cracks as I ease myself up and the pain in my shoulder sears across my back, but at least I'm not horizontal. My throat is parched. The room is hot and waxy. It's a cell, one barred window, bunk beds, a metal toilet and sink. Two surveillance cameras. I start to speak but Trash puts a finger to his lips. I notice how chewed the fingernail is. All that inner combustion and energy must make him a fireball of nerves. He leans over me and for one terrifying moment I think he's going to kiss me. But he whispers "I've worked out there is a small dead zone by the sink where they can see our backs but they can't hear us if we speak quietly. When you feel OK I'll help you over there and pretend to help you wash up."

I close my eyes, count to a hundred, and then swing off the bottom bunk bed. Trash helps me to the sink and turns on the tap. I'm thinking of Lot and Emma, but first things first.

"What happened?"

"You went ballistic. I thought they were just going to shoot you but Jez cracked you on the head and then they kicked you a bit until you were out."

"What about you?"

"I watched."

"Right."

"Jez is with them. He took us for suckers."

"Not hard to do. All those people. Diluted to feed vegetables."

"I think it's worse."

"How could it possibly be?"

"There's a second factory, as we saw. When we were brought here I watched more bodies being taken in there and I saw methane like storage tanks outside."

"What does that mean?"

"They're using the dead as petrol. I've wondered for a long time why there are no garages, and given that we import no oil and never drill for it, how do they make their engines work? There's some petrol around, but mostly the new engines have a convertor switch. Methane can be used as a fuel in a gas turbine or steam generator. I think all the waste products from bodies are extracted and then they are boiled down and the fat itself used as kind of fuel."

"People harvested as manure and petrol. Including my dad."

"Your dad was a great man. I never knew my own father. I'm sorry."

"I thought we'd reached the pits as a race but this is obscene."

"They followed through the logic of things."

"That's alright then. A great comfort, Trash. That logic wins the day. What will they do with us? Don't answer that."

The door opens and they come in.

A Protector with a band of coloured strips on the chest pocket of his uniform, presumably medals for murdering children. Another Protector on his right and Jez on his left, a thin smile on his lips.

None of them wears a helmet. Disconcerting to see Protectors without helmets because you are forced to concede they might be human beings.

"I'm Superintendent Fauberge. This is Protector Davis and this," indicating Jez, "is Protector Harness, although you know him as Jez." Jez gives a little mock bow. "You are guilty of, read it…" and Davis reads from a clipboard: "The murder of two licensed Protectors, the theft of state equipment, the impersonation of licensed Protectors, breaking into…"

"Alright. Enough," says Fauberge. "All of these are capital offences. You are now on the state execution list. We have a backlog so…Davis?"

Davis looks at his clipboard again. "Wednesday. 9.20 am. Death by captive bolt gun."

"There it is. You have two days to enjoy our hospitality."

"He murdered the Protectors," I say with a nod at Jez. Fauberge looks at him. Jez shakes his head.

"Done then," says Fauberge. "Your word. His word. His counts."

"I'll always think of you as Jez, the murdering, shabby, foul-smelling prick with bad teeth," I say.

"Pleasantries are over. Enjoy your stay."

They turn to leave, but Jez turns and mouths the words "Little girl and dog" and makes a cut throat gesture. My heart lurches at my ribs, as if trying to escape. I almost blank out and see my heart as a huge bird with golden feathers and a bright eye borrowed from an angel break through the bloody hole in my chest and fly hard to the Cutty Sark and swoop down where Lot and Emma lie like small statues, and dragging a blanket embroidered with flowers and silver thread to cover them, and then biting hard into the rope that holds the chain that anchors the boat to concrete and flying up, wings and muscles strain and flex as the mighty carcass of the boat groans and heaves and splashes into the water, and the bird pulls it through mud and gravel and water to the open sludge of sea and then beyond to the horizon where the sky swallows all.

Trash and I are both shocked, but not surprised. I feel foolish to have been completely taken in by Jez. How stupid not to realise that Protectors are planted in order to weed out insurgents, or potential insurgents, to trawl for rebels and then reel them in. He did it brilliantly. The bomb manufacturing, the pretence. And I was the one who asked him to come and he pretended to be reluctant. He played me so well. Killing the Protectors to show he was on our side. Clever and psychopathic. Seeing how far we could get to show cracks in their security.

"I'm sorry," I say.

Trash looks quizzical. "It's been interesting," he says, then after a thought, "They must execute people with stun guns because it's cheaper and because they don't want metal in the body if they're going to mulch it down. Cost effective and practical."

"Thanks, Trash. I feel so much better knowing that."

I'm tired beyond sleep. I lie on the bunk. I can feel him thinking above me. Maybe living entirely in the head the way he does is a good thing sometimes. It exempts you from the heartache of life. The sheer difficulty of getting through. I thought I was beyond the pale of most ordinary human feeling, apart from Dad, but something in me has broken open and I feel I am seeping out. It wouldn't surprise me to look down and see myself reflected in a puddle that is me.

An hour later the door opens again and Davis and Jez, as he is to me, enter. "You're wanted," Jez says to Trash. I get up but Jez holds up a hand. "Just Brainstrust." And they take him out and close the door. Surely not yet? They said two days. Perhaps they want to keep us separate. Perhaps they want to know how he fooled so much of their security and communication system. I hope they don't torture him. I almost want to pray but God has long departed this world and I'd only be talking to myself.

He returns a few hours later. Gets on his top bunk and says nothing.

"I was worried," I say. Nothing. "About you. I thought they might execute you." Nothing. "Trash, I do exist. What did they want?"

"Oh, just to talk. How did I know this? How did I work that out? You know they're listening to us and watching us now."

"It doesn't seem to matter much now. Does it?"

"I suppose not. You know what I'd really like right now?"

"A superhero to break in and rescue us?"

"A game of chess. I've just thought of an opening move that I don't think anyone has ever tried before."

"Alright then."

A night of fitful dreams. Dick Riding Bess in the rain and sleet but never arriving. In any case the flint and powder for his pistols soaked and useless. The weather too bad for coaches, the very trees huddling into themselves against a devil blasted world. And he wonders as he traverses the relentless night if a time when all the buccaneering heroes and adventurers will be hunted down, or disappear from ennui and the burden of comfort or despair.

The door opens. Superintendent Fauberge and Protector Jez enter. Jez holds a white Protector uniform.

"Rise and shine and welcome to the guild. Your uniform," says Fauberge and Jez holds out the brand new uniform. Trash swings off the top bunk and takes it. I stand up and look at Trash. He seems nonplussed.

"What's going on?" I ask.

"They offered me a job," and to Fauberge, "What is it again?"

"What is it, Superintendent? You're not some fucking slob in a garage now. And not poncing about with some greasy bitch like this on god knows what stupid bound to fail cunt of a project."

"What is it, Superintendent?" Trash says.

"You are a Protector of the guild in the service of peace as stipulated in the constitution of Dorado. The powers that be have decided that your knack with tech stuff and communications might be useful. Indeterminate period of probation subject to termination, and I mean termination, at any point."

I'm speechless. Trash has already taken off his old Protector uniform and is putting on the new one with a gold epaulette. Fauberge opens the door, then tuts at Trash and looks at me. "Aren't you going to say goodbye. Chivalry's not completely dead, you peasant. Good manners."

Trash turns to me. "Bye, Ali."

They go and the door closes, locks click.

I am numb. The hours plod by like death's metronome.

13

In the dark I go over and over it. How I was all consumed with knowing what happened to Dad and this blinded me to the futility of trying. Driven by feeling not fear and thought, which protect us from our kamikaze selves. I would like to kill Jez, but underlying that is a desire for self-annihilation for being so gullible. I assume Lot and Emma are gone. Lot to become manure or methane fuel and Emma to the garbage. My fault. Lot seemed to have prescience, yet she could not foresee her own death. I lose everyone that is important to me. Is it me cursed or that I live in a dead and dying world that will gorge on everything until, like a bemused snake turning on itself in a feast of auto cannibalism, it eats itself?

And the enigma of Trash? I can't blame him. He is given a chance to live and he takes it. Apart from a few strange detours into ordinary human feeling, he is an entirely rational person, more interested in things than people. It shouldn't be a surprise that he accepts life and work rather than a shoddy slaughterhouse death out of some dubious notion of loyalty. And loyalty to whom? A woman who only used him because he has an exceptional technological brain. Yet still I feel betrayed, but as dawn arrives in a clogged sky I realise that I have only betrayed myself. Perhaps all through I was really seeking death. To be with Joe and Chloe in a heaven that I know doesn't exist. Alive, at least they speak in my dreams and imaginings. When I am gone there will be nothing. Perhaps nothing is better. A sweet oblivion. Half in love with easeful death.

Next morning the door opens. It can only be five in the morning. There is no watery dawn as yet. Too early for my execution, unless they have brought it forward.

Protectors Davis and Jez.

"Get up. It's time," says Jez.

My body has healed but every joint feels a hundred years old. It will be good, I realise, to have an end to weariness. Davis has a tray holding a mug of water and bread roll. He puts it down. I drink some of the water. I don't want the bread. We leave the cell and walk along a long silver steel corridor, then up and down stairs. Finally we come out on a platform. It is a similar factory to the one I saw a few days ago but a different rust brown colour. This must be the methane unit. Behind is a lorry full of bodies. These are put on a belt that takes them to the metal tube chute that feeds the great vats. The smell is gut wrenching. Am I to be slaughtered here?

"Just my little joke," says Jez. "You're not really being processed today. Lot of the regular staff are ill, so you've got a reprieve. Honest day's work."

"Ill? Is the virus even here in Dorado?"

"Not your concern. All you need to think about for the next ten hours is: bodies off the lorry. Bodies into the feeder tube. When the vat's full stand well back because the chemical spray will waft up and blind you. You get used to the smell but chances are you won't be here long enough to know that."

"What if I refuse?"

"I'll push you down the chute alive. It won't be pleasant."

I join two others, a young woman with hollowed out eyes and an older man with a persistent cough, and start heaving the dead from the lorry and into the chute. At first I think it will send me mad, but I summon Joe and ask him to talk to me, to take me away with his talking. Joe tells me about wood. Different kinds. Softwoods from coniferous trees. Fir is an inexpensive durable wood. It stains badly but can make good buildings, floorboards and painted furniture. Pine - good choice for furniture, flooring and wood carvings. It is attractive, inexpensive and stains well. His favourite - Cedar – beautiful fragrant wood that is naturally resistant to rot and insects. Good for outdoor furniture. He had planned to make a swing love seat for us, but big enough for Chloe to sit in too. Hardwoods from deciduous trees. All have their own beauty. Birch – An attractive inexpensive wood. A harder wood that makes fine furniture. It can be difficult to stain. Cherry – one he loves to work with. It has a smell that takes you into fine orchards. A gorgeous wood with a white or reddish colour, easily workable and ages well. Ash Mahogany Maple Oak Poplar Teak Walnut. I can smell them, have the feel of their rough and smooth surfaces. Joe says – remember this, wood never dies. It carries all that happens and the memory of itself in its grain and texture and fibre. Even if you burn it the ash floats the ghost of itself into the air and earth. Ashes to ashes, dust to dust, things return to themselves. Everything returns home at last.

And then I summon Chloe and we ride awhile with Dick and Black Bess upon the heath dreaming of gold coin and ruby rings, pendants, Brazilian diamonds, choker necklaces with sapphire and amethyst studded aigrette, chatelaines, Fabergé imperial china eggs, stomacher brooches inset with pearl and ivory and onyx and spots of gold and silver. The riches would take us far to South America where we would live by the sea in a house of bamboo that let the salt breeze into our piratical dreams of adventure and victory and wealth and love. Always love.

And I come to as someone prods me in the back. Tears are rivuleting down my cheeks. My hands are waxy with the skin and stench of the dead. The great vats are like bloated metal insects digesting their bounty of flesh and blood and bone and gut and hair and teeth. Fra Angelico's Last Judgement of the devil chewing on the dead in a boiling pot of the damned. I understand that these ancients, Bosch, Van Eyck, Giotto, and later the Chapman Brothers, were not painting some vision of hell, but knowingly or not, a vision of the future on earth. They simply saw further than anyone else – to now.

In my cell I force myself to eat some bread and sluice it down with water. I close my eyes and fall into a blank dreamless stupor.

Sometime in the night I wake up to the sound of breathing and a stale halitosis. Jez is by the bed, close to me. He touches my cheek.

"You do anything and I'll bite your eyes out. I swear you will not enjoy anything you do to me," I say.

"You are mine, you clunky cunt. I will watch when your heart bursts and your brain finally caves in. Then you're mine. And call me Protector Harness,"

"Alright then. Jez."

He wants to rape and batter me but he's too smart to damage a worker. He licks his hand and wipes the damp palm over my cheeks and eyes. He leaves. I vomit in the bucket and lay in the dark trying to imagine the sounds of the sea when it was alive.

The next day is worse because when I summon Joe and Chloe they only appear in fits and starts, as if they are so horrified by what I am doing on that platform, greasy with the dead, that they cannot fully show. So I have little respite and the dead that keep coming and coming and I push down into the vats stay with me. The wide open eyes of a young girl with a terrible gash in her side, like the spear wound in Christ. I pull an old man from the lorry and a hearing aid plops out by my feet. A skinny man who, bizarrely, has an erection. Pregnant women. Teeth occasionally clatter at my feet and I kick them away. Some bodies already decomposing and I vomit frequently. I hope I don't come across my Dad's body. Or Lot's. The dead are not peaceful here. Not a single face at rest. As if the horror and disfigurement of pain and violence continues its story way beyond passing, and will exist forever to condemn us all for the world we have made and broken.

After a few hours I long for oblivion. This is how it works. I thought I had already been diminished beyond ordinary feeling but this is a much deeper pit to grovel in. Once you completely reduce someone they will do anything. They are no longer human and no longer care about anything. Particularly themselves. As I yank and push and pull the bodies down to the regular whoosh of hydraulic machines I long for the cattle bolt that will punch my brain like a nuclear rod and I will be gone and someone else will be pushing me down to become shit for manure or gas for fuel. I am no longer half in love with easeful death. I crave it.

That night I lie exhausted. The cell door opens and Fauberge enters. He leans against the wall and scrutinises me. He looks different, as if he has taken off a mask. He takes a small bottle from his pocket and two little glasses. He places them on a shelf and pours himself a glass of wine. He looks at me and indicates the bottle and glass. I nod and he pours a little wine for me. I wait for him to sip first and then I drink mine down in a gulp.

"What you must understand is that the real virus is hope. When people feel it they are infected, and it will destroy them. One way or another. If you were really clever you would see that this," – he waved a hand to indicate the processing plant and everything beyond – "is an evolutionary success. Because we have progressed beyond everything that people, in the old world, used to think constituted humanity. Love, despair, joy, hatred, idealism, aspirations, friendship, fulfilment, the list is long and boring. All those things are only distractions, and that was ever true, and we, some of us, see it now because we are whittled down to our utilitarian pragmatic bones. We shine. It's a miracle. There is only the work to be done today. What is the work? Whatever is necessary. That is all that counts, all that matters. It is genius in design and implementation. If you had recognised that, as you should because it stared you in the face every day, you would still be hustling in whatever brick and dirt hovel you came from, but nevertheless alive, rather than in this tank, where you will die. And soon. This is my gift to you, before you are boiled down into usefulness. Do you understand? If you do then you can shine, albeit briefly, before it is out, brief candle, out." He turns to leave and then stops. He takes something from his pocket and holds it. It is the rosewood box with onyx inlay and quartz stones that I gave to Dad. He smiles at it, then at me. "Pretty. Oh, and look, there's something inside." He opens it. A finger with a wedding ring. I know it is all that is left of my Dad. "Little memento. Yes. Pretty."

"One day I will kill you, Fauberge," I say.

"You wouldn't believe the number of people who have thought that, and a few, like you, who've said it. Guess what? No one has."

On the third day Jez and Davis arrive, with Trash. Jez looks at his phone. "Nine twenty. Let's go."

I get off the bunk and splash water on my face. My stomach groans.

"Where's my bread?" I ask.

Jez smiles at Davis. "She doesn't get it." Then to me, "New shift on the recycling, so today is your special day." He makes a fist and pretends to jolt his forehead and makes his eyes cross. He and Davis laugh. Lightning fear in my brain. I wanted this but now it's arrived...

"And why are you here?" I ask Trash. "Shouldn't you'd be busy making a missile launcher from a needle and a toilet roll."

"They thought it would be good if I saw a few executions. Closures is the proper term. I might be able to advise on the efficiency of the process. You know, speed it up a bit."

"Don't you just love him," says Jez, looking wonderingly at Trash, who remains impassive.

I am determined to walk properly, not to shake or cry or beg. I am hollowed out and hope to hope that I don't wet myself. I don't hate Trash. When you're so far on the spectrum as he is you come back on and off several times more, so it would be stupid to expect ordinary feeling, or compassion or loyalty, especially in a world devoted to stamping out those very things. I thought I saw small changes in him. He seemed to like me, and to become more engaged with life, but I was wrong. Now I just want to get the whole sorry business of life over with.

I wonder if I will see Fauberge who will come to make another little speech. It is a ten minute walk away. A barn like building made of aluminium. We are checked in by a Protector at a desk with bad acne. He looks at me and holds up his phone. "Stay still," he says. I look at him as he photographs me and then transfers the photograph to the computer before him. "Work work work," he says, "although we're in a lull. Most are coming from outside today. Culls. So all the stalls are free bar eleven and twenty two. Take your pick."

"Pick a number one to forty two," says Jez.

"Forty three, "I say.

There are stalls around three walls. Jez takes us into number thirteen. "Unlucky for some," he says with a smile. Inside is a chair with straps facing a machine that is an industrial stun gun. I see how it works. It will be moved towards me, aligned to my forehead and then a switch propels the bolt out at the speed of a bullet, which is what it is. Unconsciousness and death are instantaneous.

"So what's the process rate when you're doing it all internally?" Asks Trash.

"If we're using all forty two we can process two thousand five hundred and twenty an hour. One every four minutes. As the birth rate declines numbers are slipping but if it's true what they say, that we'll be going north for a war then we could be back to full production in a few months. Lots of little Mohammeds to keep the grub and gas going."

Davis straps me into the chair and Jez leans down and smiles at me.

"Trash here is helping with a new thermo nuclear device that pinpoints so we don't fuck up the air and everything even more. Just humans. It'll be a short war."

"You must feel honoured," I say to Trash.

"It's an interesting project," he says.

A light thud sounds a little distance away. Then footsteps as the body is taken away. Another thud, more footsteps. It's just me now.

"OK. Enough light banter. Let's do it," says Jez, and then to Trash, "You want to do the honours? Pull down the casing, steady it three inches from the forehead and then, this switch."

Trash holds the casing barrel. "Like this?" he says and in an instant swings it round to Davis, flips the switch and he falls with a perfectly cylindrical hole in his head. Then he pulls out a laser pistol and shoots Jez in the chest. Jez gasps as his uniform sucks in and I think his heart is shredded.

There is a second where everything seems to stop. I look at the smoking chest of Jez.

"That went better than I expected. I think we should go now," says Trash.

He loosens the straps.

"How will we get out?" I ask

"I'll think of something" he says.

We walk out. The Protector at the desk looks at us quizzically.

"Fuck up. Wrong one. I'm taking this back," Trash says.

"But I've put her on the system. You've got to top her. Takes ages to manually delete and correct. Where are the other guys?"

"Stun gun needs adjustments. They'll fix it."

"But that's for section one. You can't…" and Trash shoots him with the laser. He quickly goes around the desk and electronically shuts off the security camera, keys in some numbers at the monitor, and then looks up. "Sorry."

"What?" I say, but I know. I go around the desk and there is a photograph of Dad, who stood here two weeks ago. Number 400265B

We leave the building.

We walk to a small parking area and Trash slides open a van door. I get in the back. There is a new white Protector suit and helmet. I take off my stinking clothes and put on the uniform. My hands are shaking.

"We have about forty five minutes to get out," he says while I change. "You wouldn't believe the technology I had access to. It was a challenge, but not as much as I'd hoped for."

"That's a real shame. I'm so sorry for you," I say.

"I've made some adaptations that'll help. People talk a lot of martial arts bollocks about using your enemy's strength against them, but that's not how it works. Here, the strength is the technology – drones, surveillance, weapons. Though that isn't their strength, it's an entirely neutral force. Technology doesn't give a monkey's who uses it, who gets trashed, who wins. It's just there."

"So what have you done?"

"I've made it mine. Ours. Some of it anyway. Many of the drones are weaponised. I've reprogrammed them so that they fire at whoever gives the order to fire. I've also left detonators in the two processing blocks. One hour from now it will be a furnace around here. They won't find them."

"How come it was so easy?"

"I think things get sloppy when you've had it your own way for years. There's Dorado and there's the rest of us. A few insurgents but no real opposition. And in a world that's fucked what is there to take over?"

It's odd that in the catastrophe the world has become there are still the haves and have nots. The few controlling the many. Perhaps that's all there really is to the human story, and that will be forgotten once we are gone. Once everything is gone. I'm tired thinking about it and wish I could lie down somewhere and disappear with Joe and Chloe and Dad and dreams of Dick Turpin and Bess. And I would make a necklace of sea shells to remind me of Lot and Emma, whom she loved so much. Trash is still talking.

"I've got some weapons and explosives here in the van. The rest of the stuff they can reprogramme, but as I say, it'll take forty five minutes, less now. I've made this van surveillance proof. We can only be seen in reality. We can get out of Dorado and be long gone. Set?" And he presses the ignition. I wonder how many bodies it took to fill the gas tank.

"No," I say.

He looks at me.

"I want to go to the park area. You said that's where the elite live. The ones who control all of this. Who benefit. Top of the heap. I say we take whatever you have here as a present for them. Throw some fire into their party."

"Ali, it won't work. There's two of us. Against a city."

"Well, if you're not clever enough, I'll go alone."

I open the van door.

"We won't have time. To go that far in and try god knows what and then come back all this way. With an army waiting, by the way."

"I thought you were the military genius. What about the art of surprise? They will expect us to get out as quickly as we can, not go further in."

"But we won't have time to get back."

"Maybe we don't try."

I tell him to show me the map he had of the area. He'd said all the bridges were gone that led directly into Dorado, except for Putney, which was probably used for transportation to the elite, and maybe as an additional escape route. So we use that and try to get out the back way. Trash looks at his phone map, gauges distances.

"I could have thought of that," he says.

"Of course you could, Einstein. Given time. Which we don't have. And if we're still around when the processing plants blow all attention will be directed there. Confusion will help us."

Trash gives me a bottle of fresh orange juice, something which I haven't drunk in fifteen years. It takes my breath away and I suddenly want to weep for everything that has been lost. He also gives me a few protein bars. We drive west through leafy suburbs and then we approach the electrical fence around the elite area. There are gates every hundred metres or so. Trash keys in some numbers and we are through. The roads are so clean I expect to see someone sweeping up behind us. We pass a few admin buildings. A Protector looks up from a stationary motorcycle and raises a hand. Trash raises a hand back. The Protector consults the little screen on the front of his motorcycle. "He's checking us out."

"And what will he find?"

"This van is occupied by Protectors Harness and Davis." He smiles at me.

We drive down a street between beautiful apartment blocks, each separated by glorious gardens, walkways and fountains. Glass and shining steel and wall murals of scenes long gone – jungles and forests and magnificent extinct creatures – lions and bears and elephants. And walking among them an Arcadian vision of men and women wearing long robes and looking like gods. Each block, ten in all, is named. Avalon. Manu. Shangri-La. Olympus. Zion. Svarga. Summerland. Eden. Asgard. Caesars. Armed Guards at each door, surveillance cameras everywhere. This is where the elite must live. I want to get inside and see them and make them feel the kind of fear people feel on the outside. I want to burst the bubble, if only for a few of them. I want to slaughter the fuckers. A wake-up call for the gods. Whatever the cost. I've been a dead woman walking for what seems like a long time now and many things in me have died before that. I'd rather end it trying to do something and not lying down submissively. Revenge is like acid in my blood. I can smell it and taste it.

"Trash, you can go now if you like. Help me find a way in and then goodbye."

"Frankly, I don't think you'd last five minutes without me. And besides, I'm curious to see inside."

We park in a utility van area and try to think how to get inside one of the buildings. Brute force is out. Taking a Protector hostage is a possibility. Trying a back way through deliveries but this is also guarded. Trash looks through a bag and takes out a tablet and starts playing with numbers. He then takes out a phone and swipes through information pages. The phone beeps.

"OK. I've got the phone numbers of each of the Protectors at the doors. Which block do you want to get into? I'm gambling that because there is so much digital security there won't be more Protectors inside."

"Olympus," I say.

Trash tells me to wait until he is at the door and the other Protector gone. He sends a text to the Protector outside Olympus building saying he is wanted back at the front force field where there is a technical problem and additional security is needed. A replacement Protector will arrive very shortly. We watch the Protector looking at his phone and Trash gets out of the van with a bag containing weapons and explosives and approaches Olympus. A few words are exchanged and then the Protector gets on a hoverbike and leaves. I wait a minute and then take my own bag and join him.

He has all the security codes and lets us in. He disables all the security videos. Plush gold and white carpets. Hanging tapestries of fawns and angels and children. Two lifts bearing the motto *Non Nobis Solum, Not for Ourselves Alone*. We get in the lift and

Trash looks at the floor buttons. "Let's start at the top," I say. He presses the tenth button and we ascend. I take out an MP7 submachine gun and Trash has a Glock pistol in his belt and a laser pistol in his right hand. At the tenth floor the door opens and we are in a quadrangle of white carpet and tropical ferns. Turns out they are real. There are two side doors and one main front door.

"You OK?" Trash asks.

I nod. Considering I should be dead several times over by now I feel surprisingly calm. Curious to see the fuckers who feed on the rest of us like fat maggots. I press the intercom bell. A mechanical voice responds.

"Yes."

"Protectors here to check security"

"The video is not working."

"That's why we're here. Please open."

"I am sorry. That is not possible."

Trash shrugs and takes an override security device from his pocket and the door clicks open. I raise my gun and turn off the safety.

14

What did I expect? Twigs from the crown of thorns? Tears from the statue of Our Lady of Akita? These are not the days of miracles and wonder but I expected tidy opulence and velvet hangings, jewelled cushions and silver bowls of crystal fruits. We were in a huge central living area that had one entire long wall of glass that looked out on Dorado and beyond the old river. From outside it was simply a mirror. White carpeted, a dozen or so small sofas and little soft chairs. Many pictures on the walls, but of longago superheroes and cartoons – Superman, Batman, Catwoman, Bugs Bunny, Tom and Jerry, Teen Titans, Avatar, the Simpsons, Super Mario. There are also a few photographs of smiling adults in white gowns at some sort of gathering. There are nine or ten doors off this main room.

A huge TV is on facing into the room. An episode of the Simpsons playing. A sofa faces the screen. At first I thought no one was watching but then a laugh comes from the sofa. We approach either side and lower our guns. A boy of about ten, blonde and brown eyed, dressed in a white suit, is watching. He looks briefly at Trash, then at me.

"Wait. This is a good bit," he says, as Homer Simpson poisons Springfield's water supply by illegally dumping toxic waste in the reservoir. The boy laughs and pauses the programme.

"It's not Friday. Why are you here?"

"Where are your parents?" I ask, nodding at the photographs on the wall.

The boy stares at me.

"The grownups. Where are they?"

"Who else is here?" Trash asks.

"The others, of course. Shall I call them?"

"Yes," I say.

He presses a button on the TV remote and a buzzer sounds throughout the room and beyond. Within seconds doors open and more children enter. Some twenty in all. They all wear white and are immaculately turned out. They all look between nine and eleven. Their skin is pallid. Eyes bright. Clean. Too clean. They all look at us. A little girl says to us "Why are you here? It's not Friday."

"What happens on Friday?" I ask.

The kids look at each other and a few giggle.

"You know!" Says the little girl.

"Tell me anyway. Like it's a game."

"You come in to clean, take dirty clothes and bring new ones. Check our temperatures. Make sure we are clean. Bring food and games and vitamins and things to think about."

"Things to think about. Special things," I say.

"Of course. Like why we are the new breed."

"Children of the new dawn," says a little boy.

"Children of the sacrifice," says another.

"The great sacrifice," says another. "Everyone knows about it."

"What was the sacrifice?"

"Everyone knows," chorus six or seven of them.

"We're new. There's a lot to learn. Remind us," Trash says.

The children look at each other.

"It makes us sad," says a fat little boy.

"Sad is not bad," says a little girl.

The boy thinks about this, says, "Our mothers and fathers lived here. They were superior. Like we are. Then they got the virus. When they died the Chief Protectors looked after us. To make sure we grow strong and true."

"The new breed."

"Children of the new dawn."

"Children of the sacrifice. One day we will able be able to rule and put childish things away."

"One day soon," says the boy on the sofa, who has been watching us intently.

"I'm sorry your parents died," I say. "I know what that feels like."

"They live on in us," says sofa boy.

"Of course," I say.

"You still haven't said why you are here," says another girl.

"There's been a breach of security. We're Protectors, so that's what we're doing. Protecting you," I say.

"Why don't we recognise you?" Says a boy with small green eyes.

Sofa boy stands and goes to one of the rooms and returns with his hands behind his back. "We don't recognise you because you are not proper Protectors. You are terrorists who mean us harm. I see it in your eyes," he says, and swings his arms around, which hold a Sig Sauer P460 handgun. He points it at Trash and fires. Trash is flipped over by the impact. The boy steps forward and turns to me. I already have my MP7 aimed at him.

"Don't shoot," I say.

"Kill them both," says the boy and fires at me. His shot misses me by a whisker and implodes the TV screen. He steadies the gun with both hands and aims again. I fire a round above his head. The other children freeze but I can see in his eyes he means to kill me. He closes one eye and then slams back against the wall as a laser punch burns a hole in his chest. I look over at Trash, propped on one elbow. He has a shoulder wound that is pumping blood.

I see that one or two of the children are thinking of darting back in their rooms, perhaps to get more weapons. I fire another burst above their heads.

"All of you. On the ground face down, arms above your heads. I will kill every last one of you if I have to."

A few look at each other. The others are frozen. Then, almost as one, they lie down. I wonder why none of them are crying. It is as if something has been switched off inside. The lights out inside them. I step towards the shot boy. His heart is visible, still beating, but then stops. I keep my MP7 trained on the others and back up to Trash.

"I had no idea it hurt so much to get shot," he says, grimacing. The wound doesn't look ugly. The bullet went straight through his left shoulder. He can still move the arm. While he keeps his gun trained on the now completely passive children, I look in some of the doors until I find a bathroom. There are painkillers, bandages, gauze and saline solution. I grab a handful and go back, tear his uniform open, clean the wound and pack gauze into it and bind it tightly. He'll need the painkillers later, but he fumbles in his pocket and takes out a small packet of syringes.

He takes the protective cap off one of the syringes and smiles at me. "I stole them from supplies. A cocktail of opiates and amphetamines, so you get a few hours of pain relief plus you think you'll live forever. No drowsiness." He plunges the needle in his arm and seconds later closes his eyes in the sweet relief of junkie paradise.

"Give me a minute," he says. "You notice the photographs?"

"Yes. All adults. No kids."

"And the kids look spookily like…"

"Some of the adults in the photographs. The kids are clones." We are both remembering several viruses ago, was it Covid 27 or 28? – That only infected adults and drastically reduced the population. Even the first, Covid 19 was almost exclusively confined to adults. In these confined spaces, luxurious as they are, the virus would be no respecter of status. Their parents must have made provision to have themselves cloned before they died and now these cuckoos will be the new elite in a few years' time. The ultimate vanity of the wealthy and powerful – immortality. To breed their own tribe of elite people. Like gilded birds of a rare order. Except they are just flesh and blood children like any other. Like Chloe. Like Lot. The world allows for cruel choices and arbitrary privilege. Chloe, chopped up out of all recognition and out of all possible lives and selves that could have awaited her.

Children of the new dawn. Children of the sacrifice. Children of science. What is it to be a clone? Are we not all clones? The sperm and the egg, the fluids and muscle and tissue carried through the pregnancy like little codes and messages, then to burst into the world, a cryptogram of ciphers and possibilities and secrets all locked in the cells that make us who we are? DNA, the biological postmen who deliver us to order. Is conception not a form of cloning? But there are nature's quirks that perhaps trip our very natures into an unforeseeable path. Genghis Khan or the goatherd, Florence Nightingale or the tavern whore, the trickster or the martyr, circumstance and nature battling it out for supremacy in the path of the self. To clone is to replicate. But in replicating something is it in turn not influenced by the shapes and fears and horrors of the world? Is it congruent only with its template? All I know is that looking at those children sent a pitying shiver down my spine. I feel a bit sorry for this over privileged little bunch of experiments but my sorry tank has grown pretty low.

I turn to ask Trash what he thinks our next step should be.

Then Armageddon arrived.

The blast is mind numbing. My cheeks wobble, my teeth rattle and my eyes feel as if they will explode. A wave of heat and light as the long glass wall cracks so that it seems we are in a giant iced spider web. The building itself groans in its concrete cradle. A pause as if the world is taking a breath. Plaster flakes from the ceiling. The air smells wrong, as if a giant cookout has gone horribly awry. I punch a hole in the cracked glass with the butt of my machine gun and look down at pandemonium. Criss crossings of vans and hoverbikes and running as

Protectors and other people decide whether to go towards the source of the blast or run from it. The recycling plants, those factories of hideous death, look like twin volcanic craters that have decided on one last party time. Black smoke and fire eruct from both and are already brewing a toxic cloud that will doubtless drift around the world for weeks to come.

"Sure you used enough explosives there, Trash?"

"Didn't need too much. Don't forget we were in methane heaven."

"We need to get out. Try to make use of the confusion."

Trash looks at the still prostrate children, all wide eyed in terror. "What about them?"

"We set them free."

"They don't know free. It will freak them out completely."

"Welcome to reality."

We shepherd the children out. I get in one lift with ten and Trash in the second lift with another ten. A girl with big blue saucer eyes looks up at me.

"That man shot David," she says.

"David shot that man," I say.

"And he was going to shoot you."

"Yes. He was."

"Why?"

Apparently because I'm a terrorist."

"Are you?"

"No."

"What are you?"

"Terrified."

"What's happening now?"

"We're setting you free."
"What do you do when you're free?"
"You hope for the best."
"Is that what you do?"
"No."
"Why not?"
"Just shut up."

We reach the bottom. We could use these kids as a shield to escape, but I don't like the thought of doing that. Best to hope that if we set them running it will create a diversion in what will already be chaos. Trash opens the front door and we let the kids out. They look about wildly at this new reality of noise and sensation. Sirens sounding near and far. The sky raining ash and sparks. Vans and hovercycles going in all directions. Protectors running. A few gunshots sound far off.

"Scoot. Run!" I shout at the kids. They huddle. Terrified. Then the boy with green eyes sees a screen on a wall at a street corner. A hologram woman is talking. Looking paradoxically calm. The boy points. "Look. TV!" He runs towards the screen and the others follow, like little white sheep. A passing van stops and a Protector jumps out. He points an automatic weapon at us. "What the fuck are you doing?" He says.

"We got them out. Terrorists inside."
"What about all the others?"
"Still inside the building."
"OK. Most of us are on fire and containment duty. You two guard the building. We'll try to round up the children."

He turns and then stops. He looks back at us. He takes out his phone and looks at the screen, then back at us. He's checked us out. Somehow he knows. He walks back to the van, a little too nonchalantly. I look at Trash. He nods and I fire a volley at the van as it is about to leave. I know I got the driver because the van lurches and his head cracks bloodily onto the windscreen. The other Protector gets out the passenger side and starts shooting from underneath the van. Two of the children have run back from the TV to try and get inside Olympus again. They run between us and the van and the Protector's bullets find them, lift them both off the ground and dump them like bloody marionettes on the concrete. The white of their clothes and the red of their blood is like some sacrificial offering. Purity and sacrifice. Clone blood. Whose blood is it?

We run back inside Olympus and Trash code locks the doors. We're pretty bulletproof inside but who knows what high velocity weapons they have and they aren't going to leave us here, not with a building I now know is full of children who constitute the future of the elite humanity, if you can call it that. It's a nest of tyrants to come. If all the cloned kids go, that means a new world order. Who will be at the top of the pile? And what will be left to lord it over anyway? A decaying heap of reduced humanity and disease.

We position ourselves behind an upturned steel reception desk, that commands a good view of the front. The other three sides of the building on ground level are concrete. The glass walls start on the third floor so they will need hydraulic ladders to get that high and try to enter. Within minutes there are ten Protector vans and some thirty Protectors outside. Drones are hovering outside like a squadron of giant mosquitoes. Two of the drones back away and start firing at the Protectors and I see at least two fall. Trash's reprogramming works. The drones disappear. Already a few Protectors are now using distance lasers to cut through the glass.

"I reckon we have about twenty minutes unless we stop them," Trash says.

I point to some ventilation grilles at the front, either side of the large front doors. Trash uses his laser gun to cut through one of the grilles, but then the power in the gun outs. I use my machine gun on the other. We take our weapon bags and position ourselves at the grilles. I have a small window but which gives me a good panoramic view of the road facing Olympus. I reload with another magazine and fire out. The Lasers stop as Protectors take cover. Then two Protectors come forward with bullet and laser proof shields, with hand held laser guns. Trash whistles and I see he has taken out his grenade launcher. I do the same. We load up and he raises three fingers. One two and we launch. Trash scores a direct hit and Protector and shield explode in electric flames. Mine misses and instead hits a Protector van, which rocks on the impact and then bursts into flames. I load again and this time the Protector and shield are barbecued.

Standoff. They fire. We fire. I wonder what the children in the building are thinking. They must know something is very wrong unless they are all hypnotically glued to screens. I am drenched in sweat. My hearing is affected, as if reality is once removed, and sweat stings and mists my eyes. I never knew war was such bloody hard work. In some way I don't understand I am also exhilarated, as if years of quiet, oppressed depression have been lanced, like a plague boil, and I'm giving some back at last. I understand now that humanity is a paper-thin skin under which the beasts long to get out and blood their teeth and claws. Three Protectors run diagonally to get a different angle, firing at Trash's position. I pick up my Glock pistol and rapid fire. I get two in the legs and one in the chest and neck. He's gone. I fire at the two on the floor. I get one in the head and see his eye explode and he writhes and twitches. The other crawls away.

We have been here for perhaps fifteen minutes but it seems like hours. Then all changes. A tank appears in the road. It's a beautiful machine, old school but looks barely used. Someone has spent time putting a loving shine on it. Almost a shame to try to destroy it. It turns adroitly in front of the Protector vans. Trash and I load grenades and fire. One hits the traction and the tank bobbles a little. The other hits the barrel but bounces off and rolls away and explodes. Then Olympus rocks as a shell hits the front doors and explodes. I guess from the impact it was a 105 mm. My ears thrum. The glass has cracked but held. Then the barrel swivels and aims at my firing position. I roll away with my bag just in time as a shell is fired. The grille area shatters and a metre-wide hole appears. I have tiny tears in the uniform on my right leg, and Rorschach blood stains already spreading.

"What did you say about not shelling the building?" I ask

"A minor miscalculation. All great minds get a few details wrong on the way to perfection."

"If we stay we're dead," I say, as another shell blasts the hole even wider.

15

Trash gestures me to follow. We go to the lifts. He tells me there were three below ground floors, which is unusual. One for utilities, one for parking, and the third? He has a hunch. We get in and descend. Three levels below ground is a dark area with many forgotten electrical goods, freezers, air con units, washing machines, given over to rust and decay. A giant poster showing Olympus in in all its shining glory. Three little carts that look like golf carts but given that golf courses disappeared a generation ago they can't be. And electric bicycles and three hoverbikes. He checks and the golf cart batteries are dead but two of the hoverbikes still have some juice, which is surprising. If things like that are here that must mean they have somewhere to go. We look around, using small torches from our bags. I notice a seam down the centre of the Olympus poster and tear it. Behind the poster is a door. Trash comes to look. We tear the whole poster away and look inside, at a tunnel. Dark and damp, it looks like rat heaven; I shine my torch and the tunnel curves away after about a hundred metres.

"Makes sense to have an escape route for the last of the elite," he says.

"But a tunnel to where? It might lead us into a bigger hornet's nest."

"We won't know unless we try. If we stay here we have no chance. Best case is it takes us below the river."

"Alright then."

We push freezers against the emergency stair door until it is packed tight. Trash goes to the lifts, places an explosive charge in each one and then sprays paint all over the lift as an accelerant for fire. He keys in a two minute timer and then presses the ground floor button on each. The doors close and the lifts ascend. We may not know what is at the end of this tunnel but we sure as hell won't be followed too quickly, wherever it leads us. We both have our bags with us. The hover bikes have lights but to preserve the batteries we use our torches. As we round the bend we hear distant thunder behind us, probably the lifts blowing, but perhaps the tank shredding the front of the building. The tunnel has a long straight run. After a few hundred metres my hoverbike slows, falters and dies. We try both riding on Trash's but it's slow progress. Finally we abandon it and walk. Our steps echo and it is slippery with moss and damp that drips from above. Trash's shoulder seems to be holding up so I don't ask how he is. It would only annoy him. The rhythm of walking in a crisp marching beat to some purpose we don't yet know. To try and survive, I suppose.

I have a wave of feeling for the life that used to be, when I had Joe and Chloe and, in my work, the sweet comfort of machines. The satisfaction of an apparatus using mechanical power and having several parts, each with a definite function and together performing a particular task. The litany of screws and belts and joints and finely polished metals that cohere to make a small world that is useful and aesthetically pleasing. How easy to understand why Newton's clockwork god was so appealing: a

Creation of unified parts all obeying the laws of physics, such as: an object will remain in a state of inertia unless acted upon by force, and for every action there is an equal and opposite reaction. These are precisely the things that Trash and I have lived recently, inert until acted upon, and reacting against what is, I now know, a hideous machine of tyranny. We are cogs playing our part in the Newtonian model. The virus has triggered the worst in humanity, and has now been weaponised, and the lacerating irony is that it was the plague that spurred on Newton to his miraculous thinking. How far we have fallen.

I let myself fall back into the respite of thought. It serves to keep me from thinking of the horror of everything now. In 1665 the black plague created the new laws of physics. Cambridge University was closed for two years, and student Isaac Newton spent the whole time in lockdown at home studying complex mathematics, physics and optics. Using a crystal prism, he discovered that white light is made up a spectrum of colours. He also developed the concept of infinite-series calculus, the kind of startling maths that engineering and statistics scholars used thereafter. By 1666, Newton had even laid the blueprints for his three laws of motion. During the next two decades he studied how those laws of motion related to the Earth, Moon and Sun – a concept he called "gravity."

Urged on and funded by astronomer Edmond Halley, he published his seminal work in 1687, the *Principia*, probably the greatest science book ever written. Across the pages of the *Principia*, Newton breaks down the workings of the solar system into "'simple'" equations, explaining away the nature of planetary orbits and the pull between heavenly bodies. In describing why the Moon orbits the Earth because the Earth is so much heavier, he changed the way people saw the universe. So four hundred years ago the plague led to a breathtakingly revolutionary set of ideas that changed all we thought about life and the universe. In our lifetime the new plague has crystallized a truly disgusting way of diminishing life and using people as manure and gas. That's progress for you. At least we have thrown a spanner in the machine that is us now.

Another explosion trembles the tunnel.

"We have well and truly screwed up the whole thing," I say.

"Not many people can say that. Well done us. Maybe only for a while."

"How long before they are up and running again?"

"It'll be hard. For one thing I know they exist on a constant supply and demand level of fuel. It's surprisingly on the hoof. They need a lot of bodies, which is why they sometimes let out the virus again, like a mad dog on a long leash, except they can't always control it. To repair the whole recycling will take a lot of machinery and a lot of materials that need delivering. If they don't have the fuel for that they're in trouble. Perhaps they'll start small just to get going."

There is also the food production. Without fuel for artificial lights, and no compost, plus the fallout from the explosions, existing crops may ruin, and people in Dorado will, perhaps, to survive, have to imitate the scavengers they rule. See how the fuckers like that.

Something is rushing at us from behind. A formless, coagulating shadow of malevolence skittering its way. I take out my machine gun. It's coming fast.

"What is that?" I ask.

"Not that. Them. Rats."

Jesus. Hundreds of them, no doubt escaping the carnage we have wrought. Now I can make out hundreds of red eyes, like pinpricks of fire. The noise is a demented lunatic chatter as they get nearer. They are big bastards, some of the half a metre. More like dogs. I have no idea what to do.

"Ali, flatten yourself against the side of the tunnel. Point your torch at them and turn it on and off as fast as you can, and whatever you do, don't stop."

I do as he says and he stays the other side of the tunnel. The rats are moving incredibly fast, probably ten metres away. I start flashing my torch at them and he does the same the other side, both of us walking backwards. I want to close my eyes but force myself to concentrate. The rats keep coming but there is some squealing now and the pack condenses so they are running in the middle of the tunnel. They start to rush by like a hideous band of banshees locked in some ancient purge that will end in blood and teeth and pain. Several run over my feet and I feel a bite on my shoe, but then the torrent of rats carries it on. I keep flashing the torch. The sound of tiny feet and the squeal and rush of air make me feel sick. I gag but keep flashing the torch. Finally they are gone. I realise I have stopped breathing and take in a lungful of putrid air.

I look in amazement at Trash.

"How did you know they avoid flashing lights? How could you know that?" I ask.

"I know so many things," he says.

"OK."

We come to the end of the tunnel. There is a curved double door ahead. A hole in it where the rats have escaped. We still have our Protector uniforms on, so decide to try and bluff it out, pretend we are helping secure the tunnel for any elites. I push open the doors and we climb some steps and stare down the barrels of three automatic weapons levelled at us. Trash takes out his ID. I show mine too. We are south of the old river now.

"Do you know what's happening?" He asks one of the three Protectors.

He shakes his head. "Communication's out. Are you deserting?"

Trash laughs. "Oh yeah. Down a sewer full of rats to come to this shithole paradise. Really clever. We're securing an escape route in case it gets worse and we need to get the elites out this side of the river."

"What happened over there?" Asks another Protector.

"The devil came and blew a hole in the world is what happened. No one the fuck knows. Terrorists. A worker goes apeshit. A few Protectors turn. Accident. Take your pick, but both recycling plants blown to hell and back." And we all look across at the great angry mushrooming cloud that has darkened the sky and is raining fine ash on all. A terrible beauty is born.

"We need to scout a safe house for them. Orders are you do what you're doing anyway. Guard the tunnel. Extreme vigilance from now on. OK?"

The Protectors look at each other. "OK. Good luck. You might try a mile or so south where things thin out. Easier to protect and guard."

Trash acknowledges and we walk on.

"You're good at this," I say.

"I'm good at so many things. Except pain, and that fix is starting to wear thin. I'll need another soon. Where do you think we should head?"

"Back to the Cutty Sark."

He looks at me. It's not often I surprise him.

"Why go back to the Sark?" Trash asks. "She's gone. They killed her."

"Then I want to go to remember her there. Say goodbye. And besides, we have no other pressing social engagements. Other than survival."

I reason that it's not really going out of our way. We have no idea what lies South, other than rumours of mutated Covid tribes. West is unknown. North means going back through Dorado and further north are the tribes. If we go back East at least it's to a world we know. We can hunker down for the night and then try to find wheels the next day. When ordinary life is a dream long dispersed small things become the only lifeline to the next moment, the next day. Keep making small decisions otherwise you may as well lay down and weep and die. It is about twelve kilometres back to the Cutty Sark, hugging the old river. We should be there by early evening. We start out on the A320 past Battersea Park on our left. The pandemonium in Dorado is ever escalating. There are sirens and even gunshots, which is curious. Who is firing and who are they targeting? It looks like a John Martin depiction of urban apocalypse. Whorls of smoke and fire and dust and confusion. Cracks in the sky and fissures in the fabric of life itself. I hope entropy and turmoil will unfix Dorado from the world.

This also means we have a greater freedom of movement because all attention is fixed across the old river. We are just two soldiers in motion. Two hours later we are a few minutes shy of the Cutty Sark. I wonder if Lot was carried off screaming and crying and holding on to Emma, or if she retained her impassive look to the end. A sense of loss bites into me.

It is mostly deserted near the Sark. We get aboard and go up to the 'Tween deck. The tarpaulins lie crumpled. I was dreading finding their bodies, so assume they were taken. We put down our bags and I check Trash's wound and clean it and change the bandages. This is a man who less than a week ago would rather die than let anyone touch him. It is healing already. I think he will have restricted movement in the shoulder, and discomfort, but nothing comes free. We both start at a scratching from the panelling a few metres away. Rats must have got into the space behind the inner panelling. The whole carapace will crumble in a few years. Then a voice. *Shhh.* My heart leaps. We look along the panelling. There, towards the rear of the boat, a drilled hole in one panel, which means you can pull it out. Perhaps for storage. I put my finger in and pull and it comes away easily. I look inside to the left and then to the right. It's dark but a small white foot is visible, toes cramped and curled.

"Lot?"

"And Emma," she replies.

"Of course."

We sit on the tarpaulin. I feel such sad gratitude they are here it makes me feel physically sick. We have half a bottle of water, three biscuits and some apples that Trash stole from the Protector stores. Lot has never seen an apple and stares in wonder at it. "Like a jewel," she says, then her eyes widen as she looks behind me at…

Fauberge and three other Protectors. He smiles. The other three point their weapons at us. Were we that easy to find, or to follow? We're not soldiers, we're a couple of idiots in dishcloths.

"You," I say.

"Who else?"

"What now?"

"The inevitable." He looks at Lot. "She can quicken. I see that. So it's a waste. But also there's too little of her to be of use in a melting. So…" He reaches into a canvas bag and takes out a gleaming machete. He smiles at it, almost in wonder.

Emma starts barking. One of the Protectors aims his gun at her, but Lot puts her arms protectively around her and muzzles her with kisses. She glares. "Fauberge," she says, almost to herself.

He wavers momentarily, surprised. She knew his name, as if it was written on the air for her. He quickly recovers. Still looking at her he holds out the machete to me. "Take it, or I chop her now."

I take the machete. He looks at me.

"You do it. It's fitting that you do it."

"Why. Because you're a psychotic who wants a sick thrill?"

He groans. "Oh. No no no. I thought you were intelligent. He's clever," – this at Trash – "but like a robot is clever. Which is probably what he is. You, I thought, were more sophisticated. These are end days. We are the privileged ones. Here at the epicentre. Dorado. Fuel, food, weapons, an elite. We can quicken. We are exploding stars that dazzle before they disappear. Beyond," - he waves a hand at the rest of the world – "well, you know already. You live there. Vermin. It doesn't matter what happens to them. They really are of no consequence. That is the insight. People are of absolutely no consequence. We know that, and it is precisely that which makes us exceptional. God knows, even some of us aren't worth the paper we're printed on." He turns, takes out his gun and shoots one of the Protectors in the head. The other two Protectors look at each other briefly, think better of it and continue to hold their guns, one aimed at Trash and one at me. Fauberge laughs. "You see? Nothing. No revolt in the ranks. No heavenly chastisement. The freedom to do what the fuck. Kill her and you might get a taste of her power. Only for a few days, admittedly. Until we get the processors up and running again, then you are juiced. Do it. I guarantee – it will give you a true taste of strength. You will be quickened like a goddess. It's an aphrodisiac for the soul. Shine dazzle blaze bloom skyrocket gleam glimmer glisten. You will quicken. Now kill her. If you don't it will be a hundred times worse for her. It will not be aesthetic. Bit by bit I'll pull her apart. Fingernail by fingernail. Toe by toe. Eyes. Nose. Tongue. Teeth. Limb by limb. We'll be here all day. You will never be free of me, one way or another."

"Gobby shit, aren't you?" I say.

Lot continues to stare at Fauberge and hold Emma tight. I raise the machete. There is something beautiful in the shape, in the light catching the steel, the Viking sweep of the blade. I exhale, steady myself and disappear at the same moment that an apocalyptic explosion on the other side makes everyone jump. In the moments that follow there is barking and blood and a confusion of people jostling for my attention – Dad, Joe, Chloe, Dick Turpin, Bess, and I realise I cannot attend to them all at once. There is only now. This moment. The soft boom of ether imploding. Life itself unravelling. Time topsy tuyvying upon itself. I return and know what has happened. I swung the machete around quickly, catching Fauberge in the mouth but he turns his head and it slices across his cheek and ear and he staggers away. Trash takes the Glock from the cross beam where we hid weapons and shoots one of the Protectors and aims it at the other, who now looks from me to Trash. I can see in his eyes he can't see a way out, and is ready to fire.

"Drop it and run," I say.

"I can't," he says.

"Yes. You can. If not you die for nothing."

His eyes flash from me to Trash. He drops his gun, and runs, he almost vaults over the side of the boat and then runs down the road.

"Tip of the iceberg?" I ask.

Trash shrugs. I think it means something has changed. We have thrown a fire cracker in the nest and now the ants are panicking, falling over each other, some trying to restore order, others wondering what the hell has gone wrong. As if to confirm it, more shots ring out north of the river. Protectors are firing on each other, or ordinary citizens have armed themselves. Perhaps word has got out about the elite kids. The new super race is in jeopardy. They are just a bunch of scared kids. Why should they rule? I hope we have created a beautiful anarchy. Perhaps what will come will be worse – pointless to believe in progress or amelioration - but at least it's change. Fauberge has gone. I look but he seems to have vanished.

"Should have chopped the bastard's head off," I say. "The Joker," says Trash, slicing a finger across his lips, and we both laugh, surprised at our vigilance. I feel no remorse or pity. I look at Trash. Something has changed and we both recognise it. We are bona fide killers. It has settled inside us. There is probably nothing we couldn't now do to anyone who means us harm. Which is just as well. We drag the bodies to the end of the boat and cover them.

I look at Lot and Emma. She is feeding Emma the last crumbs of a biscuit. It is as if the recent carnage passed her by, as if she is a gossamer fairy untouched by the hideous excrescence of the world around her. Perhaps that is what innocence is – not that you are shielded from experience but that you are untainted by it. I ask her, "What did you do all the time in that dark hole?" She looks at me. "We made a secret world." Of course. What else?

A sleepless gobliney night of shouts, fires, sirens, gunshots and screams on the north side. The violent energy of unravelling. Strangely quiet around the Cutty Sark. Trash lay on his good side, eyes open and probably solving a calculus problem. I lay absently stroking a dreaming Emma, who lay lengthwise between me and Lot, who did sleep yet occasionally whispered who knows what, too soft to catch, her landscape a phantasmal, secret world I could only guess at. At first dawn I drifted into a half sleep state in which I know with a bitter heart that where I am is not really happening.

Tell me, Mum. Do you think Dick rides Bess in the stars now?

Yes. And when you see a shooting star it is Dick firing thunder at a rich man who refuses to be relieved of his fat timepiece.

So even the night sky is an adventure?

Even the night sky is an adventure.

"We should be going," Trash says. Somehow he produces three cold cooked potatoes and a can of beans. I know better than to ask where he got them. There is smoke but less fire from across the river, as if everyone got too tired for carnage and violence and settled for mere devastation. We breakfast and try to rub the cold from our bones. I check Trash's wound and thankfully there are no signs of infection.

I wash and bandage it. He has a few painkillers left and swallows them. He says he has seen abandoned vehicles. Some are burnt out. One or two might be drivable. He asks me to come and look with him. I'm loath to leave Lot again but she says she and Emma will go into their hiding place until we return. I worry about Fauberge but he will have to wait.

A few stragglers around but clearly order is crumbling. Protectors are in what look like vigilante groups. We show we have weapons and pass with a nod. One group stops and tells us we are to meet at gate four on the North side three hours from now, when there will be an organised cull of malcontents and Dorado will be forcibly becalmed. Engineers have been summoned from the districts. Trash says we will round up colleagues and be there. We walk down a road where several dead bodies lie on the pavements, one placed on burning rubber tyres and now smoking horribly. One eye seems to follow us while the other bubbles glutinously like a dissolving jelly. The lips have blistered into wafery strips and the teeth smile ferociously. Bubbling stench of liquid ammonia in my throat. The coppery sulphurous smell of cooking human flesh arrests the senses and can never be forgotten. There is a general sense of lostness everywhere, as if the world is waiting for someone to give it a new purpose. We pass an abandoned van. Trash looks it over. The keys are still in the dash and he pockets them.

"It'll do, but whether it gets us far…Ah, now that's better," – he eyes a large four by four all-purpose ranger slowly coming down the street. The driver is a young heavily muscled black guy and two black women next to him. In the back seat a white man wearing a fedora hat. Trash steps in the road and stops it. I stand to one side holding my machine gun.

"Whassup?" Says the driver.

"Please step outside," says Trash.

"Why?"

"Because I have a gun and so does my partner."

The driver is thinking of reaching for his pistol which is in the door pocket. Trash ostentatiously takes off the safety catch on his pistol. The driver wavers, then gets out. I wave my gun at the passengers and the hat in the back to get out, which they do.

"We are requisitioning this vehicle for the Dorado protection service. It will be returned to its legal owner in due course. In the meantime you may have the use of this Protector van." He throws the keys to the black guy, who catches them, and looks disparagingly at the battered van. "But we got…stuff in the vehicle," he says.

"I'm sure you have. Class A no doubt. These are now confiscated. There are orders to shoot drug dealers on sight but in this instance, we will make a generous exception. Now get in the van and fuck off."

The little group slowly gets in the van. They start arguing the moment they are inside. The engine chugs into life and they leave, automatic gears slipping in and out of each other. I am not a little in awe of Trash. He made it seem so easy. We get in the four by four. The dashboard is like an aircraft — computer screen, communication devices, automatic drive, and controls for lasers attached to the front of the vehicle. This is a war machine. I wonder why the black guy didn't fire at us. I think we surprised them. In the back boxes of supplies. On the floor of the passenger seat is a metal box. Inside is at least a kilo of cocaine and another two kilos of crystamorph, a new drug that is cheap and lethal – brain damage guaranteed. Perhaps that's why it's so popular. I open the window and am about to heave it out, but Trash stays me.

"It might come in useful for bartering or bribes."

True. We are in no position to claim the high moral ground. Especially when there is none left to claim. We drive back to the Cutty Sark. I look around a last time, then over the side at our gleaming new four by four. A sliver of shadow protrudes from behind it. I run down, taking the safety off my Glock, but there is no one. I look all around. Someone watches me, but from where? Perhaps my increasing derangement is getting the better of me. Ten minutes later we are on the road. For twelve kilometres we make fine progress. Confusion is a great pathway and our state of the art vehicle suggests don't mess with us authority. Then we near our old potential nemesis Gallows Corner. The Covid compound on our right and in front of us across the A12 a hideous wall built from dead virus bodies and old tyres. A warning to all. Four men wearing flak jackets appear in front of it. Three have rifles and one some sort of improvised anti-personnel weapon that fires either grenades or homemade nail bombs. One of the men fires a bullet at our left front tyre.

"Tyres are bullet proof," says Trash. "The pipe bomb might do something, but it looks just as likely to blow up in the firer's face as find a target. There for show."

I get out, holding my machine gun. "Are you going to let us through?" I ask.

"Don't see many bitch Protectors," says one of them. "You grease the boys on cold nights?" They all laugh.

"Protectors have free access to all roads public and private," I say.

"You can have free access to my dick," bigmouth says, and they all laugh.

That's when I see the belt he's wearing. With the Dick Turpin badge. I feel the lemon ribbon at my throat burn and choke and demand. I disappear.

... *Something remarkably picturesque and romantic about him as he sat so still upon Black Bess in the centre of the deserted highway. He was tall and muscular, and sat in the saddle with an ease and grace as rare as it was admirable. A three-cornered black felt hat, trimmed with broad gold lace, and with a long black feather trailing from it. A cravat of spotlessly white muslin tied in a large bow, a crimson-coloured coat, very long in the waist and very stiff in the skirts trimmed and faced also with gold lace. Close-fitting pantaloons of white leather, and large black boots coming up high above the knee. We have said he was listening intently. So Bess appeared to be, for her ears were projected forwards. And neither knew that fire was coming, and blue thunder gunning from his pistols before he rode off into the misty night with booty and treasure enough to make a king proud.*

16

Trash is driving fast. Lot and Emma sit huddled in the back. I am strapped into the passenger side. Only desolate land slipping by on each side. Trash looks at me.

"What happened?" I ask.

"You went apeshit. You shot one of them to smithereens, then the others when they tried to fire back. Why? We were negotiating."

"I saw his belt."

"Ah. That's alright then. You didn't like the belt he was wearing. For a moment I thought he might have seriously offended you."

"You don't understand."

"He was one of them," Lot says. I turn around and look at her. I wonder who she is behind those unblinking darknesses.

"Yes. He was one of them."

"We should give a name to our car. It helped us get away."

"Have you got a name for it?"

"Her. Bess," she says.

"I name you – Bess," I say, and touch the roof of the ranger.

"Shit. Hellhounds on our trail," as Trash looks in the rear view mirror. I look and see at least three cars following us. The front one has a machine gun mounted crudely from a homemade hole in the roof. They start firing. The bullets arc across, some hitting the back of our ranger, now Bess, and bouncing off. "I just hope they don't have grenades," he says.

Moments later a woman wearing a streaming red bandana leans from the front car holding a grenade and trying to steady herself to throw it.

"Hold on," Trash says and swings hard right. We are off road and driving over a bumpy wasteland. A grenade explodes some thirty metres behind us. The cars turn and follow. We smash through a fence onto overgrown parkland. I look behind and one of the cars has stopped, probably the suspension gone. The machine gun is firing uselessly. Then we turn right with a giant dump on our left – cars and rubbish pile twenty metres high. The cars are still following but have fallen behind. If we keep going we will bypass Gallows Corner and eventually come to the old M25. Trash brakes as about 80 metres in front are some six cars and maybe twenty armed people face us.

"You think these are from Gallows Hill too? They phoned them," I ask.

As if in answer a volley of gunfire. Trash switches on the front lasers and fires. One of the people drops and before he hits the ground I see some of his tripes coiling out like blue snakes from his torn gut. Trash fires at one of the cars and it ignites in flames. The shooters take cover behind their cars. Trash turns left onto an overgrown path and then a rollercoaster drive over a rock strewn scrubland of briars and choke weed long ago rusted like Viking plumes from a burial ground. One of the cars behind us follows but within a hundred metres the front axle snaps. We bump and grind for several kilometres, through a long abandoned aerodrome with two skeletal light aircraft. In the cockpit of one is a dead person grinning maniacally as the papery skin on his face and head slaps gently in the breeze like ancient parchment about to turn to ash. We come to a major intersection of the old M25 and M11.

Trash stops in a field and we all drink some water. Lot has been rummaging through the boxes and found a can of coke. She holds it out to me.

"What is it?"

I flip the metal lip and the pop startles Emma into barking. I make a drinking motion and give the can to Lot. She drinks and immediately splutters through her mouth and nose as the bubbles tickle her throat. Then a miracle. She laughs and laughs. The first time. I laugh too. Emma barks. Trash shakes his head in mock despair. We check the supplies more carefully and it is like Christmas long gone. Cans of fuel. Six bottles of scotch and a crate of Cotes du Rhone. Tins of soya protein. Tins of vegetables and beans. Tins of crushed maggots in vinegar. Pickled cockroaches. Jars of snails. Soda bread. Water. Dried milk and ground coffee. A little stove. Enough to keep us going for a month. I hold one of the bottles of scotch and look at Trash.

"Why not? Been a hell of a day so far," he says. It tastes like nectar. We both have two large swigs and then put the bottle away. Now is not the time to get hammered. Lot feeds Emma snails and gets out of the van with her. I keep an eye on them. It almost feels normal, watching a little girl laugh and play with a dog, as long as you ignore the fact that we have killed four people and stolen a vehicle and been chased by psychotic crazies.

"An idea," says Trash. He says that from here we could make our way East and get back to Kessingland in the dark. But why exactly are we going back? And to what? Given that Jez was a plant and that our names will be on record then should Dorado ever get reorganized they will doubtless be keen to hunt us down and reward us for the apocalyptic carnage we have caused – why go back? It's a good question. Another thing, he says. How will the Protectors regain control? What's the easiest, most effective way?

"Unleash a new outbreak of the virus," I say.

"Exactly. I think if we go home we go home to die, one way or another."

Where then? I ask.

"Scotland," he says.

The north coast of Scotland, Trash's suggestion, is about eleven hundred kilometres away. To get there we have to drive through the spine of England and no one in their right mind would think of going to the North of England these days. It is a terrain of dark myth, a place of rumour and discord and voodoo malevolence. Back when the sixth or seventh virus came and the wars started information became hearsay and knowledge disappeared and the space left was colonised by propaganda and what was then called fake news, later to be called the New Truth. What we did know before this was that the US was ravaged by civil war, race against race, group against group, and by wars abroad it could no longer win. China and Russia made an alliance which was actually a genocidal pact against each other. Why no one dropped a global wipeout nuclear bomb is a mystery, but perhaps the virus was a pretty good second best that would allow some survivors others than cockroaches.

In the UK protests became anarchy and this became total war. The neo liberals never understood that many human beings just don't like each other, and that hatred is a powerful currency, especially if fuelled by terror, and it outnumbers love by a hundred to one. Mostly selfishness beats up love and I say that not because I'm a pure cynic, which I am, but simply report it from the front line. This is what I saw and this is what happened. It's surprising the neo liberals didn't know this too because they seemed to hate anyone who didn't think like them, and their tolerance was a spiked leash to whip everyone but themselves, so they had a great knowledge of hatred. Protestors demanded the liquidation of the armed forces and the police, which was the shortest route to anarchic destruction. They had considerable success. Once everything was looted and stolen there was only each other to turn on and claw the face from. Mosques and churches torched and then all out pitched battles on the streets between Moslem groups and mostly poor whites who felt dispossessed. Black vigilante groups and East European gangs embroiled in their own street wars, mostly to control the drug and prostitution markets that had become the biggest economy by far. Black Lives Matter became No Lives Matter in pitched battles. And everywhere the shadow of the virus fuelling more fear and destruction. The police seemed paralysed. Military bases were taken by surprise at the vigilance of groups from all sides and soldiers either joined one or other faction or died as all the hardware the army owned was stolen and distributed. The virus had created a climate of fear and lockdown so most people took to their homes and hoped the storm would pass. Instead it destroyed many of them. As the body count rose all the major institutions collapsed and health care, law and order, disappeared. Governance was done with. Dorado had a paid hardcore of ex-army and police, employed by the super-rich, who boarded up and their hired soldiers became Protectors and created the city that now is, or was until we blew the lid off it, with an elite at its centre. The Protectors were surprisingly effective at destroying opposition. They had organization and guerrilla tactics, whereas the rival gangs and impromptu armies had only murderous intent and improvised, chaotic slaughter. Society was now officially a shambles.

Once anarchy and violence and the virus had eviscerated all that was worth taking, the tribes, for that is what they now were, travelled north, where infection had killed nearly everyone, so land and housing were there for the taking. A Protector force followed and gave them designated territories in a clever divide and rule policy. Kill each other as much as you like but come south and we'll torch the lot of you. Leeds, the Yorkshire Dales, North Yorkshire moors, and the North Pennines were now a Moslem stronghold, apparently under strict Sharia and martial law, but probably a rabble of worship and executions and infighting. Outsiders were slaughtered on sight. On the other side of the M6 the former Lake District was now an area of swamps where, rumour has it, groups of cannibals lived, feeding on each other presumably, and any stragglers stupid enough to enter their territory. God alone knows where they came from. Beyond Newcastle and up to Edinburgh were tribal groups of East Europeans and blacks and ragtaggle white English, some nomadic and some in ghettoes, who spent their time either attacking each other or off their faces on crystamorph and other cheap hybrid drugs like chemimeth. It was said that even cockroaches were crushed, mixed with disinfectant, dried and smoked in the belief that you then took on the cockroach power of survival. If the drug didn't kill you first.

Beyond Edinburgh was a mystery. Getting there was like covering yourself in honey and walking into a wasp nest. So forgive me, Trash, but how do you propose we get through this garden of delights, this bed of poisoned spikes, and why Scotland anyway?

"I have a friend in the north. A place called Thurso – why are you laughing?"

"It's the idea of you having a friend. You've lived in a lock up garage for ten years talking to bits of wire."

"OK. Let's say," he searches for a word, "an accomplice. A co- conspirator. Robbie. I helped him solve a dual interface problem. He said if ever things got beyond hopeless and I could get to him, I'd be safe, and even if not I could get out to the Shetland and Orkney islands where the North Sea flows into the Norwegian Sea. The edge of the world. No one cares about North Scotland."

"The seas have gone, Trash. They are poisonous sludge. It took me hours to get a few hundred metres."

"That's the point. If you can get across them the chances of anyone else coming are small. And he knows the way. I spoke to him yesterday. I got a signal. He said to come. His name's Robbie."

"But the journey...?"

"We're dressed as Protectors. Most people we meet will leave us alone because they'd fear retribution."

"Some will, but we are talking about thousands of fanatics, lunatics, psychopaths and people who have burnt out the insides of their skulls with drugs that you wouldn't even use to scour a sewer pipe. Plus crazed cannibals and crazies who would chop off their own legs just for the fun of it."

"The cannibals are a rumour. We don't know if they're there for sure."

"And the rest? They might not all play by Queensbury rules."

"I grant the rest might be true. I admit it's a risk."

"On a risk scale of one to ten I'd say it registers about twenty three."

"How do you work that out?"

"I'm being facetious."

"I know. But why twenty three?"

"Forget twenty three."

"You started it."

"The risk factor. Let's get back to it."

"On our side. As well as wearing Protector uniforms, we have a state of the art ranger with communications, fire power, and an engine that can outrun most things on wheels."

"Bess."

"What?"

"She's called Bess."

"Alright then. And we have fuel, water, food."

"We put it to a vote."

"A vote – just you and I?"

"No. There are three of us."

We sat on the grass. I laid out the options. Back to Kessingland with its attendant risks, or Scotland, with ludicrous risks and remote possibility of safety at the end of it. Lot chewed on a twig, one hand stroking Emma's soft auburn gold ears with their long fronds of hair, she panting softly and contentedly.

"So. Hands up who votes for Scotland."

Trash raises his arm.

"Kessingland?" I raise my arm.

Lot looks from me to Trash, torn, then raises her arm, her head down.

"So it's carried by two to one…"

"No," says Lot. "There are four of us."

"Four?" I say. Lot pats Emma's head.

"Emma? But she can't vote."

"Why not?"

"Because. Because she's a dog."

"Dick talked to Bess. And she answered."

"Yes, but…how will we know what she thinks?"

Lot looks at the little dog. Their eyes lock.

"Emma. This is very important." She takes the twig from her mouth and scratches a line in front of

Emma's paws. "This is Kessingland, and this," pointing to another spot and scratching another line, "is Scotland? Which do you vote for? It's very very super important."

I'm stuck for words. Appalled and fascinated. Trash's expression shows nothing. Lot repeats herself. "Kessingland. Scotland. Which one?" Emma lifts her left paw and scratches the Scotland line. I don't know what to do. Something comically horrifically apocalyptic about the moment we are in.

"Two each," says Trash.

"So how do we decide?" I ask.

Lot looks at me. "You know," she says. And my heart drops like a stone between my ribs. I know. I take out the coin. My poor darling Chloe will decide. I try to speak but words dry in my throat. Lot takes the coin.

"Heads – Kessingland. Tails – Scotland." And she flips the coin. They watch it spin but I close my eyes. "You have to look, Ali. It's how you do it, we all have to look," Lot says.

Scotland.

17

We have an easy drive, starting on the A1 to avoid what used to be cities, like Northampton, Leicester, Nottingham and Leeds, and which may now be slum fiefdoms populated with recklessness and devastation. Occasional groups of stragglers journeying from nowhere much to nowhere at all. The odd pack of ferals staring at us slack jawed and lost. A few mangy stray dogs that bark, making Emma's ears prick in curiosity. Bess gobbles the miles, even where the road has disintegrated into rubble and we have to slow down. We skirt Leeds and drive off road through brambles until we find a dry hidden patch to eat and sleep, a few kilometres shy of Wetherby.

Emma snuffles through the area for interesting smells, Lot hums a song she has made up in her strange private universe, Trash tries to get some sort of signal that will give him good information. I open a bottle of wine and take a long swig and then offer it to Trash. He smiles and does a mock Cheers. I suddenly feel we are a real little unit. That there is something like loyalty, even trust. Letting my feelings go that way is dangerous. I must fight back the idea that we are a family of sorts. We are a trio of lost people and a dog thrown together by terrible events, and we may be ripped apart at any moment. To soften in sentiment would only weaken me and perhaps hamper my judgement and vigilance when I need it most. Something in me wants to lay down and howl tears at the moon.

The front and back seats fold back so we have space to sleep and can keep the doors locked. I lay in the darkness. As I start to drift a small hand entwines in mine. I feel a tiny jolt, a transmission of energy. I am being taken somewhere. It accelerates, and I wonder if this is the sensation of flying. Of weightlessness, and then of arrival in somewhere painfully familiar but that I cannot place. *My mind is a foreign country. I am a junkyard of wounds, an intricate taxonomy of forgotten desires. Iniquity of oblivion. There are offerings of weapons, bones, magical waters. Myriad passages where the dead trade the engines of wars. Barbecue spits of bones, ornaments. England forged in iron, shaped by weapons, instruments of measure and governance, spade and spear, chieftains bathed in silver, broiled in blood.*

I awaken with a start. Lot is looking at me, only her eyes and a halo of hair visible in the night. "It's alright," she says, letting my hand go.

"Do you know what I saw? Even the dancing words?" I ask.

She nods.

"Is it a quickening?"

She nods again.

"It came through you into me."

"And then it goes somewhere else. Like when it rains and the rain goes in the ground and little things drink it and then they become something else."

"I don't understand."

"It's alright. Go to sleep now."

And I do.

Trash says it will be best to keep off the main A1 and turn left into what was the Yorkshire dales, where we will encounter fewer people. Even though towns and cities are destroyed and are mostly wastelands and slums, and the virus spreads more quickly there, people still congregate, as if some intrinsic homing instinct forces them together. Rumours are that the Moslem areas are particularly dense around the old towns of Bradford and Huddersfield and now further north through York on up to Newcastle. Large family groups that unite with others into packed communities. So we start driving through the dales, the little villages where place names seem freshly cropped from fairy spells: Huby, Timble, Blubberhouses. Lot loves these names and repeats them like mantras.

As we drive something settles like glass shards into me. I realise it is grief for my Dad. Like a slowly spreading stain grief takes its time to soak into the cells and tell its story of loss. When I was a little girl and my Dad used to show me how to care for tools – cleaning the edge of the blade and making sure it is true, linseeding the wood handle of the hammer, levelling the planed timber - so all of these tools assumed personalities for me. Things to be treasured and cared for. Useful and beautiful, beautiful because useful. I see him bending over his workbench, welding goggles on, his hair, grey flecked on the sides, neatly combed back, soldering wire into a broken radio, work done with love, sparks flying, the wire molten, so that in all that livid fire and light and concentration he seemed to me a magician working his art upon the raw materials of the world to make something anew. Later I saw William Blake's God Creating Adam and I thought Blake should paint

Dad in his workshop. I close my eyes to let the picture become a new part of me.

We make 50km in good time and then things change. A chill in the air. Something amiss. The first sign is a number of makeshift pens, which presumably means livestock, in a country where it has all but disappeared. I look out at woolly heads bobbing behind razor wire fences. Occasional eyes, but black and not golden yellow/brown. Ripples of side movements and jostling. The wool looks sooty, dirty white but flecked with black and a reddish hue on some. Emma is standing, paws on the window ledge, the hair on her neck upright and teeth bared – and she trembles in a mix of fear and aggression. Lot strokes her and whispers in one ear, which keeps twitching.

"What the hell?" I ask no one in particular.

"Strange brew," Trash says.

"Any ideas?"

"Keep driving is my best at the moment."

Lot looks out with Emma. "A mix," she says.

A little way on are three Moslem men, two holding an animal tight and a third shearing it. Yet something is very wrong. It is a long time since I've seen a sheep, but this is unlike any sheep I remember. The wool is coarse and flies off like wire wool. The head is flatter and the eyes black, the jaws more like fangs. As we approach the shearing is done and the shearer takes a long bladed knife from his belt and slices the animal's throat. The other lets it go and it starts circling frenziedly, throat gushing thick black blood, eyes wild with boiling pain. The men stand back and watch. Trash is mesmerised and slows. The animal spins, blood spinning out like fizz from a newly uncorked bottle of champagne and then its legs give way and it falls on its side still spinning and bleeding. The men watch impassively. One touches his forehead and looks up, presumably uttering a prayer.

"Halal," Trash says.

"But what the hell animal is that?"

"I think it's a hybrid. I think someone has been messing with genes."

"Why?"

"Look at the wool. It's industrial strength. I think it's trans-species. A sheep and, I don't know, maybe a spider. Look at how those creatures move. Sort of crab-like. Think of a spider web. Tough. So you get the wool, and the meat. Bloody hell, some of them have six legs. That one has eight."

"Jesus Christ. Spider sheep."

"Imagine – if they did it with a poisonous spider. The bite would kill an army. You could just let them loose on your enemy."

"Great. Shall we just drive on?"

"I wonder where they got the technology."

I thought I was beyond shock but something in these creatures hollowed out my imagination. I just wanted to get away. I had no idea of what trouble was waiting just around the bend.

We drove through Thwaite, Angram, Keld, aiming to pick up the main A66 road, but turning a bend, the road and either side of it is blocked by mass slaughter. Some thirty Moslem men stockpiling the bodies of animals and cutting the throats of others.

Mostly spider sheep but other animals with the snouts of pigs and covered in wiry fur.

"Don't tell me what they might be hybrids of," I say as Trash opens his mouth, and then closes it again. Trash makes sure the door locks are all on. The men all stop and stare at us, bleeding carcases and animals gargling their last bubbling breaths in agony at their feet. Two men walk towards us, wiping their bloody blades on dirty cloths. They peer through the front windscreen and indicate we should get out. I shake my head. They come to the driver's side and one gestures for Trash to open the window. He lets it down a few inches, enough to speak. One of the men looks in, takes in Lot and Emma, tries to see what is further in the back. He has a thick black beard, dark eyes and a scar that passes down his top to his bottom lip.

"You lost, bro?" He asks.

"We don't get lost. Protector business," says Trash.

"What business?"

"Our business. You have a license for these animals and for slaughter?"

He laughs. "Sharia law only around here. You know that."

The other man is peering at me intently through the windscreen.

"How old is she?" The first man asks, nodding at Lot.

"Eleven. She's my daughter," I say.

"How come you this far from Dorado on your own?"

"Who says we're on our own?" I say.

The man looks at the road behind us and smiles. "You're on your own," then looking at the dashboard. "Nice wheels. Cost a packet. How much?"

"Ten million tokens. Now can you clear the road and get those animals you've been torturing away? We have business the other side," I say.

"She the boss?" The man asks Trash.

Other men have joined and we now have about a dozen around Bess, some talking. A few of them start gently rocking the vehicle and laughing.

"You do not want to mess with Protectors. You know that. There will be consequences," says Trash.

"Maybe not. We hear Dorado," and he makes a gesture as if something is igniting. "So you get out. We like this vehicle. We requisition it. Out!" He brandishes his knife and wedges it in the window so we can't close it. Two men standing in front of Bess take out automatic weapons and train them on us. I see another man a little away with what looks like an old school bazooka, which could probably destroy one of our tyres, and then we are in deep shit. Another man approaches my side holding a large rock and raises it, ready to try and cave in the window. "You get out now!" Shouts the man with the scar. Others take up the call, like an old time protest march, "Out! Out! Out! Out!" Now they are all brandishing weapons. I turn around and look at Lot. She looks terrified but resolute, and nods at me. Emma barks in fear and aggression. Trash and I take out our pistols. "Allahu Akbar!' The man holding the rock shouts and throws it at my side window. It bounces off and hits him in the face, I guess breaking his nose or cracking a few teeth. He goes down heavily, dazed and bloody, like one of their animal carcases. All eyes are on him. A moment of shock, after which anything could happen. Then someone laughs.

He walks up to join the others, a plump Moslem wearing a chunky gold ring with a large stone in it. He has small dancing eyes, a wide mouth and wears a bright emerald scarf tied at the neck with a silver clasp in the shape of a leaping tiger. A bright scar across his left cheekbone. He points to the man on the ground and starts laughing again, and others join in. The one on the ground is in too much pain to be offended. He gets unsteadily to his feet, staggers and falls over again. The plump man laughs uproariously at this. All join in. Then he comes close and looks inside at us. He turns to the man with the knife and they converse in Arabic, at first friendly, then angry, with lots of gestures and exaggerated expressions. Whatever they are haggling over, neither seems willing to back down. The man with the knife points to us and makes cutthroat gestures. The plump man invites the others to share his opinion with a sweep of an arm, and a few nod agreements. Suddenly the plump man is behind the other man, gripping him in a half nelson and with the man's own knife at his throat. He whispers in his ear and knife man nods. He is released.

The plump man taps on Trash's window. "Open the back door. I'll sit with the missy and the dog. Don't worry, I'm not a bloody paedophile. I just like dogs." Trash looks at me. I have no idea what to do. "Open the bloody door before this lot change their collective mind and turn you into kebabs. I just saved your lives. You should be grovelling at my feet like I'm a big swinging dick." Trash shrugs and releases the back door. The plump man picks up a bag and gets in. He sits next to Emma and strokes her ears. "What's her name?" He asks. "Emma," says Lot.

"Jane Austen. Good. Culture dog. I like. She smart."

"What did you say to them?" I ask.

"Them bastards. I say if they kill you we get whole bag of trouble. I say I saw convoy of Protectors few miles behind you. So I tell them I go with you and take you wrong way and then when other Protectors go I bring you back and we kill you and take your four by four. All bullshit. Like you. Bloody Protectors my arse."

"It's called Bess," says Lot. "What we're travelling in."

"OK. Bess. Whatever. Where are you going?"

"As far north as we can, and then further if we have to."

"Sounds good. I come with you. You'll die without me. Example. You heading for A66?"

"Yes," says Trash.

"OK. Bloody stupid. Why? Because my brothers have put land mines all along A66 from Bowes to bloody Warcop. Why they do this? Because they have landmines and don't want to waste. I take you on safe route."

"Why do you want to come?" I ask.

"Bloody boring in Sharia Yorkshire. Sick of it. Wear your knees out praying. And facing Mecca. We don't know if there is bloody Mecca anymore.

Probably bombed to hell and back. Pile of rubbish floating in sludge. Knocking shop for zombies. And every time virus come half the buggers die. Where Allah then? Out having bloody hairwash? No. Stuff Yorkshire. Leave it for puddings and Moslems. Everywhere stink. Plumbing up the spout. And my three wives. No bloody good. Always moaning. Say want more stuff – I say is no bloody stuff. All gone. No one have nothing now, silly bitches one, two and three. I come with you. Shave this bloody beard off. Turn left here or we blow sky high."

"What's your name?" I ask.

"Asim. I can lead you through this bloody desert."

"This is the Yorkshire Dales."

"Whatever."

"Those hybrid animals. Where did they develop the technology for that?" Trash asks.

"Bloody creepy. But I tell you what bloody creepier, man. Make your hair white. Turn right here."

Asim told us they had labs where they bred a few animals and then experimented with trans species DNA, sometimes through cloning but also by injecting different DNA into the foetus. There was a period when they experimented with crossing human and other animal DNA. Most died but he said those who lived were incarcerated, partly because they could not care for themselves, but also to protect them from people wanting to kill them as abominations which were an insult to Allah. He said there were all sorts – humans crossed with dogs, with goats, with a horse – and the purpose was to create a super breed of warriors that would take over the whole of the UK, but it didn't work and then most of the animals died out anyway, except for the few sheep and dogs they now clone as trans species. He said seeing some of the abominations still gave him nightmares. The slaughter we saw was a major event and the meat is to celebrate the Eid-ul-Adha (Festival of the Sacrifice), commemorating Abraham's willingness to sacrifice his son, who was miraculously replaced by a lamb. Strange that the one area where religious practice continues is among Muslims in Yorkshire, albeit mixed in with creating mutations. Asim said they were still required to supply people for the Hunts, but mostly they were left alone.

He was the kind of chatterbox you can zone in and out of. Travel elsewhere in your mind, come back five minutes later and pick up the thread. We drive through ghost villages – Great Asby, Woodfoot, on lanes that come and go, sometimes completely overrun with dead or dying bracken.

"We're heading for the M6," I said.

"M6 good. Quick road. Not many holes."

"But it's very close to The Lake District National Park. The cannibal area."

"Screw bloody cannibals. Is good road. If they hungry they can chew on my belly. Is too big." Lot laughed and Asim laughed with her. These two were an unlikely and strange pair, but Lot sensed he was not a threat to her or Emma.

It was easy to get on the M6 because the road had sunk in places and we drove down a scrubby slope and joined it. The middle section was mostly gone so it was a wide stretch of pockmarked road north to south. I thought if all went well we'd stop at Gretna Green and make a plan from there. After a few kilometres things became nightmarish. On the left were vaporous marshlands that had a brown mist above them, like toupees that had leapt from their heads in fright. Then a row of poles some three metres high, two metres apart but stretching into the road's horizon. On each one a human head was spiked, some long decayed and dried out but some looking horribly fresh as if still in a death agony. Hundreds and hundreds of them, all looking down on us and beyond into some region. The mood soured to something hopeless.

"The message is – enter here and this is how you'll end up," says Trash.

"I had worked that out, Trash," I said.

"They look like flowers growing. Think of this as a garden," he says. I don't even bother to answer. I knew we were all asking ourselves the same question – are we being watched? All those heads had bodies which have now been chopped, skewered, fried, boiled, roasted and consumed. Hopeless humanity. I remember reading a history of Tamburlaine and if a city did not instantly surrender to him he would slaughter everyone and make a tower of human heads as a warning. At least he had an eye for beautiful buildings, so I'd say in seven hundred years we have very successfully regressed to a point where we probably deserve oblivion. Lot had, up to this point, seemed impressively, strangely impassive when faced with horror, but something about these spiked heads, perhaps the sheer monotonous, relentless procession of them, jittered her and she stared at them and seemed to shrink inside herself. Asim patted her hand.

"You see this scar?" He said, pointing to the scar on his cheekbone. She nods. "I know you see because you are one smart girl see everything, like an angel. I tell you how I get it. One day I am walking with my dog, just like this Emma but not so pretty. In fact bloody ugly dog. One ear gone, one eye wobble and some teeth knocked out so she dribble all the time. I call her Rose because she smell like the poop people used to put on roses to make them grow. You have poop you have rose. So I walking with Rose and these three bloody fellows amble along at us. Bloody Muslim like me, big beard and always wanting to cheat you. Even worse than bloody Christian. One say 'Hey, your dog bloody ugly and smell like toilet' and he kick Rose so she yelp like this: Yeeow! So I say 'OK, fellow, now I teach you lesson' and I hit him so hard his bloody teeth fly out. Then second fellow draw knife, big bloody knife like sword, and slash me across face. This make me bloody mad so I do flying kick like kung fu man and break his nose and knock him out. Then third man I pick him up and throw him long way, maybe twenty metre, into smelly ditch where all people poop, but I don't think he ever become rose. Then I go home with Rose and we have nice drink of champagne – bottle which I hide from old times and save for special occasion. Moslem do not drink which is bloody rubbish. They drink but just don't tell. So that how I get scar. You like?"

Lot nods and smiles.

"You believe?"

Lot shakes her head. "It's not true but it's better than true so now it is true," she says enigmatically.

We travel in silence for a few minutes and then Lot says, "You had an accident in a car and your cheek got cut on broken glass."

Asim looks at her open mouthed. "You not angel. You bloody witch. How you know this?"

"It's a quickening. A gift she has," I say.

Asim stares at me and then at Lot again, and then roars with laughter, which sets Emma barking. And then we all laugh, with a long road of severed heads watching our crazy path to god knows what end.

18

It was as if a huge shadow stalking our souls evaporated as we reached Penrith and left the valley of the heads. We stopped for water and to pee and stretch ourselves. Asim and Lot threw sticks for Emma. We ate some tins of beans and green stuff that may have been spinach or seaweed in a former life but tasted salty and fine. I was eating better recently than in the past few years. Trash had found a connection to someone who was cam filming scenes in Dorado. I watched as carnage unfolded. A lot of bodies littered around, Protectors and civilians. I guess that many Protectors saw endgame coming and went rogue – take what you can and get out. Fires were burning. No one seemed in control. How quickly things ignite once you light a spark. I wondered how the elite kids were doing. If they were still alive.

"We did that," said Trash, with a rare show of pride.

"Bastards had it coming."

Trash suggested that we just drive on and chew up the miles, perhaps even get beyond Glasgow and camp for the night somewhere near Loch Lamond. The road was overgrown but surprisingly intact with the usual garbage on the sides – rubbish piles, old wheels, abandoned vehicles. Smoke visible from camp fires or battles every now and then but far enough away from the road not to worry us. We chomped up the miles. Gretna Green, Lockerbie, Hangingshaw, Johnstonebridge. The weather turned.

Low slung cumulus. Light rain and then electric blue thunder that rocked the earth. Emma howled. Lightning made everything look surreal and I wondered if we were really in a simulacrum. A howling theatre of horrors. At least the weather kept others away and allowed us a free road to god knows what. Then the storm stopped. As if mightily bored with it all. A grey, ashen calm over what was left. We passed a group of sodden Ferals standing at the side of the road, some too drenched and frozen to even look at us, the life squeezed from them.

You never know how out of date information is. All the way up to Edinburgh was, we thought, a ruined drug district with tribal groups fighting for diminishing resources and whatever narcotics were available. I knew it was a mistake to assume if we got past Glasgow and Edinburgh we would be safe – for all I knew it might get worse – but the important thing was to be on the alert now. Which is why when it came it wasn't a surprise. The further into Scotland we drove the narrower the road because rubbish and flotsam from a dying civilisation lined in ever thickening and widening seams each side of the road. The stench outside was sickening. Millions of rats swarmed. We squashed thousands who tried to cross. How could people produce so much crap when they had so little? Consumer graveyard was all around us. Dozens of burnt out cars, abandoned trucks. I looked at Trash and realised that despite the traumas, perhaps because of them, our relationship was changing. Before he had been the brilliant weirdo in the garage, not even really a person to me.

"What?" He asked, as I look at him.

"Just thinking. I'm starting to think you're the brother I wish I'd had."

He nods, but I see in his eyes what I hadn't realised. The word 'brother' wasn't what he wanted to hear. He felt something else, something that could never happen. This world wasn't for falling in love. We had evolved beyond love as far as I was concerned. Forget it.

Ahead in the road was a tiny figure. As we got closer she started waving her one free arm at us to stop. She had only one leg and a crutch. A wound on her head was bleeding freely and she looked filthy, wearing what might once have been a dress. Trash slowed down and stopped. The girl continued waving and pointed at her bloody head.

"What do you think?" Trash asked.

"I think it's a trap."

"Of course bloody trap," Asim said.

"What shall we do?" Trash asked. "I can't get round her."

"We can't just run her down," I say. "Lot? What do you think?"

"She's doing stand and deliver, but she's not a proper highwayman."

I waved at her to move aside but she just kept beckoning us and alternately pointing at her head. There seemed to be no movement in the rubbish mountains other than rats. I took a bandage from the First Aid box, and a tin of beans from our supplies, checked my Glock and opened the door. I walked towards her and stopped to check around me again. Trash was still in the driver's seat but holding a machine gun.

"Are you alone?" I asked the girl, and that's when I knew I've been stupid. She dropped the crutch, sliced the string that was holding her other leg behind her, and ran to one side. A moment's silence and something made me drop low and to my left as a volley of automatic fire goes to my right. I returned four shots and Trash had already driven between me and the shooter. I got in the passenger side. Behind us a truck that looked a wreck rumbled out onto the road and started after us, with someone leaning out and firing a pistol at us. Trash accelerated but a few hundred metres in front of us a car pulled out of the rubbish and blocked the road side on with two people firing at us. The bullets bounced off the windscreen.

"Hold on," Trash said and put his foot down. He gambled on Bess being sturdier than the truck in the road and we hit it with a force that knocked the wind from me. The side of the truck crumpled and the two people firing at us were sausage meat. We stopped momentarily and Trash put his foot down. I feared the engine would burn out but it slowly shovelled the truck around. Their driver, a woman in a red bandana got out of the truck and waited for a good moment to fire at us. She suddenly jerked and jittered and fell dead as Asim fired at her through an open back window. Emma was on the floor and shaking with Lot bent over her, whispering soothingly. It is as if I could see and hear everything even though it was only seconds. Bess strained and pushed the truck completely around and I fired a volley at it and with a grinding of gravel we were away.

"Next time you see little girl trying to stop us she is roadkill," Asim said, and then with a smile at Lot, "present company excepted."

I breathed again. Only for a moment.

"Uh oh," says Trash.

Behind us were about six cars and trucks, and more seeping out of the rubbish. Presumably all of them focused on our destruction. Given their proximity we have no time to get out and find some way of blocking the road. If we keep driving forward they might arrange another welcome in front of us, and probably this time a stronger one.

"Personally I don't want to die on the former M74," says Trash.

"Doesn't have a dramatic enough ring to it?" I say.

"Dick Turpin would go into the woods," Lot says.

I look at Trash. "Find a spot where the rubbish seems less packed and take a chance?" he asks. I nod. I can't see any other way out other than to stop and get overpowered by sheer weight of numbers. Half a kilometre on there is a small gap in the rubbish and Trash slows. I see scrubland through the gap. He looks at me and I nod. He turns at speed into the rubbish and we cleave through fairly easily, glass and paper and dead foliage and rats scattering. We bump down and for a moment I think there is going to be a ditch but Bess rights herself and we drive on. No road. It is open dead land strewn with rocks and extending as far as the eye can see. Without a state-of-the-art vehicle we would be in serious trouble.

Bess was built for this terrain. Of course, I was wrong again.

The convoy follows us. One car stalls as it bumps down and stays put. I count seven others. Over these rocks and little hills I can't see them all making it. Asim looks behind.

"Do we have plan?" He asks.

"Plan A is to drive, plan B is to keep driving," says Trash.

Despite its off road toughness it is like bouncing around in a jumping bean. The other cars are about five hundred metres behind. I look at the clock on the dashboard and calculate, by keeping a landmark in view, that it took us twenty seconds to cover a hundred metres, given that the going is precarious. I tell Trash to slow down. He looks at me curiously but does so and they gain a little behind us. I now calculate they are about thirty seconds behind. I take out a grenade and open my door a little, pull the pin and gently drop the grenade. It rolls a little but settles and I don't think they've seen me do it.

"Now accelerate."

He puts his foot down a little and we put more distance between us. I look at the second counter on the dash. Ten. Fifteen. Twenty. Shit, just when I think it's a dud there is a satisfying explosion behind us. I look and see that in the middle of the convoy two cars at least are hot metal and dead bodies. There is confusion but as the dust and smoke clears there are still three cars and two trucks, only now they fan out to avoid another grenade getting more than one of them. I am crawling with sweat and take sips of water to calm me. I turn around and smile at

Lot and pat Emma's head, her dark liquid eyes looking, it seems, inside me to seek an answer to some impossible question.

We put a healthy distance between us and the rabble, but they are tenacious. I wonder if goods and chattels are so scarce that it's worth the pursuit and casualties. Bess would be like pure gold in any barter for drugs and weapons, and it's reasonable to assume that anyone driving this beast will have other goodies aboard. Plus there is all the fun of the kill. Starving and getting off your face every night on paint peeler must lose its shine after a while. Every now and then we have to avoid small hills, but each of us realises they are piles of Covid bodies that have weathered into one dry mass of bone and skin and teeth and matted hair and rags.

Suddenly there is a teeth grinding shear of metal and high pitched shriek as something goes very wrong. Bess stutters and keeps going but with a persistent whine like some giant animal in pain. Emma's ears are pointed skywards and she leans her head side to side trying to work out what is happening. I look at Trash.

"Brake pads? Wheel bearings?" I ask.

I need to see," he says.

"I thought trucks like this were invincible. Things like this aren't meant to happen," I say.

"Most things aren't supposed to happen," he says.

The screeching is getting worse. There is meant to be a self-lubricating mechanism for the whole vehicle that renders regular servicing unnecessary. I wonder if it somehow got blocked and is causing one set of wheel bearings to rub against each other. The danger if they overheat too much is that they rupture altogether. "We need to stop," I say.

"There," says Lot, pointing. To our right is a high ridge and about half a kilometre ahead is a building just in front of it. We are slowing and the ragged posse behind us is gaining. Trash turns and the front left wheel complains loud and long. I can't believe metal can make that much noise and not break or burn out. The cars are about 400 metres behind us. I wait for shooting to start but probably the terrain is too bumpy to waste ammo. They were hoping to wear us down or for us to run out of fuel or for something like this to happen. Trash drives around the building which will afford Bess some protection. We grab weapons and as many boxes of supplies as we can and get out. The building is an ancient farmhouse, which is good because the walls are half a metre thick. A sheet of corrugated metal is propped against the hole where the back door was. We get inside. The stairs have long gone, there is a room either side of a small corridor and then at the front of the house one long room that doubled as kitchen and living area. There are two dead Covid victims leaning against each other like roaring drunks sleeping it off. One is dressed in a faded gingham frock and the other a strangely formal dark suit. The front door is intact. There are two small windows either side of the door. The signs of old fires all over the floor. Emma is both excited and terrified. She smells our fear. Luckily all my adrenalin has kicked in and I am thinking fast.

"Are you good with guns?" I ask Asim.

"Top notch, bloody hellfire James Bond Rambo Genghis Khan."

"OK, maestro, you take the window on the right, Trash and I will take the two on the left. Lot, you and Emma keep well down. No looking out, and no moving unless we tell you to. OK?"

She nods. I give Asim an MP7 and ammo, and an M4A41 assault rifle. Trash takes two MP7s and I take a 725 shotgun and a Glock. We each have three grenades. Outside the cars arrive and park in a line. I count fifteen people, ten men and five women. At least three look like bombed out space junkies, which will either mean they are useless or recklessly crazy. I see one guy shoot up by the side of a car, then tie off his arm, which is full of scabs. At least three men and two women look alert and useful. They have an assortment of pistols and automatic rifles, but only one machine gun. Whoever has that will be my prime target. They arraign themselves behind their cars; I'm glad about that because I thought they would spread the cars out, which would give them a greater variety of angles to fire upon us. Another fear is that reinforcements will arrive, or that somehow they will get behind us on the ridge and be able to fire down on us. I see that they are handing out home-made petrol bombs in old wine bottles. If one comes through the window we are in trouble. There are two holes in the roof and if they are clever they will target those. A fire upstairs with no stairs to get up and put it out will be a problem.

I look at Lot and Emma. The little dog is licking Lot's hand and she is whispering soothingly into Emma's ears. She looks up at me and I make a gesture to cover Emma's ears. She nods and does so, whispering all the time. I wonder what she is saying. Alright. Everything will be alright, my darling. I promise. We are together. God willing. God.

19

It comes sudden and quick. They all seem to fire at once and under the cover two stand and throw their home-made bombs. One hits the wall and explodes in flames, the other hits the roof, luckily missing the hole, rolls down in a fireball and onto the ground. The sound is deafening. We wait for a lull, and then return fire. The machine guns start to devastate their vehicles. If we can destroy them then their cover is gone and they either have to suicide attack us or run. Asim knows what he is doing, standing and delivering quick volleys and then ducking. We get into a rhythm of him firing and then Trash and I. One of them breaks for open ground and runs to the side. I think he plans to get wide and then double back behind us. Trash covers me while I take aim with my Glock. I fire off three rounds and miss, but the fourth explodes his knee and he falls and rolls in agony. Trash finishes him with the machine gun.

In a battle like this time plays tricks on you. You think seconds are hours. We had been fighting for five minutes but it felt like eternal war. Asim had completely wrecked one car. Occasionally they fired through one of our windows and I was worried about ricochets getting Lot and Emma, but Asim had dragged a table behind them to prevent it. Then there was a lull. They were regrouping. Two of them, a skinny man in a red bandana and a girl I thought was black but realised every inch of her was tattooed. They started the truck and then drove at our front door. Several of their number were using the truck as cover. The skinny guy was crouching low, just his hands up on the wheel, but the girl either had a death wish or thought God was on her side and sat up. I picked up my shotgun and blasted two shots at the windscreen. She screamed as the glass exploded onto her. Her face was bloody offal, shards of glass sticking out. She pulled a long piece of glass from one eye. The truck slammed against the front door and the whole wall shuddered. The people behind the truck came out and started firing almost point blank. Trash sprayed one side of the truck, killing the skinny guy. Everything happening so fast. Duck, stand, fire, duck, hope you stay lucky. A denim clad man rolled from behind the truck and got to Asim's side and threw a home-made fire bomb through the window. Asim ducked and the bottle flew past him and landed on the back wall, exploding into flames. The wall was on fire but hopefully the petrol would burn off. Smoke might be the killer but I was glad there was a hole in the roof. The man who had thrown the bomb was crouched outside and Asim leaned out and shot him in the head. He turned to me and then seemed to flip backwards as a bullet caught him in the shoulder.

I ran to Asim's side of the room and took over his window. I picked up his machine gun and looked out just as a girl was aiming at Trash. I fired a volley at her and then back at the others behind to keep them pinned down. The skinny guy inside the truck was still alive and he reversed the truck back to the others. Everybody stopped to get their breath. Asim was bleeding freely. I found a cloth and bound a tourniquet around him. I took a bottle of whisky from one of our supply boxes and handed it to him. "Whisky bloody good Moslem drink, praise be to God," he said and took a long swig.

Trash called me over. Outside the skinny guy who drove the truck had walked out and was holding his arms up. He had crazy eyes and the smile of a mad doll.

"You can't get out," he said. "We've got more people coming."

"What do you want?" I said.

He grinned. "You know what we want. The truck and any supplies and goods you've got. And the guns,"

"In exchange for what?"

"Your lives. We'll drive you further north and let you go, but we keep everything. If you stay," he made a cut throat gesture.

I turned around to confer with Trash, but he'd gone. Lot indicated with a nod that he had gone to the back. Asim was sitting on a box with his machine gun resting on the window ledge. He shook his head at me, but I wasn't born yesterday and crazy-eyes didn't inspire confidence. We'd be shot, or worse, before they'd even opened the first bottle of wine. But keeping this nutjob talking gave us a respite.

"How many of you are there altogether? And how do you live?" I asked.

"Hundreds. Thousands. We live in fine houses with running water and gardens and days of rest and nights of pleasure. We're the wonder of the north. The new Babylon. Hey, you could join us. Tonight we could be comrades and all sleep in amazement at ourselves. We are the crusade of the new Jerusalem of desire and devastation. Armies are crushed by the mere thought of us. Enemies fill their pants with fear. Word is another Covid on the way so you don't want to travel far. Hunker down with us as bed buddies. Wait it out."

I wondered how much of this crackpot bullshit he had inside him. Turned out quite a lot. He was still waffling a few minutes later when a woman with bright red hair and junkie skin walked up behind him and hit him on the side of his head with her rifle. He fell, an ugly cut already bleeding. She was in a fury. "Get up, dick brain!" She hissed and then turned on us. "This piece of shit is no longer our official negotiator. I am. Red. And if you don't come out of here in ten minutes we will visit a world of pain and torture upon you. It will not be romantic. I will personally cut out the eyeballs of the kid and I will also wear your skin until it dries to paper."

"Can I have time to consider that offer?" I asked.

She held up one hand twice. Ten minutes. She went back to the others with a bleeding crazy-eyes in tow. Nothing to do but wait. I wondered if Trash had been taken short in all the excitement, or was sick. I needed him here. I turned to Asim. He was sweating with pain but nodded. I had no idea whether minutes or hours were passing. The thought struck me that we use the same verb as a euphemism for death. Life and time both pass. As if life is just a momentary stopover in something larger.

I looked out at the group. One of them was watching me through binoculars. He wore a dust mask. He lowered the binoculars and made a cut throat gesture. My skin crawled. I am sure it is Fauberge.

Trash reappeared, covered in oil. "Blockage," he said. "Fixed." The genius had healed Bess, but we had nowhere to go. We'd be followed. Eventually we'd have to find somewhere else to hide. If it was true that more of them were coming it would be harder for us. In an all-out attack we could simply be overwhelmed by numbers. Yet if Bess and our weapons and supplies were an important currency would this band of gypsies outside want to spread it so thinly? We would find out. Then the shooting started again. Trash ducked and joined me at the window.

"You're a genius," I said.

"I know."

I fired a blast from my shotgun and it took off the whole roof of a truck's front cab. Asim was swallowing his pain, as well as a lot of whisky, and fighting like there was no tomorrow, which perhaps there wasn't. The woman Red was on a personal glory mission. I knew she wanted to kill me in particular. I stood against the wall, Glock in my left hand and shotgun in my right. Then I picked up the Covid body in the suit. He weighed practically nothing. I dragged him over to the front door. Trash fired a volley and then ducked while they returned fire at the windows. I suddenly opened the door, with the body leaning against me and holding my weapons either side. They weren't expecting such rashness or such a bizarre sight – a gun toting corpse, and it gave me a second. I rapid fired my Glock and then levelled the shotgun and got a lucky shot which completely blew Red's head from her shoulders. Her torso stood, as in in stiff shock, and then toppled forward. I closed the door and the woodwork received a tsunami of bullets.

Foolishly I had the thought that if we stayed strong and Asim stayed conscious, we might survive, at least until nightfall, and then regroup. That's when I saw a dust cloud and then another dozen vehicles half a kilometre away. That could mean another thirty of forty people. We were well and truly screwed.

Our enemies haven't yet seen their support arriving behind them. I wonder if we should surrender, but the moment passes. No point running out back and getting in Bess. With sixteen vehicles and a small army against us I don't think we'd get far. I decide I'll go down defending Lot and the little dog she adores and who seems to now represent our fragility. I look over at Asim. I'm pretty sure it's the whisky that is keeping him afloat and dulling the pain. He looks at me.

"You see them?" I ask.

He nods. "More is the merrier, eh?"

We keep firing. They suddenly stop shooting and turn to the others arriving.

"Something's not right," Trash says. "Look at those cars and trucks."

I have a pair of binoculars in my bag and take them out. The new vehicles have black flags fixed to each roof. I can see that all the drivers and passengers are black, whereas the group we have been battling is a mix of colours and races. Then they start firing at each other and within seconds a full pitched battle is being fought.

"Rival chapters," Trash says.

"This could be our moment. Perhaps the only one we'll get."

He nods. "Time to check out," I say, and we grab our stuff and go through the back and into Bess. Everyone straps in. "Heads down," Trash says. We drive out the opposite way that we entered and hug the high ridge to keep as far away from our enemies. Perhaps they will be so intent on their battle they won't even see us.

We drive a good five hundred metres before I risk looking back. It will be carnage before the day is out. Then I see two of the vehicles with black flags take after us. One is a newish looking land rover. Above us purplish clouds like ugly bruises are scudding low with the promise of bad things to come. Seconds late a thunder crack and biblical rain sheeting upon us. Even with the wipers on high we can barely see a few metres ahead and the ground is rapidly turning to liquid mud. It's impossible to see if our pursuers are still there. I believe they are. We are a prize worth suffering for. I look behind and Asim is clearly in a lot of pain. Lot has her hand on his. That wound needs urgent attention.

We keep to the ridge until it shaves down to nothing. The ground is so mushed beneath us I fear if we stop or slow down too much the wheels will just spin. The storm rains start to abate and half a kilometre ahead is the wall of debris and the road beyond. Behind us only the Land Rover now. We could stop and make a fight of it but I wonder if they have phoned ahead and there are others waiting on the road. Trash has a signal and scans ahead.

"Gap in the wall on our left. Road looks pretty clear," he says.

Alright then."

We go up a small incline and then crash through knee high rubbish and onto the road. A few minutes later the Land Rover appears. I climb into the back and do the best I can with Asim's wound. The bullet is still in there but it's not infected yet. I don't trust myself to get the bullet out but we both know if it stays he's in trouble.

"Get bloody thing out," he says. His whole body is damp with sweat. Lot and Emma manoeuvre into the front seat. The First Aid box has bandages, plasters and tape, painkillers, antiseptic, scissors, tweezers, but what I need is forceps. In my bag I still have the tools I took from the dead man on the beach. Seems like a thousand years ago. I take out a small pair of pliers and disinfect them. I look at the wound, an angry mash of tissue, blood and flesh. The bullet isn't visible but must have gone near the big bone in his shoulder. I'll need to cut my way in and find it. I clean the scissors and flip open one blade. Asim grabs my hand.

"You have medical training?" He asks.

"No. But I was a good engineer. Mostly electrical engineering. Very good at urban water cycle management. So I'm highly qualified." I give him a slug of whisky and offer a wrapped cloth to bite on but he waves it away.

"I want to bloody shout!" He says.

"OK. You shout. Trash, put some music on. Loud," I say.

Seconds later Beethoven's 5th blares loudly and I cut into Asim's shoulder. It's going to be a series of choices between being careful or quick. Not easy, given that I don't really know what I'm doing. I try to see it as an engineering problem. The body is a machine. This one has a blockage and I have to get it out by causing as little damage as possible. I probe deep and Asim is practically screaming. I pull the flesh aside and wipe the blood away. I follow the trajectory of the bullet and see its flat bottom. It scraped the bone, which must have slowed it down, but the bone isn't broken. Now I know why clamps are needed because I need to keep the wound open and get the forceps down.

"Jesus bloody hell! Oh sodding buddha! God god god! What is this bloody horrible music?"

"Ludwig Van Beethoven. You are being accompanied by a master."

"Master my bloody bollocks. No bloody words. What kind of music this? Ludwig. Sounds like bloody insect."

He is becoming hysterical. I almost hope he passes out. No alternative but to get help.

"Lot. Come here."

She hops over.

"I need you to hold the scissors just like this. And take no notice of his screaming."

She takes the scissors and holds them in both hands. A thin jet of blood arcs over her face but she barely blinks. I take the pincers and push them down beside the scissors and locate the bullet, grip it hard and pull. It comes out with a wet plop. Asim screams. I look at Lot and then lean forward and kiss her on the forehead. "That was heroic," I say. "You are not going to die. I won't let you," I say. She nods, and then hops back to the front seat and Emma. I give Asim a slug of whisky.

"You get bloody child to torture me," he says, weeping in pain.

"That's right. All part of the service. Now shut the fuck up."

I clean the wound, then pack it and bind it tight. I crush some pain killer in a cup and pour in more whisky.

"Trouble ahead," says Trash.

A battered Land Rover with a black flag is parked facing us about five hundred metres ahead. Standing in front of it is a tall black guy wearing a top hat and holding an anti-tank mortar on his shoulder aiming straight at us.

"Any ideas?" Trash asks.

"He won't want to destroy Bess."

I see from the way the man's body tenses he is about to fire. Trash suddenly swerves and the shell misses us and explodes a few metres behind.

"Maybe no one told him that," Trash says, swerving again as the man tenses to fire. I grab a machine gun, lean out and fire a volley. It's enough to make the man run to take cover behind the Land Rover. I tell Trash to put his foot down and I keep firing. I don't want others in the Land Rover to get out and bombard us too. The passenger door opens and someone is going to start firing at any moment. I spray another volley, grab a grenade and then when we are almost upon them for a head on crash, Trash swerves and we rip off the passenger door of the Land Rover and crush whoever was behind it. Screeching of metal as Trash's side of Bess scrapes by, shearing off wing mirrors. I lob the grenade. It explodes once we are past and the man now behind the Land Rover is about to fire at us. I look back and as the smoke clears I see a pair of legs in fine boots standing looking at me, all else blown away from the knees up.

A minute later the other Land Rover skirts the mess and is after us again. I suddenly feel sick of this. It all seems pointless. I think if Lot and Emma weren't here I'd just want to stop and get it all over with. Asim is out for the count, which is a blessing.

"I feel sick," I say.

"Not over the dashboard, please."

"Of this."

"You watch everything slowly get out of shape. And then you realise, it's not everything, it's you."

"Yes, but then, you've always been as weird as witch wind."

"Is that a compliment?"

"It's a fact."

"There's another fact up ahead."

On the road ahead is a gold Rolls Royce. For a moment I think we're hallucinating. Then the front doors open and on the right one of the biggest men I've ever seen gets out. On the left one of the smallest, less than a metre high. The big man wears a bright purple coat and a gold chain. The little man wears a suit and tail coat. The little man starts waving his arm to one side.

"What do you think? Where are their weapons?" I ask.

"I think he wants us to drive on the side."

"Why?"

"I don't know. But I can't think of anything better to do."

Trash drives close to one side, still heading for the Rolls Royce. Two people, a man and a woman, in paramilitary uniforms, get out of the back of the Rolls and stand watching, hands behind backs. The little guy reaches inside the car and staggers out with some sort of weapon resting on a purple cushion. He can barely carry it as he walks around and hands it ceremoniously to the big man, who takes it while still staring ahead. He lifts the weapon, which is some sort of rocket launcher I've never seen before. He puts it on his shoulder and gets on one knee. For a moment I think we're heading for oblivion but from the angle he's aiming behind us. At the Black Flag Land Rover. A flash of fire. A crack of thunder and I look behind to see the Land Rover explode in flames.

"That'll make their eyes water," says Trash.

The midget and the two in uniform applaud politely, then one of the soldiers takes the rocket launcher and the little guy gets a gold crown from the car, puts it on the cushion, stands on tiptoe, and places it ceremoniously on the big guy's head, who is still on one knee. They all laugh. The world is getting stranger by the second.

We slow down and stop. We've run out of options. The big guy stands up and spreads his arms. I get out of Bess and show my palms to make it clear I'm unarmed. The guy has an impressive ginger beard and dancing blue eyes. He tips the crown at a rakish angle.

"'What happens now?'" She's thinking," he says.

"Will he tell her?" I ask.

He laughs. "Any enemy of the Black Flags is a friend of mine. Welcome to the kingdom."

"Whose kingdom?"

He indicates his crown with both hands. "I'm Rannoch. And you?"

"Ali."

"Ali. Ali Baba. Ali-lujah. Ali-minium. The wee laddie is Ericht," here the midget nods, "and my two soldiers, Roughburn and Linnhe. I tend to the view that anything and anyone south of here is garbage. Uncivilised garbage. But you are escaping north so might be worthy of redemption. You look tired. Your story is surely tortuous and painful, full of twists and caveats, but I'd be lying if I said I had any interest in it. When you are as big a character as myself there is enough material to ponder for several lifetimes. If I ask you questions it is merely the shadow of politeness. Follow us."

They get in the Rolls and Rannoch himself drives, very fast. We follow.

"What did he say?" Trash asks.

"He said he has no interest in us at all, but that we might be worthy of redemption. He didn't mention you specifically."

We drive several hundred kilometres over landscapes that were doubtless once beautiful. We pass a few Covid settlements with skull flags flying. Fires burning here and there. To judge by the occasional acrid waft they are the dead burning. Asim awakens and I give him some more painkillers.

"What happened?" He asks.

"We met with dastardly enemies but then Dick's friend and fellow gentleman of the road Tom King appeared on his golden steed and shot blue thunder through them and now we are embarked on a journey to safety," Lot says.

Asim looks from her to me. I shrug. It'll do. We reach Fort Augustus on the southern tip of Loch Ness, which is now a green sludge of choked weeds and bubbling mud. If anything is alive in it you would not want to know. Lot stares at it. We drive alongside the Loch.

"Once, they say a monster lived here. A dinosaur," I say.

"A supposedly extinct plesiosaur, a long-necked aquatic reptile which became extinct during the Cretaceous–Paleogene extinction event, also known as the Cretaceous–Tertiary, K–T, extinction," Trash says.

"Took the words right out of my mouth," I say.

Ahead is Urquhart castle, but not as it ever was five hundred years ago. A stockade has been built to create and protect a large area on the land side. High concrete walls with gun turrets. We stop and a soldier approaches us. I wind down the window. He shows me a small plastic instrument. "Covid tester," he says. He points it at me and the instrument beeps. He then points it at the others in turn. "Clear," he says. A gate opens and we drive through into what appears to be a medieval settlement. Tents, sheds and shacks. A hundred or so soldiers. A lot of weapons. Ordinary people and a few children, all looking remarkably healthy. I wonder where they get food. The Tower which looks directly from a bight in the Loch over what was once water has been restored, but also given three times the width and had many floors added to it. You can probably see the dead ocean far north if the air ever cleared.

We stop and Ericht the midget beckons us. We follow him to a side door by the tower that leads into a corridor with doors off. There is a lift so there must be more floors underground. He opens a door onto a suite of rooms.

"There's food and drink in the fridge. You're free to go anywhere but outside the walls. A doctor will arrive shortly to see to him," he nods at Asim and leaves. Asim levers himself down into an armchair. The fridge is full of good stuff – protein balls and wine. Cupboards have tins of tomatoes and potatoes and beans and even peaches. Where do they get it all? Two bathrooms and even a jacuzzi at the far end of the long living room.

The doctor is a young woman soldier. She dresses Asim's wound and says he'll be fine. She also takes a look at Trash's wound and says he'll have restricted movement but nothing too bad. She checks all our teeth and eyes and ears. She doesn't answer questions but just nods or smiles and says, "It'll be alright." Then she leaves. I'm exhausted but curiosity overrides it and Lot, Trash and I take Emma out for a walk around Urquhart town, as Lot now calls it. We watch a man making shoes in a little shack with an open front. Emma sniffs and explores, occasionally giving a person a wide berth, sensing something that only animals can. There are clothing businesses, kitchenware, electrical goods. It seems to be a real functioning community, oddly archaic. I wonder where their power supply is. There were wind turbines outside the settlement but not enough to fuel the whole community.

Then a bell rings and everyone stops and looks up at the tower.

20

Rannoch stands on a balcony at the top of the tower.

"Feasgar math," he bellows.

"Feasgar math," everyone returns.

I look at Trash. "Gaelic. Means Good evening," he says.

"How do you know that?" I ask.

"Stupid question," he says.

"Stupid question," I agree. What can you ask the man who says he knows everything?

Rannoch makes a speech about the good of the community, how they are all equal, all thriving and the rest of the world can go to hell, at which everyone laughs, and then he introduces us as welcome new residents. Smiles all around. This man certainly likes to control things. We've been here five minutes and already we are residents – clearly we don't have a choice in this. Admittedly he saved our lives. He announces a dance on Friday and all cheer. I feel as if I'm in some weird throwback commune with a Scottish clan chief who has his own personal fiefdom. Whenever in my life I had to listen to someone saying we are all equal, I smell a rat.

We sleep and eat and drink and Asim heals. We are given new clothes. It feels like limbo. I sense a storm brewing, but it may be that my paranoia and battered perceptions are simply alerting me to dangers in myself. I no longer trust my own judgement, which makes me something of a liability. Fear that I may decide something that puts Lot in jeopardy makes me irrational. I am caught out in these thoughts by Asim, looking at me intently while he sips a fine old malt whisky, for which he has rapidly acquired a taste.

"This is how it works, Ali. Remember before the new Covid that buggered everyone up the britches? Everyone scared – of left wing, right wing, bloody chicken wing, Black Lives Matter, Transbender this, equal rights that, Islam jihad, fascist Nazi gender benders, West Bank left bank Barclays bloody bank, can't say this can't say that, stick bloody mask on your face so can't say anything, then everyone scared of what they say, what they think, what they feel, what they bloody are. All bollocks. Now you running scared of yourself. Know what I say?"

"What?"

"Drink bloody whisky. Bloody bollocks to lot of them."

"That's a very wise position, Asim."

"So you want drink?"

I take out Chloe's magic coin. "Heads I have a drink. Tails I have a large one." I flip the coin. "Tails."

"Bloody good coin."

It's odd to be in what I suppose is a safe environment. To walk around without being threatened. We have been given a bag of tokens to trade with. I rediscover old joys. Throwing a stick for Emma, telling highway robbery stories to Lot, drinking with Asim, watching the scummy loch surface with Trash, both locked in our own thoughts. An odd tension underlies everything. Do we stay here for good? Here seems to have a lot going for it, whereas going to Trash's friend on the northern tip is simply a possibility that may already have evaporated.

"I don't know," says Trash, reading my thoughts. I look at him and he half smiles. "Should we stay or should we go? I don't know. Have you never wanted to take the lift below?"

"It's on a code. You can't."

"I deciphered the code. Took me five minutes."

"What did you find?"

"First level is a long corridor with doors off. I couldn't get in to the few I tried. Second floor below is smaller. Two doors. But the walls were at least a metre thick. Reinforced steel."

"Nuclear reactor?"

"That's what I think. It would explain their energy source."

He looks across the loch at the other side. A newly built structure with a cylindrical roof but with no visible signs of habitation.

"Spent fuel pool?" I ask.

"Exactly, with perhaps a pipe leading from here all the way under the surface of the loch."

"Why not have the reactor over there? It might be safer."

"But then prone to attacks from outsiders."

"So every night we sleep just above a nuclear reactor."

"It's like the skull Elizabethans kept on the desk. A reminder of mortality."

Far from being an ancient fiefdom, this was a hi-tech bunker. And then we were summoned to the Tower. Rannoch had something important to tell us. Lot could stay with Emma in our rooms.

Asim, Trash and I stand on a varnished wooden floor littered with hand woven rugs. A long bay window faces the dead loch. There are easy chairs in a semi-circle around a fireplace carved into a collage of long gone animals – lions, eagles, bears, giraffes, gorillas, crocodiles. Rannoch stands from a long oak desk and invites us to sit. He wears a red velvet smoking jacket over black and white striped trousers. Two armed soldiers stand by the door. Ericht brings in a tray of drinks. Some sort of herbal wine. Asim tastes it and winces. Rannoch drinks and wipes his beard. It tastes about 95% proof.

"How did you get into the lift so quickly?" Rannach asks Trash, smiling.

"Simple. Apply exact pressure to the call button and then try each of the number buttons and the right ones click and open."

Rannoch roars with laughter and slaps Ericht on the back so hard he stumbles forward and nearly chokes. "Love the man. Simple. You're a techno wizard. You understand computers. Electrical stuff?"

"Yes."

"Are you brilliant?"

"Yes."

Rannoch laughs again. "I love the modest egotism of the man. But enough of you. I have more important things to say. About me. As you may have seen by now, I am a visionary. The big picture. The long view. When Covid 23 reared its spindly head and society factionalised into war zones, which was entirely predictable from about two thousand AD on, I collected a few loyal acolytes," with a look at

Ericht, who bows, "and retreated here and started building. Except it wasn't a retreat. It was a gateway to the future. Self-sufficiency, our own power, renewables. I was after immortality. And I've got it. And now you, happy little band, have been chosen by providence, through me, to become part of it. I toast your good fortune."

He raises his glass. We all drink. What the hell is coming next?

"Suppose we want to leave?" Asks Asim.

Rannoch looks at him and then roars with laughter. Ericht joins in. Even the soldiers smile.

"No one gives up a chance of immortality."

"How do you achieve it?" I ask.

Rannoch looks at Ericht. "The hammer," he says.

Ericht goes to a small table, opens a drawer and takes out a large metal head hammer. Rannoch pulls up his left trouser leg and nods, smiling. Ericht raises the hammer and smashes it as hard as he can on Rannoch's knee cap. Small as he is this would be enough to cripple someone for life. Rannoch smiles, flexes his leg. Taps the knee.

"Carbon steel. Last an eternity. Sinews made of braeön. Strong as god's bones, flexible as rope, malleable as putty. I could run a hundred miles and nary a twinge."

"You're a robot?" I ask.

"No."

"What then?"

"Nothing so miraculous as the truth. Much of me is steel and braeön. Some titanium for keeping me fleet of foot. My major organs renewed after honourable service. I'm on my second heart and third liver. Which is why I can drink like a bastard."

"What about the brain?"

"Good question. Stem cell injections and AI implants. Keyhole surgery. Bright as Einstein and sharp as a blade. Shit, I can speak forty three languages. Even though there aren't forty three places left in the world."

He laughs good-naturedly. The sickening truth was beginning to sink in.

"You want to harvest us," I say.

"Good word. Harvest. Associations of abundance and growth and sun and nourishment. I saved your lives, so now you give them back. I call that a bargain. The kid is too young. She can have a very happy five or six years. May even keep her as a bride for one of my erstwhile soldiers. Or even myself."

"You fucking crazy man," says Asim.

"Think of it as becoming a martyr. You Muslims like that."

Rannoch drains his glass and pours another. He stands and beams at us. "Time and tide. No rush. You can enjoy the hospitality for a few more days. Let's say – next Monday for the harvest. We also bleed you out. We have a process for making all blood groups compatible. I have a complete blood transfusion every six months. Puts the wind back in my sails. I'm horny as a goat on steroids for a month afterwards."

Ericht takes out a notebook and writes something in it. Presumably the day on which we are to be chopped up for spare parts and bled dry. Then he gestures for us to leave. Rannoch stays Trash with a hand. "A word with you." Asim and I are led out by Ericht, who tells us on the way back to our rooms not to think of escape. As well as the soldiers the area outside is heavily mined. The road has retractable spikes so you can't drive out. He also tells us that the procedures for the removal of all our major organs will be quite painless because we will be euthanised prior to surgery. They will come for us at midday.

Back in our rooms Asim heads for the whisky. Lot and Emma bounce in from outside. I smile at them. Lot senses all is not well but through some complicated internal process decides to say nothing. She grabs a red ball and takes Emma outside again. At least she is safe for a while. I join Asim in a large whisky and we each brood. Half an hour later Trash enters. I know what has passed. I almost want to laugh because this is exactly what happened in Dorado.

"He wants you to work for him," I say.

"He wants me to work for him. Déjà vu," says Trash.

"You going to leave us in bloody lurch, science boy. Coward," says Asim.

"What is the point of us all dying? I help them I help the future."

"No. Help your bloody self," says Asim and goes off to the bedroom in disgust, stopping to spit in Trash's face as he passes. Trash wipes his face with his sleeve.

"I'm so sorry but I don't see what else I can do, Ali. And I'll be able to look after Lot. You want that, don't you?"

"I want that," I say.

Trash blathers on with more justifications and then wipes his forehead. "God, it's hot in here. Let's talk in the jacuzzi."

"You think I'm going to get in the jacuzzi with you? I know you're weird, but for God's sake."

He walks past me and whispers in my ear, "Just get in."

We go to the jacuzzi and strip to our underwear. He very neatly folds both our sets of clothes and we get in. He turns it on full so the water roars out and faces me, back to the room.

"Can you hear me? Just nod if you can. OK. There is one security camera at the other end of the room. It can see us but it won't pick up what we're saying. Certainly not me, with my back to it."

I nod.

"There are no cameras by the lifts so I couldn't work out how they watch. It's in our clothes. Micro cameras in buttons. They can see where we go, and what is said. This should be safe for a little while. But be aware. The camera can pick you up now, but probably not what you say. "

"OK."

"I want you to know, just for the record – I told Rannoch that you're the engineer so he should keep you too but he said you look in much better shape than I do so your body is worth more than your skills."

"I'm supposed to take that as a compliment?"

He shrugs.

"You're going to try and rescue us again? Déjà vu."

"Their reactor is leaking. If it's not fixed even if it doesn't blow people will start to get sick because the cooling plant can't keep pace. They want me to repair it and then start work on building another. It's mostly software, which is why he wants me. They had a good tech guy but he got exposed and died."

"What are you thinking?"

"I make the leak worse. Alarms will go off. Power will go down. Unless he's prepared for Armageddon Rannoch will have to get everyone out of the castle compound and away to safety. The road will be safe."

"You think that's what he will do? Not just save himself?"

"He's too vain. If he only saves himself he can't be King Rannoch, feared and adored. And he needs his small army."

"Where will you be?"

"I'll have to stay with the reactor."

"Dangerous."

"I'm too clever to die."

"I forgot. This plan of yours. It's pretty crap. What happens when we're outside? It could all go wrong at every juncture."

"OK. So what's your plan?"

I say nothing.

"I rest my case," Trash says.

21

Asim has become very ruminative and melancholy since he got shot and became addicted to whisky. I suppose both those things would change a person.

"Bloody Scotland. We should have gone somewhere civilised. Manchester or Wales," he says.

"Manchester is a war zone and Wales has disappeared. Mud and sheep bones."

"You know, if I were good Moslem, or even good Christian, I'd say this is Allah, God, whatever, taking his righteous revenge on us all for being such crap. On Moslems for not converting the Christians and the Christians for not turning other bloody cheek. And the Jews for killing the Arabs and the Arabs for killing the Jews."

"But given that you're not a good Moslem…"

"I just think is all bollocks. You know, none of us ask to be born. And why now? Why not hundred years ago when we'd have better time? World wars and poverty and starvation and whatnot but at least bloody TV work properly."

"You're a philosopher, Asim."

"Bloody idiot more like. I tell you, Ali, they don't chop me up without fight. I take some of them bastards with me."

"That's the spirit."

Now I knew our clothes were listening and watching I was wary of saying too much. And I didn't feel like being naked. It was already Sunday. Tomorrow we'd be euthanised. I hadn't seen Trash since he told me his plan, so I had no idea what was happening. Perhaps they heard us. Perhaps he was already dead. Like Asim, I wasn't prepared to go quietly to the slaughter, but another part of me just wanted to get everything over. I don't know if that's a death wish, or just tiredness. An old Beforetimes line came back to me, *It's been too hard living, but I'm afraid to die.*

At night Lot creeps into bed with me, Emma lying across our feet. I listen to her heart beat. I remember when my mother died and I was sitting by her and she just stopped. That could be me tomorrow. It was odd to think Lot would still be walking and talking and thinking, Emma would be barking and sniffing, and I would be gone. We are all strangers in this world.

"The thing is, to be ready," Lot suddenly says.

"What do you mean?" I ask.

"You know. Tomorrow."

I still hadn't told her, but of course, being Lot, she knew.

"Trash is going to try something," I say.

"It's like Dick waiting on the heath, in the misty moonlight, Bess snorting and pawing the ground. Then the coach comes and he has to be ready. Not hesitate. Not worry. And afterwards, fly like the wind."

"And that's what we must do," I say.

"Of course. When Dick is just going about his business, not being a highwayman, I think he tries to disappear. Walking through the town. So that no one sees him. To be safe."

"You said disappear. Why?"

"Because that's what you do sometimes. Only tomorrow, you have to try hard to do it and not wait for it to happen."

"We must all stay close," I say. "You remember Fauberge?"

"Yes," she says.

"I think I saw him."

"Like a ghost."

"That's it. Like a ghost."

"Yes. I'm going to sleep now."

And she does.

Next morning we are not a happy family. Lot hums and strokes Emma, but I'm aware she is watching Asim and I intently. He started early on the whisky. His blood will be ninety per cent proof iof they drain it. I surreptitiously write a note on a piece of paper and as I pass him the bottle I slip it along the table, hoping the cameras don't pick it up: *Be ready. Alarm.* I don't want him to start fighting the soldiers if they come for us and we all get killed before we have even a chance to escape. He screws up the note and looks curiously at me. The bearded disc of his face and the dark lights of his eyes that have probably seen as many horrors as I have, all secrets and desires and small tendernesses bludgeoned by a malevolent goblin who bestrode the world and whom we doubtless blamed for every burnt star and laceration, but when we all looked in the mirror there was only ourselves to blame. No god to spit fire at. Just us in the undoing of ourselves.

Ericht arrives with two soldiers. He nods at us. It is curiously formal, as if we are about to be presented to an ancient pope for some sacred initiation, instead of doped and butchered for our guts. I embrace Lot and she looks solemnly at me. Emma sits quietly, sensing the occasion. I kiss the little dog on her head and feel the lovely warmth of her. Asim has a last slug of whisky and then hurls the bottle at a picture of Rannoch on the wall. A guard raises his machine gun but Ericht stays him with a gesture. One of the guards opens the door and we go out into the little corridor, followed by the second soldier and Ericht. Ericht reaches up on tiptoe and puts in the code for the lift. I finger Chloe's magic coin in my pocket. We get in and go down to the first floor. We turn right and then the soldier stops at the second door on the right. It is opened from within by another soldier.

Inside is a gleaming white room with fluorescent lights and two surgical tables. Instruments neatly placed in a row on white towels. Two people, a man and woman, in white coats, are preparing small machines for some unknown but doubtless painful purpose. I see two electric saws with sharp gleaming silver teeth. My skull prickles. The woman in white looks at myself and Asim and says something to the man, then they prepare syringes. I think they are working out how much is needed for a lethal dose, given our sizes and heights. I decide that, given they have been stupid enough not to handcuff us, I will wait until they are about to strap me down, and then fight. I assume Asim will do the same. He is looking at the woman in mock lasciviousness, and makes his eyes roll and tongue loll. She doesn't react at all but suddenly I want to giggle. I smile and stifle the giggle, but the man in white looks at me curiously. I poke out my tongue and shake my head. He looks at Ericht, who says nothing. It is strange what mortal terror will do. You fall apart in a quivering heap of jelly or something inappropriate kicks in to steer you through the moment.

Then an alarm rings shrilly. The man in white drops his syringe. No one knows what to do. Ericht takes out his phone and calls someone. He listens intently

"Everyone out," he says.

The woman in white holds up her syringe. "We can still terminate them. In preparation. It will only take a minute." The bitch looks disappointed.

"Out. Now. We don't have time."

"But Ericht...," she persists.

Ericht takes out a pistol and aims it at her head. She puts down the syringe and we all march out and get in the lift. It is crowded with eight of us. Asim is facing the woman in white. He smiles at her and, when the lift starts, he headbutts her and I hear her nose break. We are too confined to do anything. The woman whimpers and holds her nose, which is already gushing blood down her white coat. She goes into shock and no one comforts her and I am glad.

"One for the home team," I say to Asim.

"What's happening?" The man in white asks Ericht.

"It's alright. Everything is in hand," he says, then turns to the soldiers, "When we get outside everyone is to leave the castle area. Make it quick and orderly. No discussions. Once outside keep walking for five hundred metres and then stop and corral people. It's high alert. We will take as many vehicles as possible. Be calm. Be firm. Deal with panic assertively."

Outside alarms are sounding everywhere. The quiet industry of the place has fractured and there is fear and an undercurrent of rising panic. Is this an attack? Who is coming? Is the virus inside? Where is Rannoch? Suddenly the man himself appears on the tower balcony. The alarms stop and he smiles beatifically at all. This man doesn't need a microphone. "Look at your faces. Oh me oh my I'm high, you're dry. Don't worry. I'm here. Your laird and lodestar, your provider and friend, your cicerone and abecedary. Rannoch. It's alright. We have a wee problem with our power supply which, I'm told, will be back to normal ASAP. Take heart, leave in a leisurely fashion. Purely as an added precaution. Nothing is more inscribed on my heart than your safety. The soldiers will protect you. Love. Benedictions." He blows a kiss and leaves.

We all troop through the main gates. I look around for Lot and Emma. They are about twenty metres ahead. Ericht is unsure whether we are to be treated as prisoners or just citizens. He doesn't want to cause panic by having us under armed escort. Everyone is reassured by Rannoch and files out in twos and threes and fours. Soldiers join them and at least a dozen trucks and cars are taking people and weapons and supplies out. This should tell people that Rannoch's reassurances are hollow wind. He has no idea how long they will have to remain outside. Some larger trucks drive through, beeping. I wonder if they are carrying further supplies, water, and perhaps tents for the cold nights if need be.

We all start congregating some five hundred metres from Urquhart castle. Lot and Emma are with us. There is a sense of uncertainty and hesitation. Rannoch's words calmed and galvanised but now we are out of the safety of the compound there is the ghost of fear stalking among us. The threat of attack. The threat of infection from strangers. I realise that these people have become oddly institutionalised. They have a herd mentality. It would be easy to stampede them. I wonder where Trash is.

We sit on the ground. Water is distributed by soldiers. Ten minutes later the exodus has dried up and we are all sitting around like a band of gypsies. Suddenly Emma's ears prick and she looks above. The staccato de de de de de of helicopter blades. Everyone looks up. Ericht is looking and talking on his phone. The soldiers are nonplussed. This tells me that it is not an attack. The chopper lands in a clearing nearby and Rannoch gets out with two soldiers. I wonder where the helicopter was kept as I never saw it in the compound. Immediately he starts barking orders and smiling occasionally at people. Grudgingly I must admit he has leadership qualities that would sit well with any army.

Lot nudges me. Just coming up the road is Bess, Trash driving alone. He pulls up and looks around. I stand and wave. He makes his way through everyone to us. He looks older, very pale, even though it has only been a few days. He smiles. Despite his need of a good dentist it warms my heart. He makes a shhh gesture and pulls a blanket around him. I realise this is to cover the cameras in our buttons and I do the same.

"Bastard took longer than I thought. I was worried that…"

I nod. I think of the hideous woman in white. "Close thing."

He leans in. "I've made the leak in the reactor worse. I've also closed the pipe to the cooling tower across the loch. It will take a few hours and then it will blow. The problem is the radiation will be instantaneous and have a wide radius, I don't know exactly how far, but even if we have a chance to run it may not be long enough. This whole area will contaminate."

"You don't do things by halves. Armageddon."

"Armageddon outta here. I've told Rannoch that I've contained the leak and it will need a few hours to stabilise. He wanted me to stay but I'll tell him that if I had I'd die and he loses a valuable asset. Not sure he'll agree but…" He looks around. "I need to report. Back soon."

As he leaves an idea crystallises.

I see Rannoch shout at Trash and then he strikes him across the face. It is a piece of theatre, designed to show everyone who is the boss around here. No one disobeys the big man. Oddly it seems to reassure people, but there is still a ripple of tension in the air. Asim is oddly quiet. I ask him if he's OK. He nods and lays down, closing his eyes. I realise he is missing his whisky. Lot is smiling at me. I have no idea why, but she opens her little pink satchel and takes out a quarter bottle of whisky. She prods Asim and gives it to him. He chucks her under the chin and smiles broadly. "God be with you, little angel." He takes a long swig and seems instantly restored.

Trash has set up a loudspeaker system and microphone. Clearly Rannoch now feels the need of added volume. He starts to talk about everything being under control and how he is the Guardian of Urquhart castle and nothing bad will happen under his watch. People are listening. They are pacified but I still sense underlying fear and trembling.

Trash returns to us.

"Rannoch has told me he's giving me an hour and then I have to go back to the reactor. All I can think is that when it blows you run like hell. And it will blow. I can't stop it now. I'll stay outside the castle and be in Bess. I'll try to find you."

"I have another idea," I say.

He looks at me.

"Chinese whispers."

22

Panic is a ripple and then a wave. Panic is a virus, easy to contract, hard to stop. Panic replaces thought. Panic gets in the body cells and ignites them into futile action. Panic is the currency of rumour and fear. Of all base passions, fear is most accursed. Panic is the stalking agent that waits in the shadows to spread its salt and sulphur in the soul. When Trash returns I tell him that this group of some seven to eight hundred people is ripe for suggestion. If we start telling people something that will panic them we have a greater chance of escape when the soldiers won't know whether to control people or join them. And what better rumour than the truth?

"We might only get pockets of panic," Trash says.

Rannoch is still talking. Is there no end to the man's hot air? It must be all those new organs and blood he's had shoved in him. Trash is looking at him.

"Something else might work," he says.

I wait and he says nothing.

"Are you going to let me in?" I ask.

He says it's a radio mic. He set it up so he knows the frequency and set up. He might be able to link up with his phone, which would also act as a microphone. He'll get in Bess and tell everyone they've been lied to – that the nuclear reactor will soon blow Urquhart Castle sky high and the whole area will be contaminated. The only chance is to run and get vehicles and weapons if you can. We all get close to Bess when the confusion starts and try to make our escape in what we hope will be panic and confusion. He says our stash of weapons is still in Bess, plus our supplies. Rannoch clearly didn't think we'd be going anywhere. It's an idea worth trying. I tell Asim and Lot what we plan to do. Asim is full of whisky bravado and ready to take on the world.

Rannoch finally stops talking. He has tried to work the crowd but it's been tough. They want to believe but outside of the castle compound the magic circle he can weave around them is shaky. There are scared eyes. Thumping hearts. Rebellious thoughts. It's an interesting logistical problem. You want people to trust you but if you tell your soldiers to be vigilant that trust starts to evaporate. People will know you only have the gun. Balancing propaganda and persuasion with force is an art. And now his authority is in question, Rannoch does not seem such a charismatic giant. But then I am partisan, given that if he had his way Asim and I would now be on a slab minus eight pints of blood, liver, kidneys and heart. And the bitch in white would still be sawing away to get a few tasty cuts for herself, no doubt.

Trash looks at his phone. "Now or never," he says.

He goes to Bess and gets in the driver's seat. It will be hard to see that it is him making any announcement. There are two soldiers a little away watching us, both with automatic rifles. A chill rain starts to fall. Clouds hang low and grey like sooty snowfall. I would love to see a summer sky again. The heat is always dull and acrid. Sometimes there is a crack in the sky where something like Beforetimes sunlight pierces through. It is a shock to the eyes and skin. I would like Lot to have a summer and see flowers grow in a meadow, Emma at her heels.

Static. A whine. Then Trash, clear as day.

"Attention. Everyone. You have been lied to. The nuclear reactor is out of control and will blow very soon. The castle will be destroyed and nuclear radiation will spread immediately."

Everyone lives only in their ears. Surprise. Worst fears confirmed. Rannoch is looking around wildly for the source, but Trash is head down and is disguising his voice. There is even a hint of Scottish brogue in the Rs.

"Your only hope is to get as far away as possible. Run, take transport if you can. Get weapons if you can. Good luck, people. Run!"

A second that seems like a minute as everything sinks in. Patter of rain. No one breathes or moves apart from Rannoch who is looking around for the source of the voice. He hones in on Bess and guesses right. Then a man near me jumps up and attacks a soldier, trying to wrestle his gun away. The gun fires point blank range and the man seems to jump in the air, his back spraying blood and tiny bits of flesh as the bullet goes straight through him. This was the green light. Suddenly everyone is on their feet and pandemonium has the mother of all parties. People attack soldiers. Some try to push into cars and trucks. Some just run. I grab Lot and we run towards Bess and get in the back passenger door. As Asim runs a soldier lifts his rifle ready to club him but little Emma jumps and grabs hold of the soldier's leg. Asim turns and punches the soldier on the side of the head. He drops the gun and Asim grabs it. Trash opens the boot electronically and Asim piles inside and Emma jumps beside him. Trash drives away. Gunshots, shouts, screams.

Because we were prepared for this we now have the advantage of a few hundred metres start. Behind us all hell is breaking loose. The Urquhart castle community has gone from quiet subservience and relative peace to bloody civil war in the space of minutes. How quickly things fall apart. Trash drives between a few dead trees and then swings back on the road where, so far, there are few running. He keeps trying but the back door won't close so Asim is exposed. He fires a few shots above heads to keep people away. A soldier gets on one knee and takes aim but Asim shoots him. His head jerks back and his neck pumps out blood. A young woman grabs his gun and runs into the dead trees where there is a semblance of cover.

A jeep appears on the road. Rannoch is in the passenger seat holding a machine gun. He starts firing but because the road is so bumpy the shots go high. Trash starts weaving and accelerating. Asim returns fire. We hit a pothole and Bess bounces wildly. With a yelp Emma is thrown from the back on the road. Lot tries to get out but I hold her. Asim jumps out and rolls in the road. He grabs Emma as Rannoch reloads. I crawl into the back of Bess and tell Trash to stop. I have a machine gun and start firing at the jeep. It stops and Rannoch leaps out and takes cover behind it. He has Ericht and one soldier with him. Asim barely has cover. I gesture to him that we take turns in returning fire to try and keep them busy. I am exposed with the back door open. I tell Lot and Trash to get their heads down. I get out and while Asim fires I pull the back door down manually and then open a side door as cover for me. What we need now is for Asim and Emma to get back to Bess, but they are a good twenty metres away.

Trash gets out and uses the other back side door as cover. I tell him that after three we both fire to give Asim a chance to get to us. He is exposed where he is. On three, we both fire and I shout to Asim to run. He picks up Emma and runs at us. He is less than five metres when Trash needs to reload. I try to spray fire but they have three guns. Asim looks at me and smiles and then gets shot in the legs. They buckle and he falls to his knees. He clings tightly to Emma. I go to him, firing. As I reach him a single bullet gets him in the neck and he starts to choke. I scream and then I disappear.

The sound is a song made by shingle and sea. It is as if the end of a wave thins to a caress and rolls the shingle to and fro, claiming it back for itself, making the stone surfaces gleam in afternoon sun. We watch, me sitting and Chloe leaning back into me with my arms around her, as if we are one strange body. The warmth melts into us.

"Like diamonds," she says as much to the glistening stones as to me.

"Some moments you just want to last forever," I say.

"And if you think that, they do," she says.

My arms slap into me. She is gone. For a moment I think, ridiculously, that the tide has taken her too. That she has become part of that immensity of to and fro that is guided by the moon. Then I realise it is much simpler than that. She is simply gone. And my heart breaks.

"It's OK," Lot says, squeezing my hand. Emma licks my eyes open. I am lying in the back of Bess, seats down. We are not driving. I feel as if I am in a painting – everything heightened in the moment. Colours shine. My blood rushes through me as if looking for an escape route, but now slowing. Trash leans around to look at me.

"What happened?" I ask.

"You went ballistic. You had two MP7s and you ran at them unloading both. The soldier just legged it, terrified. You practically carved Ericht in two with bullets. Rannoch stood up and roared but I pinned him down with fire and then you were on him."

"What did I do?"

"Do you really want to know?"

I see the boy on the beach I killed. Others now too. Eyes with the lights gone. "No," I say.

"Suffice to say no one will recognise his head."

"Asim?"

Trash looks to my right. I turn and there is a white sheet with blood spots.

"He died quick. Lot sat and held his hand. Like she's been sitting holding yours. You've been out for two hours. We're near a Loch Choire. I'm all in so I figure we stop here and sleep and push on to Thurso tomorrow early."

He tells me that the nuclear reactor blew and it's unlikely anyone within a half mile radius survived. Maybe a mile. He looks even more pale than usual. He stifles a cough. Instantly I know he is suffering from the effects of radiation. How could he not, working with a fucked reactor and deliberately making it worse? Genius doesn't shield you from the horrors we create. I suddenly feel useless. Everyone dies around me, and I can only protect myself by disappearing. At the moment I cannot even summon grief for Asim. I never told him how, in such a short time, he had become a true friend, a brother. I seem incapable of learning that there is only the moment. All else is dust and broken dreams and regret.

We pass two groups of gaping ferals and a pit full of Covid corpses. Half an hour later Trash says, "We're being followed."

"Someone from the castle?"

"Maybe."

I look at Lot. Her wheels are turning.

"A ghost," she says, which is what I was hoping she wouldn't say. We drive on and I think of Asim and his swashbuckling short life with us and how he brought an energy and even laughter to our doomed quest. Trash stops at the burnt ruins of a lodge at the far end of the loch. It seems safe enough. I build a fire. We have a good view of the ragged road stretching back for whoever is following. We are a quiet little group sipping water and eating tins of beans. It is Lot who finally says what we are all thinking.

"We should bury him before it gets dark."

The soil is soggy and feels unclean but it is easy to dig a deepish hole. Trash and I carry Asim's body, let it down and then cover it. Lot makes a pretty arrangement of stones on it.

"It's a secret language," she says. "Only people who die can understand it. He died saving Emma. He will be a hero forever."

I sprinkle some water on the stones and think of Chloe saying "Like diamonds."

Lot finds some scissors and cuts a lock of hair from the long fronds of dappled gold that hang from Emma's ears. She pinches out the strand and lets the hairs fall on the fresh earth. We stand there a long time until it is getting dark and there is nothing more to think. Let the dead bury their own dead. I never understood what the fuck that means, and still don't. We lie down. I know sleep will be a long time coming but Emma is such a good watchdog I know that if anyone approaches she will alert us. Lot looks up at the few ragged stars. Then she is looking at me intently. "In Beforetimes? There were trees and apples and the sea was alive and people had dogs and cats and rabbits to look after and things I haven't seen."

"Yes."

"So it was perfect."

"No. It wasn't perfect."

"But better than now."

"Yes."

"What went wrong?"

"We didn't realise how well off we were. People always wanted more. Or different. Or they wanted what belonged to others."

"Something else."

"What?"

"There's something else."

"The virus made us all weak. Not just in our bodies but in our minds. And I think – people often just don't like other people. And you can't make them. So to try and make everyone crowd together is like putting a lot of different species together. We were herded. No one knew where they belonged anymore."

"And then they want to kill each other. Dogs and snakes and sharks and rabbits and bears and lions and walruses."

"Yes. But the animals did it better than us, before we killed most of them. Perhaps we were like lots of different chemicals together. They react and explode. We were never as civilised as we thought. None of us. How do you know about all those creatures? Sharks and bears and things. You've never seen them."

She half smiles and pats Emma.

I think we were always fucked. We were just too stupid to know it for a few thousand years.

23

I feel it before I see. Eyes on me. I turn as if I don't know and there is a figure standing on a ridge several hundred metres away with binoculars on me. It's him – the man with the mask. If he has a weapon he could have finished me. Why is he waiting? And how is he able to follow us and know where we are? I haven't seen any drones, though if they are high enough you can't always see them. I slowly walk back to Bess and make sure Lot is OK. I tell her to stay inside the lodge. Trash sits against a wall sipping water. His skin, usually paper thin and an unhealthy pallid white, now has a bluish tinge. His lips are salt-caked. Eyes like jellied egg whites.

"You got a good dose," I say.

He smiles and coughs.

"I know now why you told Rannoch not to employ me too. You knew he might put me working on the reactor and I'd get sandblasted like you. You thought I had a better chance the way you did it. You sacrificed yourself."

"Bollocks," he says.

"Fair enough. Something else. We have company. You stay with Lot. I'm going to circle around behind. Be ready to leave in a hurry."

I go before he can stop me. I go through the back of the lodge and walk East on an incline so I cannot be seen from the road. I have taken my Glock and a hand grenade. I realise I have grown to like weapons. Their hard surfaces and the precise engineering that loads them with death. Machines are so much easier than people. They don't gorge themselves with their own vainglory futilities, just bullets. After a few hundred metres I turn right and walk adjacent to the road. When I get up the ridge there is a green Land Rover twenty metres to my right. The masked man is still looking down at the lodge through binoculars. I want to see him up close. I creep a few more steps. I have the grenade in my left hand in my pocket and the Glock in my right.

"That's close enough," comes from behind me. I turn and a tall black guy in dungarees holds a laser pistol on me. "Drop the gun," he says.

I drop the gun.

"What shall I do with this though?"

He looks at me curiously. Very quickly I take the grenade from my left pocket and pull the pin and throw it at him. He panics, catches the grenade and throws it as far as he can. I have picked up my Glock and shoot him three times in the chest. He fires his laser as he goes down but it goes wide and scorches the ground beside me. I hold my head as the grenade explodes twenty metres away. I turn to face the other man but the Land Rover is heading straight at me. I roll away and it misses me by a whisker. Then he gets back on the road and drives away. I stand and fire off two shots but more as a gesture than with any hope of stopping him. It looks like a customised vehicle so would probably be bulletproof. I go to the man I shot and go through his pockets. A bottle of water. Scraps of paper with numbers on them. A packet of toothpicks. A mobile phone. I take the phone and the paper with numbers and walk back down to the lodge. Lot is already in Bess with Emma. Trash stands looking anxiously as I approach.

"Worried about me?" I ask.

"Nah," he says.

"How do you feel?"

"Top of the world, Ma," he says.

Inside Bess Lot looks at me.

"You fired blue thunder through someone," she says.

"Yes. The third time was just for fun," I say.

One of the many bizarre things about knowing Lot is that you can say anything, even from your darkest intents, and she is unfazed.

"But one got away. I heard the sound of driving."

"Yes. He got away."

"So we may need more blue thunder on the heath."

"Let's hope not."

I know Trash will only get annoyed if I keep asking how he is, or, God forbid, try to nurse him. He takes frequents sips of water. We are close now to Thurso. We drive through Forsinard and Forsinain and since we left the loch do not see a soul. No ferals. No covid bodies. As if the land ran out of patience with humanity and simply said *No more*. No sign of the Green Land Rover. I hope he just got bored with the chase. We stop to stretch our legs. I show Trash the slip of paper with numbers. He says they are co-ordinates and checks the satnav. The numbers correspond to places we have been.

"What does it mean?" I say.

"It means he's been tracking us."

"Drones? Hacking our satnav?"

"I don't think so," and he stops Bess. He looks at the dashboard. He gets out and starts examining the doors and windows, the bumpers and then underneath. Twenty minutes later he shows a small silver disc, like a battery.

"Behind a wheel axle. Tracker. Who do you think?"

I know exactly. It is as if his face is in front of me. I hear him say, "You will never be free of me, one way or another."

Trash decides to keep the tracker and lead a false trail. We turn west and drive along the coast for about twenty kilometres and stop at a tiny place called Skerray. I take the tracker into a tumbledown cottage that smells of things long ago rotted and gone. I am going to put it beneath an old metal sheet but when I lift it there is a volley of squeaks and a flurry of cockroaches the size of small dogs and a dozen or more rats run out and away. One has a leg missing and has trouble getting away. I catch it and put my foot on it while I look around and find some old rags. I tear a strip from one and wrap the tracker inside and then tie it around the rat's neck and let it go. It hops and runs in a skewed fashion. Hopefully it will keep Fauberge busy and by then we'll be away and he'll lose our trail. A rat hunting a rat. They deserve each other.

We drive back along the coast, a constant wind tugging the scrub and heather, some of which actually looks alive. I wonder if it is still possible to grow things this far north, or anywhere. The sea winds will have helped, blowing away infections and pollution. Harsh landscapes help if you want to be free of humanity. Farr, Brawl and Portskerra, tiny places without habitation that once had farms and sheep and fishermen who spoke in poetry long forgotten. This has always been rugged country, long before we ruined all. We arrive in Thurso mid-afternoon. No one has been following us all the way from Skerray, so I am hopeful. As we come into Thurso on our right is what was once a caravan park. Most are burnt out husks now but a few are intact, though without windows. Some on wheels where the rubber has rotted down to the metal and others are static, on breeze blocks. I guess it's another rat and cockroach holiday site. The whole town seems deserted. In all our recent drives and wanderings I've never felt less threatened. The clouds are so low it's oppressive, as if they weigh too much and the skies are just letting gravity do its work. The beach on our left looks oily, glutinous, and the sea the same dead colour I am used to on the East coast. Thick poisoned goo, but there is something different. I tell Trash to stop and get out to look. The merest swell, more the hint of movement that quickly exhausts itself. Nevertheless more of a tidal movement than I've seen in years. In Norfolk it was sludge realigning itself, but this looks like possible natural motion.

 We drive through broken narrow roads to a junction of Shore Street and Marine Terrace. We park outside the Marine, once a hotel, and a peeling sign still declares: *Luxe B&B with sunroom and Egyptian linens*. Trash and I get out. Curtains drawn. A Marie Celeste feel. Then a man comes out of the front door holding an axe. He's in his fifties, bald but with mad brillo pad tufts of hair either side and a beard that probably has mice nesting in it. Quick dark blue eyes.

"Trash?"

"The same. Good to finally meet you, Robbie. You can put the axe down."

"Ach. I was doing a little interior decorating. Chopping up my last stick of furniture for a fire. You look shite, Trash. Are yous dying?"

"We all are. Just at different rates. This is Ali. Lot. Emma."

"Pleased to meet yous all. Come in. I've got shite all to eat but some home-made brew that'll blow your pants off."

Robbie's place probably hadn't been cleaned since Robert the Bruce. He wasn't lying about the axe and his last bit of furniture. A chair lay on the concrete floor smashed to bits and a desultory fire flickered in the grate. Otherwise the room was empty and cold. He offered us a swig of his gut rot from a demijohn but we all refused. He said we could bed down where we wanted, so we looked around and chose a large room upstairs with a small adjoining room. We had enough blankets and clothes in Bess for warmth. Robbie said he trekked a few miles along the coast to get water from an underground spring that miraculously hadn't ruined. He had a bicycle with a small handmade trailer attached. The one room that was a surprise was his office, where he had several laptops, vid screens and signalling devices. He was like a Scottish Trash and they instantly fell to tech talk.

Lot, Emma and I went to the beach and again I was struck by the faintest of movements in the sludge. A salty smell rather than putrefaction. To my astonishment there were some nettles growing. I pulled down my sleeve and pulled up several handfuls. They had bugs attached but they would make good protein and there was iron in the nettles. We walked the streets looking for anything of interest. I found a few old wooden window frames and broke them into small pieces and put them in a foraging bag I had brought with us. We went to the caravan sites and looked inside a few. I found a couple of gas canisters that still had something in them, and a box that contained lubrication oil and a tin of grease. I took them. Emma had her nose down and found all kinds of interesting things to explore beneath the caravans, and numerous rats were startled from their beds. In one caravan on the floor was a photograph of a family – parents, two children, and a dog. It was curled at the edges and had been stepped on a lot over the years, but Lot looked hard at it. When I turned to leave I saw that she surreptitiously put the photograph in her pocket. In another caravan was a drum that hadn't been broken. I hit it and Lot was delighted with the sound. She banged out a rhythm and decided to keep it. The absence of covid bodies was a good sign. Everywhere was wrecked but not diseased. There were several abandoned motorbikes with what might be perfectly serviceable two stroke engines if you looked beneath the rust. At the edge of the caravan park was an old school children's fairground. Lot had never seen the like and she sat in a two-seater duck on an electrical arm and was entranced. Amazingly it worked and the duck slowly rose up and down and around as the central winding machine cranked on and took her on a roundabout ride. Each time she came into view her expression was even more blissful. I glimpsed the child beneath the mask she had to wear to survive. Emma ran in circles barking and wagging her tail. For a while, life seemed simple. When Lot got out of the duck she looked at me and said, "Is it OK to say I love you?" I felt I might choke, swallowed hard and took a breath. "It's OK, Lot. And I am honoured by it." In truth I felt only loss, a dislocation from all that had been taken. The shadow of ordinary human life and love haunted me.

A faint sun glimmered its setting behind distant hills. We went back to the Marine and I stoked up the fire with the wood I'd found. I found a filthy pot, swilled it out, and put in the nettles. It was very rare to find something to eat with iron in it. Then I added beans. We sat companionably, Emma watching the fire, Lot quietly tapping her drum. I noticed she occasionally took out the photograph and stole a glance. Trash and I drank wine. Robbie was companionable enough in a bizarre, uncoordinated way, occasionally offering some piece of information or asking a question, and then lapsing into serious drinking. The more sloshed he became, the less he pretended to be interested, though he did evince a warmth for Trash, who looked increasingly ill. I tried not to think about it. It was best to take each hour as it came, and none of us knew how many tomorrows there would be.

Lot slept peacefully in the small room, doubtless dreaming of ducks and drums and families, Emma by her side. I settled down next to Trash on clothes we'd piled up. We covered ourselves with an old tarp. The night was cold and he was shivering. His chest rasped. I turned and put my hand on it and felt his heart thump. He tensed.

"It's alright," I said.

Awkwardly I peeled off my clothes and put his hand on my left breast. I kissed his neck. I started to undo his shirt.

"Help me out here," I said.

Like first time teenagers we managed to get his clothes off. He looked at me. "Is this a sympathy fuck?" He asked.

"Of course it is. You don't think I'm actually going to enjoy it, do you?" I whispered.

"That's alright then."

Later, a pale clouded moon stared at us mournfully through a filthy window. We were both warm, his breath on my cheek. His raspy breathing slowed into a deep somnolent sleep. "Good night," I whispered, but he was somewhere else.

24

The days rolled on and thunder came and went. When the rain stopped I foraged with Lot and Emma. The little dog was brilliant at finding bits of wood. There were more nettles and even scrubs of seaweed that cooked well enough. I watched the sea constantly for movement and tremor. Some days there was nothing. At others it carried the ghost of a swell, a faint echo from somewhere else. A possibility. Something was forming in my mind but as yet was all mist with no discernible shape. I let it lay there without probing. The dead sludge of water had a strange fascination. There is a violent beauty in the immensity of the death of this world. A terrible beauty is born, the poet said. The mushroom cloud, the tsunami, the fractured buildings with scaffolding thrust like bones from a shot limb, a wondrous chaos of dust and smoke, the vegetable protrusions of disease with colours from a goblin's palette – purple, green, mustard. Sores that weep the only tears left to people in their glorious ruin. It is the Fall writ large. Sometimes I got confused between what I saw before me and my own thoughts, themselves a ruined landscape. One morning I stopped in my tracks. A figure was shuffling towards me along the beach, carrying a basket and, bizarrely, wearing a fireman's helmet. Lot stopped and looked and Emma ran towards the figure. When she reached him he stopped and petted her. She rolled on her back and he tickled her tummy. I took this to be a good sign. As he got closer I could see he was probably in his seventies, weathered, wearing an old oilskin and wellington boots. In his basket were what looked like a few shellfish and some scrubby seaweed. His face was an ancient bed of brown wrinkles. He kept his eyes down and I realised he was going to walk straight by us. He seemed completely unfazed by our presence.

"Hello," I said.

He stopped, looked up at the sky, then at Lot and Emma, then at me.

"Aye yourself."

"I didn't think there was anybody else around."

He grunted and spat.

"Nice dog," he said. "I miss a dog. Must be six months since I saw the last. Don't suppose you'd sell her."

"No!" Shouted Lot. "You can't just buy animals."

He looked at Lot and his face changed its composition. I realised it was meant to be a smile.

"Right you are, missy."

"Are you here on your own?" I ask.

"Me and six thousand ghosts. You're at Robbie's. Miserable git. But I go if I'm in need of cheapo hooch."

"I'm Ali. You've got shellfish."

"Not many around. Takes an age to find the bastards. I'll bring you a few *if* I have a good find. Hamish."

"What are the names of the ghosts?" Asked Lot.

"Andrew, Hennie, old Jacob and young Jacob, McAllister, mad Jane and her twins, Livingstone, and all the others whose names have drifted on the wind."

"Dick. And Tom King. And Bess."

"Aye. Them too."

And he left, trudging his lonely path to wherever he lived.

In heavy rain we stayed indoors. Robbie spent time in his office and then would go out for hours at a time.

"Where does he go?" I asked Trash.

He shrugged. "I think he just walks. Communes with himself. He told me he hears voices."

"What do they say?"

"I didn't ask. I think they're private conversations."

Sometimes at night we just lay there, listening to the wind rattling the windows. Once a chimney stack fell off and we were both out of bed looking for weapons. It showed that this respite was gossamer over a seam of fear and apprehension. Sometimes we fucked but neither of us talked about how things had changed. There were days when I thought he was recovering, but then he would shiver and I would see how thin he was. I guessed he had acute radiation syndrome, given that he seemed to get cramps and I would catch him rubbing his sides, and he was often sick, which suggested internal organs had been affected. He must have received a level of more than five hundred millisieverts but, as yet, it wasn't proving fatal. I knew that most people who die from radiation sickness are killed by infections or internal bleeding as the white blood cells died. It could take weeks, even years in some cases. Trash would know all this far better than me, so we never spoke of it. Most of what went on between us was subliminal. That was fine by me. I had no hunger for discussions about romance or mortality. Yet we had become something in spite of ourselves, as if some puppeteer was experimenting with us to see what worked and what didn't.

"What do you think about us?" I ask one night when we've just made love.

"I think we're doing OK. As long as we keep vigilant and can find supplies."

"I mean you and I. Us."

I feel his bafflement. "Is that a woman type question? Where no matter what answer I give it will be wrong? And I wish I'd kept my mouth shut."

"Yes. That type of question."

Silence.

"What do you think about us?" He asks.

"I think we're two monumental fuck ups who are three roadblocks short of knowing a good relationship if it came up and knocked out our front teeth. I think we are destroyed personalities bent and warped by a dying world that couldn't give a liquid shit whether we fuck or kill each other. I think we cling to each other occasionally in the dark because we have reached the end of our miserable selves and know not where to turn. We are Sodom and Gomorrah, doomed outposts in a wilderness of pain where no god resides and there is only the tortured shreds of feeling we are barely capable of mustering at the best if times."

A silence. "Fair enough. Goodnight," he says.

I'm starting to like this man.

Lot kept away from Robbie. When we were on the beach one day I asked her why. She watched Emma running and chasing some imaginary beast and then looked out at the putrescent goo that extended to the horizon.

"Did Dick know that one day he would be caught?" She asked.

"A good question. I think he did."

"Then if he knew, why didn't he go away?"

"Where would he go?"

"Far across the sea. It would have to be in a big boat, because he would take Bess."

"Perhaps some people only have one story. They get trapped in it. They can't change things."

She looked at me, then ran off to play with Emma.

When it came it was both a surprise and half expected, because Robbie was drinking even more, and seemed on edge. It was also a perverse relief because I was starting to tire of fearing the worst. Let it come. The stupid thing was not to have weapons close by. Apart from handguns by the bed, and a Glock I took when we went out, Trash had hidden the rest beneath some floorboards. It was early evening, a grey sky day of heavy cumuli and the promise of storms to come. I was strung out but tired, almost dozing, sitting against the wall watching desultory flames flicker in the grate. Trash was on his laptop. Lot and Emma cuddled up before the fire, Lot telling the little dog whispered stories, Robbie drinking his gutrot and smiling whenever I looked at him. That's how I knew something was wrong. He never smiled at me. He looked at his phone and then at Trash.

The door was flung open and two men came in, both armed with light hand guns. Emma barked. One of the men pointed his gun at her. Lot put her hand over Emma's snout to quieten her. The masked man entered, also armed with a handgun. He looked at each of us in turn but spoke to me. I knew now it was Fauberge. There was a strange red-rimmed light in his eyes.

"At last. All's well that ends well," he said.

One of the men bound our hands with duct tape and went through our pockets. He took Chloe's magic coin and flipped it to Fauberge, who smiled at it and pocketed it. I will kill him and my only regret will be that I can only do it once. Robbie was left free, and looked both ashamed and expectant. Trash stared at him.

"What did he offer you, Robbie?"

"I'm sorry, Trash."

"What did he offer you?"

Robbie looked at Fauberge.

"Tell him," Fauberge said.

Robbie licked his dry lips, took a swig, and looked at Trash. "Arcadia," he said. "I'm going to Arcadia. Couldn't turn it down, could I?"

Trash laughed. I shook my head.

"You want to go now?" Fauberge asked.

"Aye."

Fauberge looked at one of his men. "Take him to Arcadia."

The man opened the door.

"Don't I need to pack a few things? I mean, I've not got much, my computer and a few odds and sods."

"You will have all new things. Clothes. State of the art technology. Good whisky. That's why it's called Arcadia. Lennie will drive you down to Edinburgh. There is one flight a week to Arcadia. This time next week you'll be sitting in the sun with a scotch and ice in your hand, a new white fedora hat on your head and a smile on your face. And knowing that you've served justice. These two are killers of the first order. Wanted criminals. Go."

Robbie stepped through the door. A minute later we heard two shots. How easy to fool someone with the promise of a dream. The man called Lennie returned and gave a nod to Fauberge, who smiled at Trash, then at me. "Happy now?" He asked. "The betrayer betrayed. A certain symmetry about it. You're probably wondering what next. It may have occurred to you that to put myself to all this trouble for mere personal revenge would be foolish. I could just pay someone else to hunt you down and kill you. No. There's a price on you two. A fortune in fact. In Dorado, which you made an admirable mess of, there in the smoking ruins is a skeletal group of chief Protectors, high rankers, and a few surviving kids. Children of the New Dawn. They formed a power nucleus. They have weapons and supplies. A fortune in tokens. There are other power groups trying to oust them, and once word got out about the devastation of Dorado all manner of Covid people and insurgents started thinking of trying to grab a little power. They got rid of most of them, though."

"How?"

"Released a new strain of Covid. It was not a pretty sight. Stink of it. Had a bubonic strain, so boils, blackened skin, blood rotting in the veins. Very colourful. It certainly stopped a few power grabbers in their tracks. The problem with releasing a new strain is how to put the genie back in the bottle. Not my problem. The point is you have become celebrities of a sort. The new little power group has offered a million tokens and a land mass somewhere safe. They want you alive, though, so they can broadcast your confessions and executions. They believe it will set an example and enhance their status. I got the commission."

"Because you'd put a tracker on us, so you had the best chance of finding us," Trash said.

"Exactement. So you two are going back south tomorrow morning." He looked at Trash. "You'd better not die on me," then looking at Lot, "the girl is no use. Nor the dog."

"If you hurt either of them I will rip out your eyes. You don't even have the gall to take off your stupid mask and show us what a mess I made of your face," I said.

For a good five seconds he wanted to kill me, but greed won out. He took off his mask to reveal the bottom of his nose missing and a deep ugly red slash across both cheeks that had been badly stitched and now looked like a second clown's mouth.

"An improvement. It feels good to see you like that," I say.

He took a bag from his pocket, emptied some crystals on a window ledge, crushed them with the heel of his gun and snorted them. That explained the light in his eyes.

A long uncomfortable night. My bones ache. I am a wasted vessel. No ideas how to get out of this. Trash is too ill to think. He shivers constantly and I am worried he will die in the night. Fauberge and his henchmen take it in turns to nap. Trash coughs and Fauberge gives him water. He wants him to live so he can collect his booty. Every hour he has a long snort of crystal. It keeps him awake and wired. Perhaps it will induce a seizure and at least I'll have the pleasure of watching him die. The rain batters the hotel and there is a wind that sounds like it is angry with everything. I feel glad the weather is like this because it is something to listen to other than my own ragged thoughts. The one bulb hanging from the ceiling is on all night, and I look over at Lot and try to say things with my eyes to her that I should have said before. That she has become very special to me. That she deserves better than this world. That despite myself and the damaged soul I am I love her. My main concern is for her and Emma in the morning.

  We are taken to the bathroom when we need to but the door is kept open. Sometime in the night Fauberge clearly sniffs up a double dose and loses it. He stands in the middle of the room and points up. Then he slowly rotates, occasionally looking at each of us and espousing what I recognise from the Book of Revelation:

"Fear not; I am the first and the last: I am he that liveth, and was dead; and, behold, I am alive for evermore, Amen, and have the keys of hell and of death. There was a sea of glass like unto crystal: and in the midst of the throne, and round about the throne, were four beasts full of eyes before and behind. And the first beast was like a lion, and the second beast like a calf, and the third beast had a face as a man, and the fourth beast was like a flying eagle. And the four beasts had each of them six wings about him; and they were full of eyes within: and they rest not day and night, saying, Holy, holy, holy, Lord God Almighty, which was, and is, and is to come."

Lot is awake, staring at him in fascination. He senses a captive audience and addresses her, as if casting a spell. He is shouting now and everyone is awake.

"And in those days shall men seek death, and shall not find it; and shall desire to die, and death shall flee from them. And the shapes of the locusts were like unto horses prepared unto battle..."

To Fauberge's amazement, and mine, Lot continues, but quietly, almost whispering: "...and on their heads were as it were crowns like gold, and their faces were as the faces of men. And they had hair as the hair of women, and their teeth were as the teeth of lions."

Fauberge's mouth gapes. His scar looks swollen and sore even in the half light. He stares at Lot.

"How the fuck do you know that? How the fuck?"

She shrugs. He crushes some more crystal and offers it to Lot in his hand.

"Go on. Treat yourself. You're like me. This helps," he says. "Go on. Your dog too if she wants."

She shakes her head.

"I don't need it. You do. Because it's bigger than you. You think it's you but you don't know the words. You only say them," she says.

A look of fury on his face. He aims his gun at her.

"No!" I shout.

He stops, looks at me, spits, and goes outside, kicking Lennie properly awake as he leaves. He rants outside, then goes quiet. When he returns an hour later he is subdued. He looks ragged. He crushes some crystal and restores himself. At first grey light he studies the sky from the open door. There is the smell of a storm coming but he is anxious to make a move. He checks his phone but there are no weather reports now. We are given water and something he calls porridge but I suspect is boiled grass and uncooked maggots. My stomach heaves. Lennie is outside packing their own truck and comes inside.

"Someone coming," he says. "Old geezer with a weird hat and carrying a bucket."

Fauberge turns to me.

"It'll be Hamish. A friend," I say.

"Are there others?"

"Loads," says Lot. "He lives with loads of people. And they have much better guns than you. A cannon. Boom boom boom."

"Shall I waste him?" Asks Lennie.

"I don't want to get bogged down in a war here. Not with a storm coming. Just let him come. Hide your weapons. Do nothing unless I say. Untie them. Put the girl and the dog upstairs. Strangle the girl if she tries to run."

"Hamish will want to see Lot and Emma," I say. "They're good friends. And he loves the dog."

"Alright. They stay. But anyone tries anything and I'll kill you all."

"What about your precious tokens and passport to freedom?" I ask.

A knock at the door. Fauberge looks at me.

"Come in," I say.

Hamish enters. He is not wearing his helmet. Without he looks older, his grey hair long and straggly with streaks of faded ginger, his skin deeply grooved and weathered, like ancient leather. Emma runs to him, tail wagging and rolls over for him to tickle her. I sense he takes everything in.

"Hi Hamish. Good to see you," I say. "These are some friends arrived yesterday."

Fauberge and the other two nod at him. Trash, still slumped on the floor, raises a hand.

"Aye. Robbie?"

Gone for a walk. What's in the bucket?"

"Some snails. You boil 'em down, add salt and you've got a bit of protein," and he plonks the bucket down.

"We've been hearing about you. And all the others," says Fauberge.

Hamish looks at him keenly. My brain freezes.

"Andrew, Hennie, old Jacob and young Jacob…" says Lot.

Hamish darts a look at her and smiles.

"Aye, McAllister, mad Jane and her twins, Livingstone…" he says.

"Dick. And Tom King. And Bess," says Lot.

"Aye, them too. They's all asking after ye. And says come up whenever you like."

I could kiss her. Hamish looks at Fauberge and smiles.

"Best be making my way back. They'll all be wondering what I'm up to," he says.

"Hamish. Would you take Emma? She needs a walk and she'd love to see them all again," Lot says.

Fauberge looks at Lot. Then smiles at Hamish.

"That OK?" He asks.

Hamish puts on Emma's lead. "Fine. Be nice to have her for a bit. I'll make my way then."

He leaves with Emma. Fauberge goes outside and watches him walk away. When he returns he looks at Lot.

"Sassy little bitch, aren't you? Prophetess. We'll see how smart you look when I put a bullet in your brain. See what visions and scriptures pop out then."

"If you hurt her, I'll kill myself and Trash. Somehow I'll do it, I swear. Then you don't get your prize," I say.

"And if I let her live you'll come quietly? No fuss. No dramas."

"Yes."

"Let's pack up."

25

Forty minutes later our hands are tied with duct tape again and we are ready to leave. By now Trash is almost unconscious. Lennie half drags him out to Bess and puts him in a back seat. He immediately slumps back, and dozes. Lennie gets in the driver's seat. Fauberge is taking both vehicles. Lot sits in the front of their vehicle with the other man and I am put in the back with Fauberge. He takes a long snort of crystal. Then sneezes, looks at me and laughs aloud. He is coming apart but isn't there yet, so is probably more dangerous. He will make bad decisions. I am concerned for Lot. There are black clouds scowling. Rain is becoming heavier by the second. Already the roads are becoming waterlogged. We all jump when a double crack of thunder booms so loud my ears hurt. Screams of wind tear against the four by fours. Rain pounds the windscreen as if it is a living banshee determined to get inside and wreak its havoc. The rain suddenly intensifies and seems solid, coming down in metallic sheets of silver grey. A telegraph pole crashes behind us and into the Marine. A surreal light momentarily illuminates everything through the rain as lightning snakes down far out on the dead ocean. The gods have declared war and are throwing everything that heaven will allow onto us.

The driver turns around to Fauberge.

"I can't see shit. Maybe we should go back inside until this passes. The roads will be a nightmare."

"Your face will be a nightmare if you don't turn around and shut up. Don't whine."

Slowly it abates and there is a crack in the clouds where a single thin shard of light points down a little in front of us, as if showing the way. The roads drain and start to steam. The steam rises like a stage mist. It is like being in a ghost world. The lightning takes its broiling rage south and the thunder follows. After a few more minutes we are able to see ahead.

"Let's go," says Fauberge.

We drive down Beach Road and turn left onto Smith Street and will head across what was the River Thurso. Ahead someone walks into the road and faces us, like a figure in a dream, especially as I can't see his feet as they are shrouded in a low mist steaming from the road. It is Hamish. He has his fireman's helmet on and old wellies, and a brown drizabone wax full length coat. He reminds me of an old marshal in a western, standing his ground one last time on Main Street for the final shoot out with the bad guys. The driver sounds the horn. Hamish raises his left arm, his right nonchalantly behind his back. The driver slows.

"What shall I do?" He asks.

"It might be a trap. If there are others with weapons I'd rather we just get out of this dump. Accelerate," says Fauberge.

"But…"

"But but but. Knock the old fucker down and keep going, whatever happens."

The driver accelerates. I feel the engine drink up the fuel injection and surge forward. Hamish stands his ground, unflinching. He is no more than four metres away when there is a sudden lurch and the front of the vehicle jolts down, throwing us all forward. Lot was belted in so she is OK but myself and Fauberge crash forward. I have my taped hands in front of me so this cushions the blow but Fauberge hits the back of the headrest and I hear his nose crack. The driver lurches forward and twists his neck.

"Shit!" says Fauberge and holds his revolver pointing at me while his free hand assesses the damage to his face.

"You're even more of a freak now, Fauberge. If your nose isn't set properly you'll be sniffing sideways for the rest of your life," I say. "You'll have to snort junk through your ear."

His eyes flash hatred, but something in him has gone AWOL. By my reckoning he has gone at least thirty six hours without sleep and he has uploaded a mountain of junk through his nose. The driver gets out, rubbing his neck. He holds up a rubber strip full of tyre spikes that had been laid across the road. Hamish stands watching. The driver shrugs at Fauberge, wanting to know what to do. Fauberge points his gun at Hamish through the windscreen. The driver nods, takes out his gun and steps towards Hamish. As he raises the gun Hamish's right arm comes from behind his back holding a pump action shotgun. He fires both barrels at the driver, hitting him in the chest. The impact lifts the man off his feet and slams him against the four by four.

There is a second of surprise, then Fauberge gets out of the vehicle and uses the door as cover to fire at Hamish. This is a stupid mistake. It leaves me free to get out the other side using both bound hands to open the door. He should have stayed with us and forced Hamish to make another move. I look behind to see if Lennie is going to start firing but what I see stops me in my tracks. Lennie's red and panic-stricken face as he struggles to breathe. From behind him Trash has looped his taped hands over his head and is strangling him. I find it hard to compute. I thought Trash was near death, so either he was bluffing extremely well or he's had a shot of adrenalin. He was so ill that I can't believe he can sustain his hold on Lennie. Hamish fires at the door behind which Fauberge squats. It shatters the window. I shout to Lot to get down and I run back to help Trash. By the time I reach Bess Lennie is kicking out wildly and gets his legs from under the dash and kicks the windscreen. He has both hands on Trash's, trying to free the grip. His gun is on the floor. I open the door, pick up the gun and fire point blank into his liver. His whole body jumps as the bullet shatters and ruins him. He gurgles a scream and starts to go into a seizure of shock. I fire again and his side starts pumping blood. I hear the shooting behind me and now I am anxious about Lot. Lennie's tongue lolls a horrible swollen purple and his eyes are distended and blood red. He subsides and is gone. I take a knife from Lennie's belt and cut Trash free, then he does the same for me. I drag Lennie out of the car and he slumps on the pavement, his dead carcass still pumping blood.

"I thought you were dying," I say.

"We're all dying. I put it on a bit," Trash says, and then starts coughing.

He says something else but I am already running to the vehicle in front, where firing has stopped. Hamish is a little away, on the ground, where he tried to take shelter behind a low wall. The doors are open. Lot is gone. I look on the floor of the back. I shout her name. Nothing. Fauberge has her. He knows a sure way to get me is to take her. He knows I'll come, and it gets me into open ground. I go to Hamish. He's wounded in his side but with any luck it has missed his kidneys and liver. Too low for lungs. The shotgun is on the ground beside him. I look at him.

"Thanks," I say.

"But I lost my bloody helmet."

"We'll get you a new one. I have to go."

"Aye. You have."

I look at the shotgun. He nods. I take it, go through his pockets and load a new magazine. It has seven rounds.

I scan as I run. If he thinks there are others around he won't go far because his plan is to get me back, not run away from me. The danger is in how far he is prepared to go with Lot to reel me in. He was as high as a kite but the comedown, unless he keeps sniffing crystal, will make him volatile. He may lose all original intent and just want the pleasure of wasting us. I run along Smith Terrace, past the holiday park, and stop when I hear something. The fairground. The merry go round. I turn and my heart misses a beat. Lot is sitting on the duck, slowly going up and down and round. Fauberge stands in the centre, smiling at me. He stops the machine and Lot stares down at me. Fauberge has his pistol trained on Lot and I see that both her hands and feet are bound. I walk as close as I dare.

"Simple pleasures. Family holiday. Fairground. Who would have thought that the world could go so horribly wrong? A merry go round apocalypse. You know what I was before Covid?"

"Pimp? Drug dealer? Paedophile? General dickhead?" I say.

"I was a doctor."

Despite myself I laugh. Fauberge laughs too.

"I know. How absurd. How ridiculous to want to heal the human race. Pointless project. Now, arms dealer – there's a profession of social usefulness. Or euthanasia programme director. But doctor. Poor career choice. Except. Everything has its upside. For example, with this," and he takes out a surgical scalpel "I could remove half of little Lot's organs and she'd still be alive. Conscious of all that is happening. I could take out her eyes, her tongue, and she'd live. Isn't that a miracle? And I might do that if I lose you and Trash. So it's in your interest to keep me happy."

"You realise that this reward, tokens, a free pass to a safe place of your own. It's bullshit. They'll probably just kill you too. And if there is a new Covid strain spreading the chances of making it back are remote."

"Let's say I'm an optimist."

"What about the others here? They'll be coming to look for Hamish."

He assumes a mock thoughtful look.

"I'm starting to think these others. They're phantoms."

"Your toy boys are dead. Just you. That long drive. You're already wired. You really think you can make that journey on crystal alone? Your brain will fry by Manchester."

"Never underestimate the power of the will. Superman, that's me. Nietzschean superman."

"That's what all dopeheads think on the way to the big crash."

"Enough banter. You're done. There are others coming. I just got here first is all. You know the deal. She lives if you comply. Gun down."

I put down the shotgun.

"And the handgun."

I take the Glock from my back belt and put it down. Fauberge aims the gun at me and lowers it.

"Afraid I have to wing you, given what's happened so far. It's a question of whether it's both kneecaps or just the one." He takes out Chloe's magic coin. "Heads one knee. Tails two. Are you feeling lucky?" He flips the coin. "Lucky girl. Heads. Right or left?"

"The one in the middle," I say.

"I think the right."

He takes aim. I close my eyes. I promise myself I will not scream, no matter what pain it brings. I will not give the bastard that pleasure. A loud gunshot and I buckle slightly and realise I have stopped breathing. I open my eyes and for a second am unable to register what is happening. No pain. How can that be? Did he miss? I touch my intact knee and look up. Fauberge is staring incredulously at the stump of his right arm, an open mess of bone and sinew and gore. On the ground a little a metre away is his hand still clutching his gun. Weirdly the hand is twitching, as if still trying to pull the trigger. I am aware of Trash walking into view holding a laser gun. Fauberge staggers a little and clutches the merry go round handle with his good hand. Slowly, the ancient machinery wheezes and grinds into life. I run at him and jump like an animal, see his eyes as red pools of alarm. My mouth opens and I shout, but it is a jungle sound, arching back through time to a world of hunt and lushness and beautiful death.

    Then I disappear.

26

We are sailing. I am amazed that we could own such a vessel. Wooden with billowing white sails in a fresh westerly wind. Chloe stands on the deck looking at the foam crested waves that roil and whip at our sides and laughing at the salt spray from each broken crest. She points at Joe, who stands at the prow, one leg on a raised plank and wearing a joke Admiral's hat, one arm behind and one tucked in his shirt like Horatio Nelson. He takes out a cardboard tube as a telescope and in a mock theatrical sweep scans the horizon. The prow of the ship is a wooden carved horse's head, the mane splaying out like mermaid hair or waves in a dream. It is a piece of Joe's finest work, carved and honed and planed and varnished with the love of the craft. I know it is the head of Turpin's Bess. We are bound for somewhere but I cannot remember where. It doesn't matter. Then from nowhere a swell of panic begins in my stomach and I taste something salty. I can't breathe and I realise my panic is in not knowing if we are playing a game here or really bound for somewhere. Chloe looks at me and shakes her head, as if I have spoilt the moment, wrecked the adventure. I try cry out to her but my mouth is cloyed with something that disgusts me.

When I return it can only be moments later. The merry go round is still revolving slowly and squeaking as if in pain. I am standing and my jaw aches, my mouth is wet, but something is wrong. I taste blood. I spit it out and there is soft tissue too. I wipe my mouth and my hand is covered in blood and a mushy, fleshy saliva, and a thin trembling piece of what looks like gossamer pink piping. I grip the rail of an ancient alabaster unicorn, paint peeling on its once golden horn. Draped across its back is Fauberge, his bloody stump of an arm across his chest in what looks like some benedictory gesture. His throat has gone, just an open sore of blood and flesh, his eyes wide open and staring redly at the sky in horrified wonder. I spit out what is left of his throat in my mouth and feel sick. I turn and heave out what little is in my stomach. Then I turn back and for reasons I will never fathom I lean down and kiss him gently on the forehead. I look in his pocket and take out Chloe's magic coin and press it against his forehead. It leaves an imprint of a head. He will take that wherever he goes next. I look in his pocket and take out a pretty rosewood box with onyx inlay and quartz stones that belongs to me. I don't look inside.

Trash stops the merry go round.

"Good shot," I say, trying to hide how eviscerated I feel.

"Lousy shot. I was aiming at his head."

I look at Lot but something tells me not to get close. Despite being a changeling with all kinds of gifts, she has seen the beast too many times and needs time to accommodate it. Just as I now need to let it leave me. I am not sure how many more times this can happen before I stay in whatever dark cave I go to. I realise I am streaming tears and wonder why. I think it is for all of us. Whoever we are and whatever we have become. I close my eyes and let the breeze cool my thoughts.

Hamish is tough. He has gone back to the Marine and bathed his own wound and is binding it when we return in Bess. He also has Emma with him, who runs in delirious circles at the sight of us and restores Lot to herself. He says that he put her in an abandoned boat shed where he kept his shotgun. He says he knew things weren't right because Lot would never have asked him to take Emma and the reciting of imaginary names was clearly a message to him. I said the dressing on his wound needed changing every few hours and that he should stay with us. He smiled and said he'd think about it.

"Have you seen it?" he asked.

We all looked at him.

"The swell. That was one almighty godstrike of a storm and it made the change."

We all go out and walk to the beach.

"Look," Hamish says, pointing out at the horizon.

I wonder if I am still dreaming or lost in myself. There is the grey-brown sludge of sea, dead and unmoving, but perhaps eight or nine hundred metres out there is a difference in texture and colour. A trick of the light. A difference. A scarred strip of sunlight dazzles from the horizon pointing inland like a crazed finger looking for a pulse. A tin flash in the sun dazzle as if the dead water has cracked open like a wet egg to reveal a secret life lurking below. As I look a world seems to dance before me, or is it behind my eyes? Light lancing forrards, beasts like shadows in glass, lynx purr and smell of heather, eye glitter of dancing bright, the drowned swimmers and fishes rise up like branches of light, fish scales over groin muscles, sinews of Poseidon come alive in a wave wreckage, black azure and hyaline, waves the colour of golden wine. As if the ghost of something is recovering. Lifeless sludge is now sinewed water.

"Is it real?" I ask.

"The storm was blue thunder. It shot blue thunder through the sea. But instead of killing, it woke it up," says Lot.

Hamish laughs, rubbing his shoulder. "Ach, lassie's right there. The storm was a wakeup call." He does a little hornpipe in the sand. "Thunder and lightning, very very frightening, made the lady dance," he says. Lot joins him in the dance, and Emma runs around them both, barking in joy and confusion.

"What do you think?" I ask Trash.

"If it's a mirage, it's a bloody good one. It's not a hologram because where would it be coming from and why? I think that perhaps there was a dormant life, at least seawater, way below the surface, and the storm has broken the caked layers above it, or that torrential rain and wind has blown in something fresh from God knows where. Either way, it's a bloody miracle."

"So maybe now it's a good time to tell you my mad idea."

He looks at me suspiciously. He's right to do that. I would.

He listens intently as I explain. The abandoned rusting motorbikes in the caravan park had started it. There were some decent two stroke engines. I thought I might be able to adapt something to make a powerful outboard motor. Panels from the caravans were light and durable. We could fashion a boat of some sort and attach the outboard. It would have to be strong to get through the glutinous porridge of the sea and I'd have to make a water or air cooler so it didn't overheat and find some way of stopping it from sludging up. The boat would need a prow that was sharp and strong to cut though everything. The biggest drawback was that as far as we knew all oceans were ruined and even if the boat worked we might simply end up trapped in a giant pudding into which we would eventually sink, as if it were a swamp. But now when it seemed there was a clear spot out there suddenly it was worth considering. I realised I was talking too animatedly, and because I was nervous he would simply think it a ridiculous idea and we would be stuck here for whatever presumably short time remained. I thought his rejection might finish something in me for good. With the new Covid infecting people, the infighting in Dorado, I thought that another giant step had been taken in the destruction of the human race. Even a corrupt centre is a centre and now there was no glue, even fear, to make things cohere. I also thought that when Fauberge didn't return others might come. We could wait it out or at least die trying something. I knew I needed to keep busy. I was an engineer. I needed to make things and see if they worked.

    He walks away a little and looks again at the horizon. The silver and gold sunlight flashing on water was still visible. He coughs a few times, and turns to me.

"Or skis?" He says. "Like a kind of catamaran so it doesn't have to plough through the sludge below the surface but half glide on it."

I run and hug him. Momentarily he looks horrified, then surprised, then pleased. Fucking in the dark was one thing but a hug in the sun was clearly a whole new level of intimacy for him. We discuss the possibilities. I feel an enthusiasm that shreds my tiredness and sends a few of the demons in me scurrying into shadowy corners. I knew they were still there but they could wait. Hell, maybe it was even them that had kept me going this far. Maybe I should be grateful to the little bastards.

Back at the house we went into more detail and drew up a list. I would do the engineering and Trash would do the electronics and build a touch screen control device. Ideally we could find an old outboard casing and I could use this as a carapace for the new one. Hamish seemed to be a decent handyman and in his youth had his own fishing boat, so he could help construct the frame. As we talked a little colour seemed to return to Trash's pallid face. Then he would have a coughing fit and I feared the worst. I knew that sometimes at night his breathing became ragged and he would get up so as not to wake me. I suspect he was also coughing a little blood but he would never tell me.

Trash insisted we build two motors, one as back up but also to give us the option of travelling further without recharging. This made sense. I needed a gearbox and brushless DC motor, preferably a high specification Parvalux or Maxim motor, 48V with automatic battery charger. I still had my toolkit, and would need a hacksaw, power/battery drill, lighting, workbench, soldering iron and good multimeter. I kissed Hamish when he said there was a workshop in a side street where there was a lathe. If we could get power there it might still work. I also thought that with a bit of improvising I could use a laser pistol as a cutting tool.

Two days of foraging later we laid out everything we had acquired in the living room. We also had four decent 12V car batteries, three from Fauberge's vehicle, which had two spares, and a spare from Bess. Trash was already close to completing two LED touch control computers that could also be controlled long distance with a phone. We had several dozen panels from old caravans to make a carapace, some axles from caravans that I could bolt together to make the two long crosspieces and then some fibreglass hollow pipes from the fairground that could form the two long sections running parallel to the main body. It would look like a giant insect. A beast of the deep. Hamish also suggested an aluminium mast and some improvised sails as back up to the motors, using old curtains from wherever we could find them.

Lot asked what Dick Turpin and Bess looked like. Something in her tone told me this was important. I stopped repairing the casing of a power drill we found in a hut at the fairground. I gave her the full Romantic hero.

"He was tall, with curling black hair and dark eyes that flashed fire. Pale skin and a strong chin and aquiline nose. If he had an earring and bandana he could be taken for a dashing pirate. He was muscular, and took great pride in his clothes – shiny black boots but with no spurs, because his love for Bess forbade ever causing her pain. A bottle green frock coat with velveteen buttons, and sometimes a bright red coat that showed his fearlessness at being seen, velvet dark grey breeches, and matching gloves. He walked with strong purpose and only ever stole from the rich and proud. Bess had a magnificent head and a mane so black it shone and dazzled as it flew in the breeze on a midnight run and caught the rays of the moon over the heath. Her eyes like liquid coals. And the love she had for Dick was unsurpassed. These two adventurers were the talk of every town in the kingdom."

A few hours later she had made stencils and drawings that were frighteningly good of Dick Turpin and Bess, and which she wanted to use to decorate the boat, using tins of paint we had found at the fairground, many of which were usable once I thinned them down. I felt in awe of Lot, who could endure so much and retain her wonder at things. The four of us had become a working unit, a peculiar family of ragtaggles, and I realised that it didn't matter if we failed and that it was only these moments that we stitched together through industry and affection that did.

The sky had changed after the storm. Low pearl cloud banks that foretold of weight and pressure, but behind them a presence, as if the sun had decided to concentrate on earth and make a last apocalyptic change. Occasionally a cloud would break up and a laser beam of light strike the earth and sea, searching for something. A greeting, a welcome, an apology. As a believer in nothing but what the day brings I tried not to read signs in this, but I was aware Lot often stopped and looked up, as if a voice no one else could hear had whispered, summoned her. At such moments she would touch the yellow ribbon and her lips moved in silent prayer.

Emma sat outside sniffing the breeze and often her ears pricked on high alert. I looked and saw nothing but she seemed to know there was something around that would not be ignored. Little did I know that it wasn't to be Gabriel on golden wings or a Second Coming but something slithering out of the darkness seeking a mirror to its own pain. A heady mix of anticipation, industry and uncertainty affected us all. I wondered if we were building an ark or a coffin.

I decided the battery would be separately mounted and connected via flexible electric cable. Then I had to mechanically connect the electric motor to the donor outboard engine. I measured all mounting holes on top of the engine, and the mounting holes on the electric motor, and designed a transition plate. Using a movable clamp to stabilise it and an improvised shield, I used the laser gun to cut the plate out of 10 mm thick aluminium. Using the lathe I turned down the end of the 11mm spline and put an 8mm thread on it.

This screwed perfectly into the 8mm female thread on the motor shaft, and a lock-nut completed the union. Now the motor, donor engine and driveshaft were all connected. Trash did the electrical assembly from there on while Hamish and I worked designing the main hull and the side sections. The caravan panels were fairly flexible but not durable so we created a frame for them from thin metal poles and then sprayed with a waterproof paint. Hamish had the idea of melting tyres to create a rubberised insulation, which worked after a few failed attempts at getting the temperature right and we basted on the rubber with plastering tools.

I also fashioned a generator. A crank handle attached to a spinning wheel I got from the fairground. It wasn't hard to attach the wheel to a rotor and then a stator to collect the energy and transfer it to one of our batteries. I tried using an old cordless drill to spin the wheel but it kept slipping. It would take time to refine. We decided to take as many tools as we could and Trash had the idea of making a small tub-like boat which we would pack with supplies and tow with our main vessel.

We were there. We carried all the pieces outside to erect it. We couldn't be seen from the road behind the Marine so it would be safe until we had a test run. It took a day of cursing and errors before we had assembled our giant machine, which now resembled some prehistoric jumble monster with a central bulbous body and angled metallic arms and legs and sinews. Lot christened her Bess Two and began painting her in bright colours and adding her stencils. Trash suggested more calmer colours that would act as camouflage but Lot gave him a withering look that silenced him. We erected our mast with the sails as a back up. As evening approached we realised we had finished. Surprise and jubilance. Hamish did a little jig, Emma barked and

Trash and I shook hands in mock ceremony, then he embraced me. "We've done something here," he whispered.

We went inside and opened a bottle of wine.

"Where are we going to go?" Lot asked. "Over the sea and far away?"

It was a good question. Probably we'd all had vague ideas but we had never properly discussed where we might go. Hamish galvanised us. He spread out some old maps and pointed with a stubby dirty finger as he showed us.

"Here we are. Then there the island clusters. Two archipelagos. Orkney and Shetland. This bubby here, Fair Isle. Then here," and he drew a line, "the Faroes. Never been there meself. Slap bang betwixt Norway and Iceland."

"How about we just work our way North? Start with the Orkneys and then the Shetland isles if we need to," I said.

We agreed. One step at a time. Tomorrow we would put Bess Two through her paces in a test run. That night I lay next to Trash. His breathing quietened after a while and he reached for my hand, then turned and stroked my cheek with feather fingers, and kissed my eyes with butterfly kisses. My stomach knotted. I turned my head away.

"What?" He asked.

"I'm sorry. I'm not ready for tenderness. It doesn't sit well with the pit of snakes inside me. I need to protect myself. In fact it makes me want to punch you in the face."

"Fair enough," he said, and rolled over. The great thing about Trash was that you didn't have to labour the point.

Making Bess Two, the boat, or whatever it was, had been a welcome respite from reality. Things felt better when I could lose myself in calculations and measurements and surface textures of wood and steel and plastic, reassure myself with angles and dovetail joints and making bolts coil and turn like poetry. Now it was done I had a sense of deflation. What if it was all in vain? I remembered the hell of a job I had getting a boat out to the oil rig. Suppose we get stuck? Suppose our calculations are wrong and the thing doesn't work. We should have done resistance tests in the sea to check what voltage engine we needed. We hadn't really done a proper weight and flotation calculation. The questions and doubts buzzed until the buzzing became a soporific spell that wove itself around me in the darkness.

And as they rode into the night, Bess's nostrils flaring and the steam rising from her and trailing back like comets as she picked up pace, Dick hunched low in the saddle and whispered to her, "Atta girl, That's me lovely Bess, best horse in the world, fleet of hoof, clear of eye. We fly like the wind because you run with angels of the highway to fire and protect you, me girl."

And he laughed outright at their plight, the local constable and three of his men behind him, pistols cocked and ready to blow blue thunder through him, though Squire Creasey had requested that Turpin be taken alive, that he could watch him humiliated in trial and finally dance the hornpipe at the end of a rope, soiling his britches and gurgling like a strangled chicken. And the Squire would take Bess for his own horse and bend her spirit to his whip and will.

"Not yet, not yet by a long straw," said Dick aloud, and the silver plate and wine cups he had taken clanked in the canvas bag tied to his saddle. And people will sing his praises for generations. Someone will take up the pen and write: Turpin was the *ultimus Romanorum*, the last of a race, which—we were almost about to say we regret—is now altogether extinct. Several successors he had, it is true, but no name worthy to be recorded after his own. With him expired the chivalrous spirit which animated successively the bosoms of so many knights of the road; with him died away that passionate love of enterprise, that high spirit of devotion to the fair sex, which was first breathed upon the highway by the gay, gallant Claude Du-Val, the Bayard of the road—*Le filou sans peur et sans reproche*—but which was extinguished at last by the cord that tied the heroic Turpin to the remorseless tree.

"'Cos he was caught, one dreadful dark night," said Chloe.

I held her close, could smell apples and bubblegum, and we watched her mobile of Dick and Bess pinned to the ceiling slowly turn in the star silvered night.

"He was. But he never wavered. A brave face to the world even at the end."

"What happened to Bess? Did she go to the loathsome Squire Creasey?"

"No. She would rather die than be whipped by that plump toad. No. It's a mystery. One night she was there in the stable. Next morning, gone."

"Where?" Chloe asked, her thumb creeping into her mouth.

"To join Dick, of course. To ride through the stars."

When Chloe finally slept I went to the window and looked out. A fire burning in the distance. Things unwelcome to come.

"It's coming," I heard Chloe say, but when I turned, she was asleep.

"It's coming," Lot said gravely, looking down at me. She was standing on the bed, legs straddled. As I fumbled out of a heavy dark sleep she seemed like an angel of the apocalypse come with dread and dark visitations.

27

"It's coming," Lot repeated.

"That's what I thought Chloe said in my dream, but you probably know that," I said. "Do you know what it is?"

She turned and walked out. Trash had gone to check on Bess Two. I got up, the anxiety already churning in my veins and the skittery remnants of the dream still flitting like bats in my mind. Sure as hell seemed as if something was coming. All I could think was to get up and go to work. We needed to give Bess Two a trial run. The weather was bleak. Purple clouds like bruises. A fog and poor visibility. Bad sailing weather, but increasingly it felt as if we had no choice. I wondered if that vision of light on the water had been a collective dream. We all so wanted something to be out there that we willed it into our horizon. I ate some beans and checked our stores. Plenty of water but food was running low. We would have to hope that wherever we landed had grubs and worms and bugs otherwise we'd be in trouble. In a moment of wild optimism I'd thought that if there was sea water anywhere there might be edible life there too, but you can't eat hope. I decided to have a last forage along the beach just before we left to see if I could find snails or kelp or weed. I asked Hamish where the best place to look was and he said he'd come with me. We had already loaded the spare tub with much of our equipment and tools and dry clothes in plastic bags. I started cleaning our cache of weapons.

Emma's barking from the beach had an urgency to it. It bespoke warnings and fear. I stopped cleaning and took a light machine gun that I found in Fauberge's vehicle, an old M2409. The weight suited me. Easy to handle and reliable. I ran down and stopped dead when I reached Lot and Emma. Three hundred metres away in the fog, in a perfect line across the beach, were perhaps fifty flaming torches, apparently suspended in mid-air. Lanterns from a nether world, as if a ghost army had been summoned from some fiery pit for a last reckoning at the end of things. They were big, perhaps a metre and a half tall, and a light breeze made the torch flames sway in unison, like snakes to a charmer, a formation dance of living fire.

"This is it? What you meant?" I asked Lot.

She nodded, still looking at the torches. Hamish joined us and stared.

"Seen anything like this here before?" I asked.

He shook his head. "Not in my life."

I had a sudden memory flash of reading about the last druids of England in Anglesey, the banshees, running along the beach in their ragged robes and shrieking their final song, torches flaming, as the boats arrive in the mist bearing Roman soldiers who will slaughter each and every one of them and nail them to giant oaks. The end of a line, death of a culture in one swift brutal cut. Whose end was being planned here? Fauberge said others were coming, but who were they?

"It's children," Lot said.

"What?"

"It's why we can't see them. They're holding the giant torches in front of them."

I looked again. I stepped forward. I took out my binoculars. I saw a few pairs of feet, a few hands gripping the torches. She was right. No magic here, but kids standing holding giant flames before them. Ferals don't behave like this, in paramilitary union; they were sprites of spontaneous uncoordinated chaos and malevolence. This was an army awaiting a signal. Tin soldiers in thrall to some hidden hand. Did they mean to attack or just frighten us? Who was in charge? No point in asking what they wanted. The answer was, as everywhere – whatever we've got. As we had our standoff in the grey morning I suddenly realised what they were doing – checking us. They wanted to see who came to look at them and how many we were. It was a clever tactic. No way of knowing if they were armed. Then, as if from some hidden signal they started to slowly recede. The whole episode had the reek of organised malice. We watched until the torches became pin pricks in the gloom and then disappeared.

"What do you think?" I asked Hamish.

"I think they's be coming back. Not from anywhere round here. So my way of thinking is that things is getting so bad and people are moving up until there's nowhere else for them to go, then theys'all turn on each other like as not."

Signals were poor here so Trash hadn't been able to get much by way of satellite. In any case whatever we were allowed to see would not be what is happening. The only news we had was what our eyes and ears told us. I watched until I was sure the children had gone and we returned to the Marine. I feared an attack. The sooner we were away the better. We dragged Bess Two down to the shoreline and into the sludge that reeked and swilled like a congealed pudding. She was heavier than I'd imagined, but in foul weather that might not be a bad thing. And unless there were pockets of the sludge that acted like a swamp and sucked us down, the thickness of the Dead Sea might buoy us up. Then we dragged down the little supply vessel and tied her on. We pulled her into the sludge. We all got on the boat and distributed our weight. Myself and Trash one side and Hamish, lot and Emma the other. The controls and outboard at the rear. Hamish had found some old plastic oars and we strapped those to the boat. I thought the outboard might churn up the sludge onto us so had made two mud guards from old caravan panels. Some weapons and supplies in the centre and the rest we were towing in what we now called the Tub.

"God bless Bess Two and all who sail in her," said Lot.

"I'll drink to that, lassie," said Hamish and produced a small tin flask that probably contained something stronger than nuclear fuel.

"OK. Bon voyage," said Trash and used the keyboard to start the motor. We sat in anticipation. Nothing happened. He tried again. "Shit," he said.

"Trash. You are a genius. I know this because you've told me. Now start the bloody motor."

Nothing.

"I don't understand. How can I possibly have got it wrong?" Trash said.

"Is there an override? A hand crank?" I asked.

"Of course not. I knew what I was doing," he said.

"Alright then. And it's not working,"

He glared at me. His professional pride was wounded. Lot was looking along the beach, her dark eyes oval like a beautiful bird's. I turned and the flames were back, approaching. I felt they probably meant business this time.

Once out of the fog they are a strange sight. Over fifty flaming torches with children's legs beneath them. What chills me is that they all step in unison, as if to the beat of a silent drum. Trash is still fiddling with the keyboard. I've never seen him so annoyed. Professional pride, as well as possibly our lives, are at stake. We have to do something.

"Hamish, you and I with the oars."

We each take an oar and start trying to push the boat out, as we are still in the shallows. It was one thing in a small rowing boat on my own, when I went out to the rig what seems like a hundred years ago, but this monster with four people and a dog, provisions, tools, weapons and towing a laden tub, is another level. We barely move an inch. Lot jumps out, up to her waist in sludge, and starts to push. We move half a metre. I am sweating heavily now, willing this thing to move. I curse the sludge. It is everything that has held me back, dragged down the ones I loved, crucified what I once called myself but is now a stranger to my anfractuous self. Even now, when I have people that matter around me, I feel I am still walking with ghosts. We are now about three metres out. The children come. They line up on the beach a metre before the sludge. Then a figure I recognise breaks rank and holds his torch aloft. He walks along the line, then turns and looks straight at me.

"Surprise surprise, look in my eyes," he says. It is the cloned boy who wanted so badly to kill us. The head concho kid from Children of the New Dawn in Dorado. I thought he was dead.

"How did you know where to find us?" I ask.

"There were odd reports. Random drone images. Mostly I used my intelligence, gleaned from my father who was a genius, and my mother who had the tenacity of Job. You did a very bad thing. A cunty thing. And bad things have to pay. Especially very bad things."

He sounds older, mature even, but then suddenly childish. Adult sensibilities in a child's frame. I wonder if that is what happens with clones. DNA just sparks off and these kids evolve in jumps and starts. It is creepy.

"And what's your intention now, genius?"

"My intention is to kill you. More importantly I want you to suffer first. We had a new empire in the making, a new elite, and you ruined it. Children of the New Dawn, the Golden Dawn. Why did you have to ruin things for us? You witch. You stinker. Everyone loved us until you came."

"You were just a bunch of spoilt runts. Not even proper kids. Just clones. Replicas. How unoriginal is that?"

He smiles. He knows I'm playing for time, goading him into some rash outburst which he is too smart to fall for. I suddenly realise something.

"You have no weapons."

There is a slight change of expression, a flicker of lost composure. He recovers. "Ah but I do," and gestures to his little army. "These are my weapons. I've trained them. It was like winding up clockwork puppets. Interesting really that so many ferals are practically braindead. But useful. I may let them eat you. Slowly."

He tuns to his little kamikaze army and points at us. "Bring them to me," he says. Slowly the kids advance, still holding their torches.

"Trash!" I say.

"Alright, alright. I'm getting there," he says and there is a slight whirr in the water, which then dies. The kids are now in the sludge, but it is hard going. They want to form a semi-circle around us but it is too arduous. A few drop their torches. A few have got the knack of raising their knees high to progress and are within a metre and reaching out to our boat. I take out my Glock but I really don't want to shoot.

"Get back. Don't listen to him. He's using you," I say, but the zombie, sleepwalking eyes tell me they will keep coming. One is almost touching the tub and I see he has the little finger missing on his right hand. I wonder how he lost it. He skirts the tub and touches the boat; the motor suddenly thunders into life and a great swill of sea sludge pelts the kids, making them scream and some of them fall. The guards I made protect us. The motor turning is one of the sweetest sounds I've ever heard. It works like a pebbledash sprayer as we slowly chug away, and the kids now resemble creatures from the sludge lagoon, or camouflaged miniature warriors. They are in disarray, some dropping their torches, others trying to wipe their eyes clear and making them worse. The feral with the missing finger is hanging on to the boat with one hand. I hit it hard with the butt of my gun. He lurches back in pain and tries to keep his head above the sludge, and fails. There is a plop as his head disappears and he is sucked down. The leader is on the beach screaming at them to keep going, keep going. Now he is a child again in the full throes of a tantrum. I smile at his rage, but then feel the horror shine down the back of my neck as I realise the kids are so automaton they will obey. Already a few more are up to their necks and still trying to follow us, spluttering and gagging. This will be a mass suicide. I aim at the screaming kid on the beach. Maybe if I take him out the others will stop coming, but I feel a tug at my arm. Lot.

"Don't. It won't help. They'll just keep coming anyway," she says, twirling a finger around her head to show their collective dumbness. I can let him be, a Canute like figure with a kingdom about to vanish. Some of the kids are in over their heads now and dying, thin arms projecting like bony church spires waving in a storm. I know that the psycho on the beach will find a way to follow, and I'm tired of being hunted, hounded, and wrecked, so I get an M4 A41 assault rifle, take careful aim and get him clear in the head. It explodes in a starburst of blood and brain. A good clean shot. I know Lot is looking at me. I can't help her just now and move to the front to check our course. As we continue to move, the prow of Bess Two slices a passage in the glutinous muck like a knife through mousse. The ski like wings keep us buoyant. A minute later the kids are all gone, and there is just a litter of torches and a slight movement on the surface of the sludge where the living are working hard to become the dead beneath the surface. "I had not thought death had undone so many. Sighs, short and infrequent, were exhaled," I whisper to myself, but Trash hears.

"That corpse you planted last year in your garden, has it begun to sprout? Will it bloom this year? Or has the sudden frost disturbed its bed?
Oh keep the Dog far hence, that's friend to men, or with his nails he'll dig it up again!" He smiles, never failing to surprise me.

"Well done with the motor," I say.

He mock bows.

We chug on, set keel to breakers, forth on the sea that God and the devil himself has abandoned, and that knew only itself and an indifference to all.

28

We make slow progress and swap motors as the first is overheating but within an hour the Orkneys are in sight. Tall sandstone cliffs, beaches, rocky outliers. Emma stands on the prow like a mindful captain scanning the future, her fronds bronze and gold in the pale light. I pass out plates of sea snails and stewed seaweed, and cups of water. The absurd thought occurs that I am a waitress on a cruise. I wonder if ludicrous thoughts are a release of pressure or a sign that total mental collapse is just around the corner.

"We're on a quest," Lot says.

"Yes. I suppose we are," I say.

"To find a treasure."

"Yes."

"What is it?"

"What?"

"What treasure are we questing?"

"Fresh water. Things to eat. Somewhere to stay without being hunted."

"And like in Beforetimes. Trees and apples and the sea alive and people had dogs and cats and rabbits to look after and things I haven't seen. Not perfect but better."

"Exactly." This little foundling breaks what is left of my heart.

Hamish suggests skirting Hoy and the smaller Graemsay and then going starboard to the mainland. The two lochs, Stenness and Harray, he says are brackish but with the storms there may even be fresh water that we could boil. He says it has been several years since he's had news from the Orkneys, so whether they are inhabited is anybody's guess.

"I have no idea if my brother is alive, or if he is, if he's still on the Islands," he says.

"You have a brother there?"

"Aye. Rory. Miserable get, so we called him Happy Rory. Not a good word for anyone. Could'na stand the get. If anyone's alive it's him. Too bloody stingy to die, like a good soul."

"You're close, then?" I say.

He smiles.

"Aye, Cain and Abel. Chalk and cheese. Grand spoot catcher, though."

"What's a spoot?"

"Razor clam. Long, thin shellfish. You walk backwards at low tide, get 'em quick with a knife before they react to your footsteps. Rory got good because he was too bloody mean to buy his grub."

He told us that in Rousay and Wyre Sounds there had been rich maerl beds and seaweed forests. Maerl is a group of coral-like seaweed species growing, unattached on the seabed. Protected by this were sponges, peacock worms, little fish and shrimp. Gobies and crabs hunted there and were themselves grub for larger fish and diving seabirds. There were Blue-rayed limpets and topshells that grazed the algal slime that grew on the fronds. And shelly beaches and wonderful grassland, called links. Lot listens, rapt by the magic of names and things unseen. I realise that every moment for her is an education. She listens, feels, thinks, and lets the world and her own mind speak to her. Depressingly there are no gaps in the sludge, no hint of living water. We turn starboard between the island of Graemsay and the port of Stromness and on to the mainland. No sign of life or growth. None of us will voice the disappointment we each feel. On our starboard side we see standing stones defiant against weather and plague and humanity, stoic and solid.

We chug on through a small inlet where the road has crumbled, and on into the loch of Stenness, then hug the coast. We stop at a cracked and faded sign that says *Maeshowe Visitors Centre. Closed.* It seems foolish to leave the boat unattended so Trash stays and we get out. I take the M4 A41 assault rifle and my Glock and Hamish takes a shotgun. Emma barks wildly and runs in circles. If anyone is here they'll certainly know we have arrived. The Visitor's Centre is a shell. Some stairs leading up to a first floor. Downstairs just rubble and dust. "Hello?" I call upstairs. Nothing. We wander on. We approach a scrubby hillock with a rusted wire door. I go inside, my pistol in front. Smell of ruin and damp. It has all the welcoming ambience of a morgue. Yet I feel things have happened here. Mysteries. I shine a torch and look around. Lot stares entranced at the walls. She reaches out to touch and something in me senses danger.

"Lot! No!" I shout, but too late. She touches the wall and instantly starts shaking as if in the throes of a fit. Her eyes roll up and her mouth foams. I run to her and pull her away. It is as if her hand is stuck to the wall and there is a spark as I wrench her hand free. "It's all right. I've got you," I say and hold her tight to stop the violent shaking. Slowly she returns but her eyes look through me, as if she has seen a distant shoreline of some unimaginable horror.

"Agi. Barn. Illr. Leave hí eðdeyr," she says, but not in her own voice. It is deeper. "Leave hí eðdeyr. Leave hí eðdeyr."

"OK. OK. Come back. Come back," I say and slap her across the cheek. She chokes and takes a gasp of air as if she has been underwater. I lay her down. Hamish crouches next to us.

"What is this place?" I ask.

"Viking Cairn," he says. "In the eleven hundreds. Group of Viking warriors sought shelter from a heavy snowstorm."

"Led by Earl Harald, Christmas 1153," Lot says in her own returned voice.

I look at the runes on the walls. Graffiti from nearly a thousand years ago. The human need to make images, narrate, give things meaning.

"How do you know that?" I ask. She stares blankly at the wall. "What were you saying?" I ask her.

She turns her big eyes on me.

"Not me. He was talking."

"Who?"

She looks at the wall again. I can see marks and runes and signs and an etching into the stone of a dragon.

"What did it mean? What you were saying," I ask.

"Let's see," she said, and opened her hand. There in a bright red weal as if burnt with a branding iron is the head of the dragon, turning back so its right eye seemed to be looking at something. An exact replica of the one on the wall. She looks at it intently. "Maeshowe Dragon. It says: Danger child bad. Leave here or die. Leave here or die. Leave here or die."

Emma growls and I hear something. A pebble rolling. Something move. As I turn I see a shadow flit across the entrance and then disappear. I click off the safety on my Glock. I go first, then Lot, Hamish behind her. Outside the brackish light makes me squint after the darkness of the cairn, but I cannot see anyone or anything. Could there be animals here? The whole island now seems full of foreboding. Rocks project like rotting teeth, clumps of dead heather are tumours, air a dead weight upon us. All I can think is get back to the boat and leave. Lot seems to have forgotten her strange ordeal and is throwing a stick for Emma.

"What just happened?" I ask Hamish, not expecting an answer.

"Islands are strange places. They carry the past. Maybe the Orkneys don't want any more intruders."

"What about your brother? You're not curious what happened to him?"

"No. Fuck him."

"Alright then."

We trudge on and I feel the place closing around me like a barbed glove. Something in me is recoiling. We turn a corner and go down the slope to where Trash is cleaning the motor and tightening the ropes on our provisions.

"Anything?" he asks.

"Ghosts and dragons and Vikings is all," I say.

He looks at me strangely. "Where's Lot? And Emma?"

I turn. Shit. How could I not have noticed? "Lot!" I call. Nothing. I run back up the slope. Desolation landscape. "Lot!" "Lot!" Trash and Hamish join me. Both have their guns. "Let's retrace our steps. Maybe she went back to the Cairn. Trash - best if you stay with Bess Two in case she comes back." I run back to the Cairn, Hamish puffing behind me. I know she won't be there but it's the only thing I can think of. It's deserted. I look at the dragon on the wall and have an overwhelming desire to shoot it. To erase history and all violent, pointless, bloody roads to this day where nothing makes sense and everything is broken. Fuck the whole world.

We go back outside and scan every direction. Nothing. How can a girl and a dog disappear in such a barren place? And why would they want to? It isn't like Lot to play games like this. She's seen too much danger and turmoil and carnage in life to seek the cheap thrill of scaring those who care for her. We walk down to the loch, then return. I wonder if we've missed something. We go back in the Cairn and I trace the dragon on the wall with my index finger. A skittering of feet behind us and there is Emma, stressed and wide eyed, unable to bark or whimper because someone has put a leather muzzle on her. There is also a cloth strip trailing from her leg. I bend down and stroke her head. "Alright, it's alright, girl. Good girl. Good Emma." The dirty end of the cloth is damp. I guess she has bitten through it and escaped from wherever she was. I undo the leather muzzle and she takes a gulp of air and barks, eyes shining at me.

"I think we have our guide," says Hamish.

"Where is Lot?" I ask.

The little dog's ears prick up and she looks to the exit.

"Find Lot, Emma. Good girl." And she is off. I jog behind her, Hamish behind me. Emma runs up the hill, looks behind to make sure I'm following, turns a bend and heads towards the visitor's centre. A minute later I am there and wait for Hamish, who is puffing and cursing to himself. We go in the centre and Emma is slung low on her haunches at the foot of the stairs looking up, her lips curled back to reveal perfect white sharp teeth in a gesture of fear and aggression. I take out my Glock. Hamish comes beside me, his shotgun raised. We look at each other. He shrugs. Up is the only way.

I creep past Emma, who stays low at my feet, and Hamish a little behind to cover me. Suddenly I am sweating heavily, not because of who might be waiting but at what they might have done to Lot if she is there. If she has been harmed I am already starting to feel something in my head open, that door to dark places where I disappear. I take a deep breath and blink to keep the feeling at bay. I am sure my mouth drops open when I get to the top of the stairs. I was half expecting a band of island warriors with claymores and blue face paint. What greets me is a pathetic waxwork bunch of elderly ragtaggle ruins of people who look unhinged. Lot is seated, tied to a chair, but looking calm and untroubled. There are two elderly women. One in rags, the flesh hanging from her jowls as if she is melting. She holds an ancient revolver and points it at me. The other is cross eyed and toothless, skin long ago turned to a cracked mud landscape. She holds a pitch fork out at me. A skinny man in a filthy black suit made for someone three hands shorter than him, no socks and old trainers with no laces, one with his toes poking through. He grips a long handled broken kitchen knife in one hand and a sawn off shotgun in the other. A small man, bald but with a ludicrous combover of wiry salt and pepper hair on his dome, is next to him staring fiercely at me and holding a rusty machete. Between the two men on the filthy floor a sheet laid out, as if for some arcane ceremony. Another man has his back to me and is looking through a window frame down at the loch. What chills me is next to the sheet on the floor. An old camping stove lit and a large filthy black pot with a broken handle bubbling water. If I am right about their intention I am going to find it hard not to kill each and every one of these desperate rags. They all stare strangely at Hamish.

Hamish holds the shotgun ready while I go to untie Lot. The little man with the machete takes a step towards me and raises the machete. Hamish fires off a shot and the noise is deafening, bouncing off the walls. Too quick to see the little man's arm flies off, splatters against the wall and lays in shreds on the floor, the finger bones still clutching the bloody machete. The little man stares in horror at his stump, sinews and bone and veins a bloody tangle. His mouth open in a silent scream. No one knows what to do. The toothless woman smirks and covers her mouth to stifle a giggle. The man in the ridiculous suit steadies the shotgun at me. He ignores the small man who is on the floor writhing in agony.

"Best put a tourniquet around that arm otherwise he'll bleed out in about five minutes. Not that I give a fuck," I say.

The man looks at the giggling woman. She waddles to the man on the floor and, still smirking and stifling a giggle, tears a strip of rag from herself and starts to bind the bleeding stump tightly. The man shrieks and she laughs outright, slapping her side. The standing man points at Lot with the knife.

"She got the mark," he says.

"What mark?"

"Dragon. She carries it on her, so in her too. We wanted her. Protect us like. Soul like that. Very rare. She carries the ancient."

"So, sanctimonious prick that you are, thought you'd eat her to get some of that power?" Says Hamish.

The man looks genuinely puzzled.

"Not just eat. Sacrifice. Honour blood. Like the bible. Sacrificial lamb. Honour spirit. Take her into us."

Lot looks one to the other, taking all this calmly. Her inner life must be the strangest universe anyone could know. Hamish scoffs and spits.

"She comes with us. We're family," I say, and at this Lot looks at me and registers surprise.

"She stays with us. For us," says the man and, with a speed I wouldn't have thought possible, moves the knife to Lot's throat and stands behind her.

"If you harm her you have no idea what I will do to you and these other throwback retards," I say, and take a step forwards. I kick the bubbling water over the man on the floor's bloody stump and he screams long and loud. The mad woman goes into a paroxysm of giggling that almost makes her choke.

"Seems we have us a standoff," says the man at the window and turns around for the first time. I almost drop my gun. It is Hamish in different clothes.

29

Hamish at the window looks at his double next to me, and says, "Thought I recognised your turdy tones. There was I hoping you was dead and you turn up here against the odds just to remind me what a shitebag of lavvy-heided wankstain you is."

The resemblance is extraordinary. They are twins. The man with no arm has passed out, which is a blessing in terms of noise. The giggling woman has stopped and is busy running a dirty finger along her gums, as if looking for something, like a tooth. The other woman still holds a revolver at me. Our Hamish looks at me, and then back at his double. "Meet my brother, jobby-flavoured fart lozenge that goes by the name of Rory, though even our dear mother, whose funeral this fuck-bumper didna come to, preferred to call him a scabby walloper with balls no bigger than mouse snot."

"Family. Best thing on this earth. You didna tell me you had a brother, Rory," says the man with the knife at Lot's throat.

"Nae muh brother," says Rory. "Ma said she found him hanging from a sheep's arse."

"Moving and emotional as this sibling reunion is, we should go, Hamish." I say.

"Aye, sooner I get away from the stink of this gobshite lard stabber the better I'll breathe."

"You'll no be taking the girl," says the man with the knife. "She was sent. To minister to us."

"Sent by whom?" I ask.

He looks towards the window. "Them. The old ones. They comes to us in dreams. Now they've sent her. It's a gift. We canna say No. It would be impolitic."

"You were going to eat her, you fucking broomstick," I say.

The mad woman starts a fit of giggling and holds her crotch, as if about to wet herself, which she probably already has. If I could get a clear shot I'd take the man out but even if I got him his hand could jerk the knife into Lot.

"I have a wee suggestion," says Rory. "A solution to this imponderable."

We all look.

"Me and this bellyband lavy-lickin bastard fight. To the death or near as dammit. Winner takes the girl and nae questions asked."

The implications sink in. We watch these two bite, claw and scratch the bones from other. Immediately I don't like it. For one thing too risky. I don't trust any of this band of mugwumps to fight fair. Two, Hamish might lose and I'd have to start killing anyway in the hope of saving Lot.

"This is not a good deal, Hamish," I say.

He glares fire at me. "Yous think I canna beat this pissy spineless tadger?"

"No. It's just too risky," I say. "For one thing, I don't trust this lot."

"Theys'll abide by it. True and fair, won't yous?" Rory asks his merry little band. The man in the suit nods. The mad woman giggles. I see by the puddle at her feet that she has indeed peed herself. Revolver woman nods assentingly. The only sane presence here seems to be Emma, who sits watching and listening attentively.

Hamish looks at me. His face is an unnatural red, flushed by a hunger to do violence to his last living relative. I can think of no other way.

"OK," I say. "Let battle commence. Queensbury rules."

"Queensbury can shove his rules where the bugs fuck," says Rory.

Hamish puts down his gun. We clear the centre of the room. The man with the knife continues to hold it to Lot's throat but backs slowly to a wall, taking her with him. The unconscious little man is dragged by Rory to a corner and placed slumped on a chair. I stand in a far corner, Emma next to me. I know that what is happening is laced with disastrous possibilities but can think of no alternative. I shudder slightly too when I realise there is a dark part of me that is intrigued to see these doppelgängers have at each other, as in some ancient gladiatorial ritual of sibling hatred so fierce it glistens and borders on love. Cain and Abel. Romulus and Remus. Is there something fundamental in wanting to annihilate that to which we are most bound? The raw pain of intimacy and belonging that makes us want to smash its fragile strength just to shed all notions of belonging and responsibility, to be truly, dangerously free of affection and kinship because they claim something of us that is too painful to bear? I wonder at the human heart and its longings for the sheer ecstasy of release from confinement and restraint, to feel nothing but its own brief fluttering and single flight, like a hawk that is the only shadow in the clear sky, utterly intense in its own being, or the wave that knows only its frantic rush and breaking on the rocks. There is no other god but the self in its brief illumination. God was always adored in his singleness and if we were made in his image it is this longing for lone shining and being that aches in us, everything concentrated in this diamond bright moment that is both breathing and transcendent. The salmon leaping, the whale diving, the comet tracering the night sky, the star imploding, the lizard feeling the stone hot beneath its feet, the hermit's breath in the night, a breeze drifting leaves, all the little universes that are beautiful only in themselves. If we are at the end of things, at least for us as a species, it is the palimpsest of these moments of singleness that will remember us.

There is no wary circling, no formalities, no handshake. Just a moment they both recognise and they are at each other like deranged angels of malice. Rory tries to get a grip on Hamish's throat while Hamish rains side blows to Rory's ears. Rory rears up and headbutts Hamish square on the nose, which breaks and instantly fountains blood. Hamish kicks Rory in the groin, which he clutches and stoops to recover, giving Hamish time to put his hands together in a double fist and pound Rory's head until he is on his knees. He grabs Hamish around the knees and they both tumble to the filthy floor, sending up a dust cloud as they roll and curse and spit and bleed. Rory rolls on top and pins Hamish to the floor and then crashes his head down to bite the face, but Hamish turns his head and Rory bites into his right ear, sinks his teeth and pulls off an ear lobe, tossing his head like a dog shaking a creature for the kill. He spits the lobe across the floor and tries to bite again, but with an immense heave Hamish pushes Rory off and over and frees himself. He stands quickly and as Rory tries to get up, one leg crooked on the floor and one straight behind he jumps on the crooked leg and it snaps at the ankle. Rory roars in pain. Hamish cracks his boot down on the leg again and the bone splinters through just above the ankle like a bleached spire. Rory manages to stand, his weight on the good leg, and Hamish runs at him, but Rory shifts to one side, grabs an arm and twists hard. Hamish grimaces as his arm is twisted. I can't fathom how the arm is not breaking, but I see that Rory's grip is wet with blood and spit and he cannot get enough leverage to snap the bone. Both men are breathing heavily.

Rory gathers himself into another attack and, half hopping to avoid standing on the broken leg, comes at Hamish with a roar. I see then that he has a knife from somewhere, presumably his pocket. He slashes in front of him and Hamish ducks but not quickly enough and the blade slices across his forehead, which opens and a curtain of flesh drops, and blood fountains down blinding Hamish completely. He falls to his knees and then rolls away, wiping furiously at his eyes and spraying blood across the room. Some lands on Lot's lap and some on Emma's paws in front of her. He reaches into his pocket and pulls out a filthy rag and binds it quickly around his head. Rory hops towards him but Hamish steps away and spits in his hands and then rubs his eyes, which are bloody and streaming. He blinks furiously and can see enough to know Rory is about to lunge at him again. He moves to his left and then grabs the hand with the knife and bites deep into the joint between thumb and finger. The knife clatters to the floor and Hamish kicks at the broken leg hard and knocks the foot at right angles to the leg. He makes a fist of his free hand and drives a knuckle deep into Rory's left eye. Rory starts to collapse but Hamish holds him close under his arms and they dance, face to face, across the floor, and then Hamish lets Rory down a little and smashes his face several times into the corner of the free chair. The teeth all break off at the gum and then the jaw collapses altogether. Hamish smashes the head down again and drives the corner of the chair deep into Rory's right eye. He lifts the head and the eye has disappeared into his head; he smashes the head down until Rory's nose is flattened into his skull. There is no face left to speak of, the architecture has gone and there is only fractured bone, glistening raw tissue and dribbling tendon. With no nose and a bloody cave of bone and teeth and flopping tongue he cannot properly breathe.

Hamish lets him go and he crumples to the floor like a piece of destroyed offal. Hamish breathes deeply and looks down at what little is left of his brother. Then he gets to one knee, looks searchingly at Rory and whispers "Good night, brother," and kisses his forehead. The imprint of his lips is like a bubbled mouthpiece shining in the blood. Hamish stands and looks at me. "We're done here," he says.

I move to untie Lot. The man with the knife hesitates and then drops his hand. I free her, squeeze her hand and then back away. The woman with the revolver looks as if she is about to shoot. I turn my gun on her. "Don't," I say.

"We had a bargain. We won." The mad woman simpers. The man left standing gestures to the woman and she puts down her gun. Hamish is at the top of the stairs, now holding his shotgun, but barely able to walk. I get to the top of the stairs, Lot in front of me and now with Emma. Some still small voice makes me turn and the man holds the shotgun pointing at me.

"I canna help it," he says.

"I know," I say, and fire off two shots. The first in the chest and the second in the head as he goes down. I turn to the woman but she has no intention of trying anything. There is no fight left here. Even the giggling has stopped.

Ten minutes later we arrive at Bess Two. Trash looks us over and whistles through his teeth. "Had a good time then," he says.

I nod.

"See what happens when you don't have me there?" He says.

"Babes in the wood," I say.

He starts the motor and slowly we chug away, and Hamish curls into a foetal position away from the rest of us and begins to cry softly, like an abandoned baby.

30

We have no plan now and are too exhausted to do anything but lie down, each in our own thoughts, the chug of the motor and the slurp of the glutinous sea, as we go north. Through the Orkneys, past Skaill and Birsay and beyond, the Shetlands eventually visible on our right, Norway somewhere beyond, a constant wind and the rain skeeting in, poor visibility as if even god doesn't want to look at the world. I wonder if Hamish will die from his beating and some deep private grief that I can only imagine, and Trash too, coughing while radiation does its work deep in his cellular self that is only poor, fragile tissue not built to withstand nuclear assault. Perhaps we will all die on this strange craft and that is what is meant to be.

And then there is a great jagged scar of light across the sky and an ear drumming clap of thunder. Emma howls at the sky and then puts her paws over her head in blind terror and Lot smothers her in protection. The sky is alight and the air is electrified. I think of Blake's *Ancient of Days*, Urizen crouching in a circle with a cloud-like background and his finger pointing down and sending fire as an act of violent creation. It is an image of terror and awe and majesty. And then Urizen striding through a darkened space, exploring his dens, mountain, moor, & wilderness, with a globe of fire lighting his journey. I understand the primitive need to anthropomorphise the world and beyond. Lightning and thunder are anger, so someone, something, must be furious with us, and must be appeased by a sacrifice. Now we are the sacrifice, the lost souls in the last of days. The boat rocks. Trash is blinded by rain and we are moving slowly and blindly towards nothing. How pathetic we must look.

When sleep comes I welcome it like death itself. The end of thinking and the beginning of a dream.

She is running along the beach, heels kicking up golden sands, and I think we are all animals designed for play and rest and growth. She turns and laughs and I wave. Joe will be in his workshop, the sweat shining on his back on this hot day, planing and shaving wood until it reveals something that is beautiful and useful and still has the smell of the forest because wood never really dies. Then that other smell that makes my throat burn and my stomach churn and I turn to see it flopping out of the sea, dark and moist and spraying foam. It is black and wet and what chills me most is not knowing where the head is. Is this just appetite itself, the whole thing slavering like a giant mouth? It grows as it emerges, taller than two men. What is this thing beneath the skin? Breastless, formless, leaned backward with a lipless grin, jellied glue in sockets meant for eyes, and thought that clings around dead limbs tightening its lusts and luxuries. I am incapable of movement while it comes to claim me, but suddenly she is there. Her. The sun dancing in her hair, life shining liquidly through her eyes. 'Mum! Mum! It's alright. It's only in your head. See? See!' I turn and there is the white tumbling surf and the grey blue beyond it spreading its silk to the clear horizon as if the sky has pencilled a perfect line.

I open my eyes and shiver. Lot sits next to me, Emma beside her, her head in the girl's lap. Hamish is inert and still coiled, hopefully asleep. Lot looks at me. "It was in your head," she says. "Yes," I reply. "Only in my head. Sometimes it's hard to know where one ends and the other begins."

I stir and sit up. Mist. The storm has brutalised itself away, yet the air itself seems to remain in shock.

"Where are we?" I ask Trash.

"My reckoning, the Faroe Islands are a spit ahead. Can't get any signals so it's partly guesswork."

"And the rest is pure genius."

"Yes. Something else."

"What?"

"Not sure, but every now and then the mist has broken."

"Mist doesn't break."

"OK, so you tell me what I saw while you were snoring away in lala land."

"Sorry. Tell me what you saw."

"The mist seemed to break," he said, emphasising the word *break* just to put me in my place. I think again of Blake's Urizen and how the divine finger cracks reality open to let something else through. I'm prepared to believe everything and nothing because all my steering lights have disappeared.

"Look," says Lot, pointing a hundred and fifty metres ahead. There are strange little seams of brightness on the sea sludge, as if someone has placed jagged pieces of light on the surface.

"Something floating in the sludge?" I wonder.

"No. Hang on. Je-sus," Trash says.

"It's certainly not Jesus. What is it?"

Trash peers intently. He suddenly has the flushed look of an excited little boy. His grey pallor has gone. "It's light reflected. Look, there are sunspots through the clouds, and if it's reflected below that means…"

The possibility is too much to hope for.

"There is clear water," I say, not daring to believe it.

"Must be."

We chug on. I hardly dare to look. Hardly dare to believe. He is right. There are patches where the mist looks broken, as if someone has snapped it off and a different dimension appears. We get to one of the light shapes in the water. We look and hardly dare to believe. A break in the sludge and it is sea water. A murky emerald green but liquid with the promise of movement. Trash dips his hand in and the surface breaks. He smells his hand and then licks it. He dips in his hand again and then splashes the water at Lot. She opens her mouth in delight. Emma barks. It is a champagne moment. Living water. There are more patches and we delight in putting out hands in and splashing. I keep looking for other signs of life – seaweed, possibly even fish, but it is important not to hope for too much. Let this suffice for now. I find I am crying and wipe away the tears with my sleeve.

"Land ahoy!" Shouts Trash in a mock pirate voice.

Appearing in fits and starts in the light that suddenly appears and then is eclipsed, the Faroe Islands, part of the Kingdom of Denmark which may or may not still exist. Probably not. Trash tells us it comprises eighteen rocky, volcanic islands between Iceland and Norway in the North Atlantic Ocean, connected by road tunnels, ferries, causeways and bridges. Hundreds of islets and skerries around the main eighteen islands. And suddenly we are out of the mist, as if we have passed a threshold. It feels theatrical, like stepping from behind the curtain and into the dazzle of lights. I look at the southernmost part of the Islands. I blink and squint my eyes, because I am not sure if what I am seeing is real.

At the southernmost tip is a thin strip of rock trailing like a lazy stone finger, but there are more patches of light reflected on the water around it. Further back is a lighthouse. Trash passes me an old map. The place is called Akraberg. Around the lighthouse are patches of green. The colour is so sweet I can almost taste it. I see something else and grab the binoculars. At first I think it is flotsam blowing in the wind but the movements are swooping, regular. A huge gull circling the lighthouse and crying and I think it is one of the most beautiful delights I have ever seen. I realise I'm trembling. I give the binoculars to Lot and point. She looks. Her brow creases. She looks at me inquisitorially.

"It's a gull. A bird. A dinosaur," I say excitedly.

The word triggers something in her. She looks again, then at me. "So it knows things, from the very beginning?"

"Yes. It knows."

And I know Trash is thinking the same thing. If there is one bird there will be more. And that means a food source. And fresh water. And if there is grass it means the earth can grow other things. The possibilities begin to multiply. Subpolar oceanic climate. Mildish winters. Cool summers. As we get closer I see other birds. Trash is intoning names: common eider, common starling, Eurasian wren, common murre, black guillemot. It sounds like a litany or a poem. As we land I see a small group of puffins with their beautiful comical heads looking at us from a piece of heather. I take the rosewood box with onyx inlay and quartz stones and float it in a little pool of sea water. From somewhere a tiny whirlpool starts and the box is taken down and away.

"I love you, Dad," I say. "Welcome home."

I wake up Hamish, who stirs painfully.

"Wake up," I say. You don't die on me. There's too much to do." Trash looks at me and I feel a wellspring of something long buried. "Goes for you too, Trashy. Don't you dare fucking die on me. Not now. Work to do. Daughter and little dog to care for." Lot looks at me as if I've finally gone mad, which I have, and it is blissful.

And the many centuries fall away until time is squeezed into a ball of eternity. Good green ground beneath my feet. I am a palimpsest of the ages. I will no longer disappear. My family is a band of ragamuffin soldiers torn and bloody from the wars, hurt beyond comprehension, but with flute and drums still marching on into the little patches of light and life that beckon us and say; Here, and now again Here, See — something stirs and breathes and refuses to die. And this is all we can finally ask of things. The next step, the next breath. And so I know my world is abundant, those to care for and protect, and there is Dick Turpin and Bess riding off for all times in their mad quixotic, doomed adventures, and there, there, the many ghosts to walk with and whisper to in waking and sleep, my father at work in his shed, all those I have been touched by are with me now and my body is no longer merely salt and ashes, but the living dreaming bone of the times that breaks and heals and goes on, because finally that is all we can do. My heart is broken in a thousand places but it beats on and I will honour it. All you have is those you love and those you have loved and who are gone from you. There is nothing else worth a pinch of salt.

The End

About the Author

An award-winning writer of film, television, stage, radio and books, from London, Steve worked as a Performance Poet, sometimes opening for John Cooper Clarke. He has had 8 stage plays produced and several one man shows at the Edinburgh Fringe – **Dick in Space** and **Ron the Plumber**, both of which received 5 star reviews. His TV and Film work includes, children's dramas, historical films, series work (including **The Bill**, **Dalziel and Pascoe**), drama and art documentaries. He has 3 RTS Awards, 2 Writer's Guild Awards, 2 BAFTA nominations, Best Film Award, Eric Gregory Award for Poetry, Best Brit Film, a Radio 4 Travel Writing Award. Published fiction includes crime thrillers, satires, political novels and children's fiction. He has also written 2 history books. Work in progress includes a new historical novel based on a true story, a memoir and a children's book. Writing has always been a matter of survival. He learnt as a child that if you could tell a joke or a story the bullies sometimes listened rather than beat you up. He also lived in a world of puppets and pets when little, which explains a lot. He lives in Warwickshire, sometimes in Spain.

- **AWARDS**

- 3 RTS Awards, 2 Writer's Guild Awards, 2 BAFTA nominations, Best Film Award, Eric Gregory Award for Poetry, Best Brit Film, Radio 4 Travel Writing Award

➤ **FILM AND TELEVISION**
- These include Children's TV Drama series, such as **The Queen's Nose, The Boot Street Band, Billy Webb's Amazing Story** and **Harry's Mad**
- TV Dramas and documentaries include **Hawkins, The Brontes, George Eliot – A Life, Turner –The Man Who Painted England, The Scarlet Pimpernel, The Bill** and **Dalziel and Pascoe**. Docudramas, including the **What if?** BBC Docudrama Series
- 8 Films include **GUY X, Eva, Elizabeth Bathory** and **The Shadow of the Sword.**

➤ **STAGE PLAYS**
- Various stage plays produced
- **Ron the Plumber** (Writer, Performer) Edinburgh Fringe
- **Dick in Space** (Writer, Performer) Edinburgh Fringe

➤ **BOOKS**
- Include a psychodrama **The Harrowing of Ben Hartley,** a satire on corporate corruption **Bottom of the List,** political satire **Behind Closed Doors,** thriller series called **A Mind for Murder: The Second Sex, Human All Too Human, The Natural Law** (achieved number 1 in Kindle Singles bestseller list)**, Beyond Good and Evil, Philosophical Investigations**
- 2 history books published - **The Boer War**, Endeavour Press 2014 and **Imperialism and National Identity in Late Victorian British**

Culture, UK and US publication by Palgrave Macmillan, Jan 2003

- **RADIO**
  - 2 plays on BBC Radio, Travel talks on Radio 4, Radio 3 talks and monologues

- **TALKS AND LECTURES**

    Talks, Workshops and Lecturing on **Writing, Film, Literature** at numerous venues, including Oxford, London, Warwick, Sheffield, New York, Europe and Asia.

Printed in Great Britain
by Amazon